#1 *New York Times* Bestselling Author!

"IF YOU'RE LOOKING FOR SENSUALITY, YOU WON'T BE DISAPPOINTED IN

JOHANNA LINDSEY."

Chicago Sun-Times

"One of the most reliable authors around. Her books are well-paced and well-written, filled with strong characters, humor, interesting plots—and, of course, romance."

Cincinnati Enquirer

"The charm and appeal of her characters are infectious."

Publishers Weekly

"First-rate romance."

New York Daily News

"Johanna Lindsey transports us . . . We have no choice but to respond to the humor and intensity."

San I

Books by Johanna Lindsey

ALL I NEED IS YOU • ANGEL • BRAVE THE WILD WIND
CAPTIVE BRIDE • DEFY NOT THE HEART
FIRES OF WINTER • A GENTLE FEUDING
GENTLE ROGUE • GLORIOUS ANGEL
HEART OF A WARRIOR • HEART OF THUNDER
A HEART SO WILD • HEARTS AFLAME • THE HEIR
HOME FOR THE HOLIDAYS • JOINING
KEEPER OF THE HEART • LOVE ME FOREVER
LOVE ONLY ONCE • THE MAGIC OF YOU
MAN OF MY DREAMS • ONCE A PRINCESS
PARADISE WILD • A PIRATE'S LOVE • THE PRESENT
PRISONER OF MY DESIRE • THE PURSUIT
SAVAGE THUNDER • SAY YOU LOVE ME • SECRET FIRE
SILVER ANGEL • SO SPEAKS THE HEART
SURRENDER MY LOVE • TENDER IS THE STORM
TENDER REBEL • UNTIL FOREVER • WARRIOR'S WOMAN
WHEN LOVE AWAITS • YOU BELONG TO ME

WHEN LOVE AWAITS

An Imprint of HarperCollins*Publishers*

**Dedicated to Vivian and Bill Walje,
my second parents**

This is a work of fiction. Names, characters, places, and incidents are products of the author's imagination or are used fictitiously and are not to be construed as real. Any resemblance to actual events, locales, organizations, or persons, living or dead, is entirely coincidental.

AVON BOOKS
An Imprint of HarperCollins*Publishers*
195 Broadway
New York, NY 10007

ISBN: 0-380-89739-3
www.avonromance.com

First Avon Books paperback printing: June 1996

Printed in the U.S.A.

23 24 25 26 27 LBC 44 43 42 41 40

Chapter 1

England, 1176.

SIR Guibert Fitzalan leaned back against the thick tree trunk, watching two maidservants pack away the remains of the picnic lunch. A man of moderately good looks, he was an unassuming man and women, even his liegelady's servingwomen, had a way of unnerving him. Wilda, the younger of the two servants, caught his eye just then. Her bold look made him look quickly away, heat burning his face.

Spring was in full flower and Wilda was not the only woman to turn her eye on Sir Guibert appreciatively. Nor was he the only man who received one of her hot gazes. Wilda was decidedly comely, with a sleek little nose and rosy cheeks. Her hair was a glossy chestnut, and she was equally blessed with a lush body.

Even so, Guibert was a confirmed bachelor. Besides that, Wilda was too young for a man of two score and five years. Why, she was as young as Lady Leonie whom they both served, and that lady was just nineteen.

Sir Guibert thought of Leonie of Montwyn as a daughter. At that moment, as he observed her leaving the pasture where she had begun her spring herb gathering and disappearing into the woods, he sent four of his men-at-arms to follow her at a discreet distance. He'd brought along ten men to protect her, and the soldiers knew better than to grumble at the duty, but it was hardly their favorite. Leonie often asked them to pick plants as she pointed them out. Herb gathering was not manly.

Before this spring, three guards had been enough to accompany Lady Leonie, but now there was a new resident at Crewel, into whose woods Leonie entered to search for herbs. The new lord of all the lands of Kempston was a matter of great concern to Sir Guibert.

Guibert had never liked the old lord of Kempston, Sir Edmond Montigny, but at least the old baron had caused no trouble. The new lord of Kempston made endless complaints against the Pershwick serfs and had done so ever since taking possession of Crewel Keep. It helped not at all that the complaints might be valid. Worse, Lady Leonie felt personally responsible for her serfs' misdeeds.

"Let me see to this, Sir Guibert," she had begged him when she first heard of the complaints. "I fear the serfs believe they are doing me a service by stirring up mischief at Crewel."

For explanation, she confessed, "I was in the village the day Alain Montigny came to tell me what befell his father and himself. Too many of the serfs saw how upset I was and I fear they heard me wish a pox on Black Wolf, who now rules Crewel."

Guibert found it hard to believe that Leonie would curse anyone. Not Leonie. She was too good, too kind, too quick to mend any ill, ease any burden. But then, for Sir Guibert, she could do no wrong. He doted on and spoiled her. And, he asked himself, if he did not, who would? Certainly not her father, who had sent her from him six years ago, when her mother died, banishing Leonie to Pershwick Keep along with her mother's sister, Beatrix, because he could not bear the sight of anyone who reminded him of his beloved wife.

Guibert could not fathom the man's action, but then he had never known Sir William of Montwyn very well, even though he had come to live in his household as part of Lady Elisabeth's dowry when she wed Sir William. Lady Elisabeth, an earl's daughter and the fifth and youngest of her father's children, had been allowed a love match. The man was in no way her equal, but Sir William loved her—perhaps too much. Her death destroyed him, and he apparently could not bear the presence of his only child. Leonie, like Elisabeth, was small and slender, fair, and blessed with extraordinary hair of silver-blond and silver-gray eyes. "Beautiful" was not adequate to describe Leonie.

He sighed, thinking of the two women, mother and daughter, one gone, the other just as dear to him as her mother had been. And then he froze, pleasant musings shattered by a battle cry, a cry of rage coming from the woods.

Guibert was frozen for no more than a second before he was running toward the woods, his sword already drawn. Four men-at-arms who'd been standing nearby with the horses chased after him, everyone hoping that the men with Leonie had stuck close by her.

Deep in the woods, Leonie of Montwyn had also been stunned for a moment by the unearthly cry. She had, as usual, managed to put a good distance between herself and her four protectors. Now, she imagined some great demonic beast was nearby. Still, her inborn, unladylike curiosity urged her on toward the sound instead of back to her men.

She smelled smoke and broke into a full run, pushing through shrubs and trees until she found the source of the smoke. A woodcutter's hut had burned. The woodcutter was staring at the smoldering remains of his home as five mounted knights and fifteen men-at-arms, also mounted, sat silently facing the ruined hut. An armored knight paced his great destrier back and forth between the hut and the men. He let out an explosive curse while Leonie watched and then she knew where the first horrible sound had come from. She knew, too, who the knight was. She moved back into the bush, out of sight, thankful for her concealing dark green mantle.

Concealment was jeopardized as her men came running behind her. Leonie quickly turned toward them, hushing them and motioning them back. She made her way to them silently, and they positioned themselves around her, then moved back toward her land. Sir Guibert and the rest of the men were upon them a moment later.

"There is no danger," she assured Sir Guibert. "But we should leave this place. The lord of Kempston has found a woodcutter's hut burned to the ground and I think he is none too pleased."

"You saw him?"

"Yes. He is in a fine rage."

Sir Guibert grunted and hurried Leonie along. It would not do for her to be found near the burned hut with her men-at-arms. How would she talk her way out of that?

Later, when it was safe, serfs could return to the woods and retrieve Leonie's plants. For now, Lady Leonie and the armed men had to be removed from the scene.

As Sir Guibert lifted her into her saddle, he asked, "How do you know it was the Black Wolf you saw?"

"He wore the silver wolf on a black field."

Leonie did not say that she had seen the man once before. She could never tell Sir Guibert that, for she had disguised herself and sneaked out of the keep without his knowing, to go to the tourney at Crewel. Later, she'd wished she hadn't.

"Most like it was him, though his men also wear his colors," Sir Guibert agreed, remembering that awful bellow. "You saw what he looks like?"

"No." She could not quite keep the disappointment from her voice. "He wore his helmet. But he is huge, of that there was no mistaking."

"Perhaps this time he will come himself and see the trouble ended instead of sending his man over."

"Or he will bring his army."

"He has no proof, my lady. It is one serf's word against another's. But get you safe inside the keep now. I will follow with the others and see the village guarded."

Leonie rode for home with four men-at-arms and her two maids. She saw that she had not been firm enough in warning her people against causing more trouble with the Crewel serfs. In truth, her heart had not been in the warning, for it gave her satisfaction to know the new lord of Kempston was being plagued with domestic problems.

She had thought to soften the situation with her people by offering entertainments at Pershwick on the next feastday. But her anxiety over the Black Wolf and what he might do next made her decide against any gathering at her keep. No, she was better off keeping a weather eye on her neighbor's activities and offering no chance for her people to gather where there was bound to be drink. They might, she knew, decide to plan something that could easily rebound on her. No, if her villagers were going to plot against the Black Wolf, she would be better off if they did so far from her.

She knew what she had to do. She would have to speak to her people again, and firmly. But when she thought of dear Alain, banished from his home, and poor Sir Edmond who had died so that King Henry could favor one of his mercenaries with a fine estate, then she found it hard to want peace for the Black Wolf, hard indeed.

Chapter 2

LEONIE handed her soap to the maid and leaned forward so Wilda could wash her back. She waved away the bucket for rinsing and instead settled down in the large tub to take advantage of the soothing herb-scented water while it was still good and hot.

A fire burned in the hearth, taking the chill from the room. Outside, it was a mild spring evening, but the bare stone walls of Pershwick Keep created coldness that seemed never to lessen. And the ceiling of her room, open to join the great hall, allowed every draft to enter.

Pershwick was an old keep, designed neither for comfort nor to accommodate guests. The hall was large, but hadn't been altered since it was built a hundred years ago. Leonie's chamber was partitioned off the dais end of the hall with wooden boards. She shared the room with her Aunt Beatrix, more boards dividing the room in half to give each lady a little privacy. There were no women's quarters, and no other chambers off the hall or above it, as there were in some of the new keeps. The servants slept in the hall, and the men-at-arms in the tower, where Sir Guibert also slept.

Rough though it was, Pershwick was home to Leonie, and had been for the last six years. Since coming here she had not returned once to Montwyn, her birthplace. Nor had she seen her father. Yet Montwyn Castle was only five miles away. In that castle lived her father, Sir William, and his new wife, Lady Judith, who had married him the year after Leonie's mother died.

If Leonie could no longer summon a kind thought for her father, no one blamed her. From having a happy childhood and two loving parents to losing both parents in one stroke was a cruel fate, and wholly undeserved.

She had once loved her father with all her heart. Now she felt very little for him. At times she cursed him. Those times occurred when he sent his servants to raid her stores for his lavish entertainments—and not only was Pershwick involved, but Rethel and Marhill keeps as well. They, too, were hers. He never sent a word to his daughter, but he reaped the benefits of her hard work, taking her profits and rents.

However, he'd had far less success in the last few years as Leonie learned how to outfox the Montwyn steward. When he came calling with his list, her storerooms were nearly empty, her hoards hidden throughout the keep in unlikely places. So also she hid her spices and cloth bought from the merchants of Rethel, for Lady Judith sometimes arrived with the steward, and Lady Judith felt she could make free with anything she found at Pershwick.

Leonie's cunning sometimes went awry when she couldn't remember all of her hiding places. But rather than give up the plan or confide her deceit to the Pershwick priest and ask his help, she convinced Father Bennet to teach her to read and write. That way, she was able to keep records of her maze of hiding places. Now her serfs no longer faced starvation, and her own table was full. No thanks were due her father for any of that.

Leonie stood for the rinsing and let Wilda wrap her

in a warm bedrobe because she would not be leaving her room again that night. Aunt Beatrix sat by the fire with her embroidery, lost in her own world, as usual. The oldest of Elisabeth's sisters, Beatrix had long been a widow. She had lost her dower lands to her husband's relatives when he died, and hadn't married again. She insisted she liked it that way. She had lived with her brother, the earl of Shefford, until Elisabeth's death. Soon after, Leonie was cast on her vassal, Guibert Fitzalan, and Aunt Beatrix felt it her duty to stay and take care of her niece.

More likely it was Leonie who did the care-taking, for Beatrix was a timid woman. Even the isolation of Pershwick keep hadn't made her bolder. Being one of the first children born to the late earl of Shefford, she had known the earl at his stormiest, whereas Elisabeth, the youngest, knew the earl as a mellow man and a doting father.

Leonie did not know the present earl, whose holding was in the north, far from the midlands. When she'd reached a marriageable age and begun to hope for a husband, she had wanted to contact her uncle. Aunt Beatrix had explained, kindly, that with eight brothers and sisters and dozens of nieces and nephews besides his own six children and *their* children, the earl would surely not concern himself with the daughter of a sister who had not married well and was now dead.

Leonie, fifteen then and closed away from the world, began to think she would never marry. But pride soon asserted itself, pride that didn't permit her to ask for help from relatives who neither knew her nor ever inquired after her.

After a time she began to think she might be better off without a husband. There wasn't the usual threat of being sent to a nunnery, and she was lady of her own keep, independent, answerable only to a father who never approached her and seemed unlikely to show any further interest in her.

It was a unique and enviable position, she told herself after those first longings for romance had been stifled. Most brides did not even know their husbands before they were wed, and were likely to find themselves the property of an old man, a cruel man, or an indifferent man. Only serfs married for love.

So Leonie came to believe she was fortunate. The only thing she wanted to change was her isolation, and that was what caused her to venture alone to Crewel to see the tourney.

Having never seen a tourney before, she was impelled to go. King Henry's policy was to forbid all tourneys except a few held in special circumstances and with his permission. In the past, too many tourneys had ended in bloody battles. In France a tourney might be found at any time in almost any place, and many knights became rich by traveling from one to another. It was not that way in England.

The tourney at Crewel was exciting at the start. The Black Wolf rode onto the field in full armor, six knights flanking him, all wearing his colors, black and silver, all large and impressive men. The seven opponents were also full-armored. Leonie recognized a few by their banners as vassals of Sir Edmond Montigny. The Black Wolf was, by then, their new overlord.

She had not asked herself why the present lord of Kempston would challenge his new vassals. There were many possible explanations, none of which interested her. What held her attention was the Black Wolf, and the lady who rushed onto the field to give him a token. A bold kiss followed as he swept the lady up into his arms. Was she his wife?

The crowd cheered the kiss, and then all at once the melee began, a mock battle in which all the contestants took part most ferociously. There were strict rules for a melee, rules which distinguished it from real battle, but the rules were ignored that morning. It was immediately obvious that all seven opposing knights meant to unseat the Black Wolf. They succeeded quickly, and it was only the swift work of his own knights that prevented him from being defeated. He even had to call them back from giving chase as his opponents fled the field.

It was over all too soon, and Leonie went home in disappointment, her only satisfaction being the knowledge that some of the Black Wolf's new vassals had apparently rejected him as their overlord. Why? She could not guess what he had done. It was enough to know that his taking possession of Kempston had not gone easily.

Leonie dismissed Wilda and joined her aunt by the fire, staring pensively into the flames, remembering the fire in the forest and wondering what new troubles the future would bring.

"You are worried about our new neighbor?"

Leonie glanced sideways at Beatrix, surprised. She didn't want her aunt burdened with this.

"What is there to worry about?" Leonie hedged.

"Bless you, child, you need not hide your troubles from me. Do you think I am not aware of what happens around me?"

Leonie believed just that. "It is of no great importance, Aunt Beatrix."

"Then we will have no more rude young knights coming to threaten us with angry words?"

Leonie shrugged. "They are only angry words. Men like to bluster and snarl."

"Oho, do I not know it."

They both laughed, for of course Beatrix knew more about men than Leonie did, confined as she had been since the age of thirteen.

Leonie confessed, "I thought we would have visitors today, but no one came. Perhaps they do not blame us for this day's trouble."

Beatrix frowned thoughtfully, and her niece asked, "Do you think the Black Wolf might have other plans this time?"

"That is possible. It is a wonder he has not already burned our village."

"He would not dare!" Leonie cried. "He has no proof my serfs have caused his troubles. He has only the accusations of *his* own serfs."

"Yes, but that is enough for most men. Suspicion is enough." Beatrix sighed.

Leonie's anger drained away. "I know. Tomorrow I will go to the village and make certain that henceforth no one leaves Pershwick land for any reason. There will be no more trouble. We must see to that."

Chapter 3

ROLFE d'Ambert threw his helmet hard across the hall the moment he strode in. His squire, newly acquired from King Henry, hurried to catch it. The helmet would need a trip to the armorer before he wore it again, but Rolfe was not thinking of that. Just then, he needed to smash things.

At the hearth across the large hall, Thorpe de la Mare hid his amusement at his young lord's display of temper. It was so like the boy he had been, not the man he was now. Thorpe had seen many such displays in the years he'd served Rolfe's father. The father was dead these nine years and Rolfe's older brother had inherited their father's title and the bulk of his estates in Gascony. The property left to Rolfe was small, but the greedy brother had wanted even that and had outlawed Rolfe from his home.

Thorpe left with Rolfe, giving up his comfortable position to follow the young knight rather than serve the brother. The years since had been very good, years of fighting as mercenaries, growing rich from the ransoms won at tourneys. Rolfe was now twenty and nine years to Thorpe's two score and seven, yet Thorpe never regretted letting the younger man lead him. Other men felt the same way, and Rolfe had become a leader to nine knights and nearly two hundred mercenaries, all of whom had chosen to stay with him now that he was settled.

But was Rolfe settled? Thorpe knew how Rolfe felt about Henry's generosity. The estate gave him more aggravation than he had experienced in years. Much more, and Rolfe would be ready to leave it all and return to France. The estate was something that existed only as an honor, for it gave nothing tangible and drained his purse daily.

"Did you hear, Thorpe?"

"The servants have talked of nothing else since the woodcutter moved into the keep for the night," Thorpe replied as Rolfe sat down heavily in the chair next to him.

"Damn me!"

Rolfe slammed a fist down on the small table beside him, opening a crack down its middle. Thorpe kept his expression carefully blank.

"I have had enough!" Rolfe bellowed. "The well fouled, the herds scattered into the forest, the serfs' few animals stolen, and this was the third fire. How long to rebuild this hut?"

"Two days with several men working quickly."

"And so the fields will be neglected. How can I wage war when my flanks are forever being nipped at? Am I to leave Crewel and come back to find nothing left of it, the serfs run off, the fields barren?"

Thorpe knew better than to answer.

"Do you want men sent to Pershwick again?" Thorpe ventured carefully. "Will you punish the serfs?"

Rolfe shook his head. "A serf would not act alone. No, serfs follow orders, and it is the one who gives orders that I want."

"Then you will have to look elsewhere than Pershwick, for I met Sir Guibert Fitzalan, and I swear that when he heard why I had come, his surprise was too real to be feigned. He is not a man who would stoop to this knavery."

"Yet someone there is urging serfs to mischief."

"I agree. But you cannot take the keep. Pershwick belongs to Montwyn, and Sir William of Montwyn has enough keeps that if you try, he can summon more men than you are prepared to meet."

"I would not lose," Rolfe said darkly.

"But you would lose your advantage here. Look you how long it has taken just to win two of the other seven keeps belonging to Kempston."

"Three."

Thorpe raised his brow. "Three? How?"

"I suppose I can thank Pershwick, for when I reached Kenil Keep today I was so furious over what happened here that I ordered the walls destroyed. The siege is finished there."

"And Kenil useless until the walls are rebuilt?" It was the only conclusion.

"I . . . well, yes."

Thorpe said no more. He knew that Rolfe had meant to use catapults only as a last measure in taking the seven keeps. It was part of a bold plan, conceived when the tourney failed in bringing the rebellious vassals to heel. The tourney had been for the benefit of those vassals, giving them a chance to meet their new lord and judge his skills. But instead of merely testing his skills with theirs, they had tried to kill him. Rolfe was therefore left in the unenviable position of owning eight keeps of which seven would not open to him.

Waging war against one's own property was never profitable, and least profitable was to destroy that property. So Rolfe recruited five hundred soldiers from King Henry's forces. Harwick and Axeford keeps made terms to surrender without any damage sustained once the bulk of Rolfe's army appeared outside their gates. The army then moved to Kenil, and now, after a month and a half, Kenil was taken.

Rolfe sat there brooding and Thorpe took a moment to wonder why Lady Amelia had not come down. She had probably heard Rolfe's voice raised in anger and decided to hide. Rolfe's mistress would not know him well enough yet to know he would not take his anger out on her.

Hesitantly, Thorpe asked, "You do see that now is not the time to attack the east? You must clean your own house before you go looking at another's."

"I see it," Rolfe said testily. "But tell me what I am to *do*. I offered to purchase Pershwick, but Sir William wrote that he could not sell it because Pershwick is part of his daughter's dower lands, left her by her mother. Blast that nicety. The daughter is under his rule, is she not? He could force her to sell it and give her another property."

"Perhaps the mother's will is written just so, and he cannot."

Rolfe scowled. "I tell you, Thorpe, I will not stand for another offense."

"You could always marry the daughter. Then you would have the keep without having to pay for it."

Rolfe's eyes, black since he'd entered the hall, began returning to their normal dark brown. Thorpe nearly choked. "I was but jesting!"

"I know." Rolfe mused thoughtfully, too thoughtfully for Thorpe's liking.

"Rolfe, for the love of God, do not take this idea to heart. No one weds merely to get a few serfs under control. Go over there and knock some heads together, if you must. Put fear into them."

"That is not my way. The innocent would suffer with the guilty. If I could catch one of the culprits, I would make an example of him, but always by the time I get there, they are long gone."

"There are many reasons for marriage, but to quell the serfs of a neighbor is not a good reason."

"No, but to gain peace where peace is wanted is," Rolfe countered.

"Rolfe!"

"Do you know anything about this daughter of Sir William's?"

Thorpe sighed with exasperation. "How could I know? I am as new in England as you."

Rolfe turned toward his men, gathered at the opposite end of the hall. Three of his knights had returned with him from Kenil, as well as a small troop of men-at-arms. Two were from Brittany, but Sir Evarard was from the south of England.

"Know you my neighbor, Sir William of Montwyn, Evarard?"

Evarard approached. "Aye, my lord. At one time he was often at court, as I was before I came of age."

"Has he many children?"

"I cannot say how many he might have now, but he had only one, a daughter, when he was last at court. That was five or six years ago, before his wife died. I understand he has a young wife now, but of children from this union I do not know."

"Know you this daughter?"

"I saw her once with her mother, the lady Elisabeth. I remember wondering at the time how such a beautiful lady could have such an uncomely child."

"There!" Thorpe interjected. "Now will you let the fool idea rest, Rolfe?"

Rolfe ignored his old friend. "Uncomely, Evarard? How so?"

"She had great red splotches covering every part of her skin that could be seen. It was a shame, for the shape of her face might have foretold beauty like her mother's."

"What more can you tell me of her?"

"I only saw her once, and she hid behind her mother's skirts."

"Her name?"

Sir Evarard frowned thoughtfully. "I am sorry, my lord. I cannot remember."

"It is Lady Leonie, my lord."

All three men turned toward the maid who had spoken. Rolfe did not like the servants to be so attuned to his conversations. He frowned.

"And what is *your* name, girl?"

"Mildred," she replied with proper meekness. Now that the lord's eyes were upon her, she could have torn her tongue out for speaking up. Sir Rolfe's temper was a terrible thing to behold.

"How do you know the lady Leonie?"

Mildred took heart at the quiet inquiry. "She—she came here often from Pershwick when—"

"Pershwick!" Rolfe bellowed. "She lives there? Not at Montwyn?"

Mildred blanched. She was beholden to Lady Leonie and would have died rather than hurt her. She knew her lord blamed Pershwick for the damage Crewel had suffered since his taking it over.

"My lord, please," Mildred said quickly. "The lady is all that is kind. When the Crewel leech left my mother to die of a disease he could not cure, Lady Leonie saved her. She knows much of the healing arts, my lord. She would never cause a hurt, I swear it."

"She does live at Pershwick?" At Mildred's reluctant nod, Rolfe demanded, "Why there and not with her father?"

Mildred stepped back, eyes wide with fear. She could not say anything bad of another lord, even one her new lord might not like. She would surely be beaten for criticizing her betters.

Rolfe understood her fear and softened his tone. "Come, Mildred, tell me what you know. You need not fear me."

"It—it is only that my former master, Sir Edmond, claimed Sir William liked—drink too well since his first wife died. Sir Edmond would not let his son wed Lady Leonie because Sir William swears he has no daughter. He said an alliance with her would gain them naught. She was sent to Pershwick when her mother died and has been separated from her father since, or so I have heard."

"So Lady Leonie and Sir Edmond's son were . . . close?"

"She and Sir Alain were only a year apart in age, my lord. Yes, they were very close."

"Damn me!" Rolfe stormed. "So she *has* set her serfs to plague me! She does it out of love of the Montignys!"

"No, my lord." Mildred risked herself again. "She would not."

Rolfe paid no attention to this declaration for he had already dismissed the maid from his mind. "It is no wonder our complaints were ignored if the lady herself is set against me. But if I make war on Pershwick, I make war on a woman. What do you think now of your jest, Thorpe?"

"I think you will do what you will do." Thorpe

sighed. "But do consider whether you want a deformed creature as wife before you rush ahead."

Rolfe waved that aside. "What law says I must live with the lady?"

"Then why take her to wife? Be reasonable, Rolfe. All these years you avoided marriage when many great beauties were willing."

"I was landless then, Thorpe, and I could not wed without a home to offer my wife."

Thorpe began to say more, but Rolfe said flatly, "What I want most now is peace."

"Peace? Or revenge?"

Rolfe shrugged. "I will not hurt the lady, but she will regret causing me any ill if that is what she intends. See how she likes being confined in Pershwick the rest of her days and her people hanged—for the slightest wrongdoing. I *will* have an end to these troubles."

"What of Lady Amelia?" Thorpe murmured.

Rolfe frowned. "She came here by her own choice. If she wishes to leave, so be it. But if she wishes to stay, she is welcome. My taking a wife will not change my affections in other regards. At least my taking of *this* wife will not. I have no duty to please her, not after all she has done. The lady Leonie will have no say in what I do."

Thorpe shook his head and said no more. He could only hope a good night's sleep would bring Rolfe to his senses.

Chapter 4

ROLFE paced in the anteroom outside the king's chamber. It was good of Henry to see him so soon, but Rolfe hated asking favors, even if this favor would cost Henry no more than words, words on parchment. Henry, on the other hand, loved doing favors. Rolfe's new position as one of Henry's barons had been such a favor, given without warning during a friendly talk the last time Rolfe was in London. The Kempston lands had come unexpectedly into their conversation, and Henry asked Rolfe if he wanted Kempston.

In truth, Henry had long wanted to reward Rolfe for saving his natural son Geoffrey's life. Until then, Rolfe had refused all offers, staunchly maintaining that keeping the son safe was only his duty. To be sure, that was not the first time Rolfe had helped Henry. But Henry was surprised when Rolfe accepted the offer of Kempston, for in truth Kempston was no prize and would have to be won at great cost. He immediately offered Rolfe something better, now that Rolfe was finally showing an interest in settling down. "Something closer to home? I can arrange—"

Rolfe put up a hand to interrupt before the king could tempt him further. "It is the challenge I want from Kempston, my lord. I could buy estates aplenty in Gascony, but I do not call Gascony home any longer, nor do I want land I cannot earn. I will take Kempston and thank you for it."

"Thank me?" Henry seemed embarrassed. "It is I who must thank you, for in truth I was loath to pay an army to secure it. Now it will cost me nothing and I will have a man I know I can trust to curb the lawlessness in that area. *You* do *me* a service, Rolfe, and this is not how I meant to reward you for all your other service. What else can I give you? A wife who will bring you a large estate?"

"No, my lord." Rolfe laughed. "Let me secure Kempston before I think of a wife."

Ironically, a wife was the very reason Rolfe was there, pacing the anteroom. His offer for Leonie of Montwyn had been flatly refused.

There were ways other than marriage to end the troubles, he knew that. He could always hire more men to patrol the borders of his land and keep her serfs out until Kempston was secured. But then, the cost of hiring enough men to patrol the whole area would be huge, he told himself.

"Damn me, she will not dent my purse more than she has already!" Rolfe exploded aloud, then saw to his embarrassment that Henry had entered the room.

"Who will not dent your purse?" Henry asked, chuckling as he came forward. "The lady Amelia? Have you brought her with you?"

"No, my lord. She is in the country," Rolfe replied, uncomfortable with the line of questioning.

Rolfe was never at ease in the king's presence. Rolfe was the bigger man by far, but Henry was the king of England and unlikely to encourage anyone to disregard the fact. He was also heavily built, with broad shoulders, a thick neck, and the powerful arms of a fighter. Henry had red hair which he kept cut short in the current shaggy fashion, and which emphasized his florid face. He was not lavish in his dress, unlike Queen Eleanor, though no one saw her often since Henry had confined her to Winchester for instigating the battles between him and his sons.

Henry was in superb shape for a man forty years old. He could outwalk and outride his courtiers and usually exhausted anyone who tried to keep up with him. He was a man of such energy that he seldom even sat down. His meals were usually taken standing up, walking about his hall. Court etiquette prevented everyone else from sitting as well, a bother much complained about, though never in the king's hearing.

After the amenities had been dispensed with and they were seated, each with a silver goblet of wine, Henry asked with a twinkle in his gray eyes, "I did not expect to see you for some time. Have you come so soon to curse me for Kempston?"

"All goes well there, my lord," Rolfe quickly assured him. "Four of the eight keeps are mine, and the other four are closed tightly, waiting to be secured."

"So the Black Wolf has lived up to his reputation!" Henry cried, delighted.

Rolfe flushed. He hated the name, certain it was inspired by his dark looks rather than by any wolflike prowess. It embarrassed him.

"My coming has less to do with Kempston as a whole than with Crewel particularly, your majesty. I have a neighbor there who has set her people against mine. I am not a man to deal with domestics."

"What fighter is?" Henry chuckled. "But you say 'her people'? Your neighbor is a woman? I can think of no widow in that area."

"She is no widow, nor wife to an absent lord. She

is daughter to Sir William of Montwyn and residing on her dower property which lies next to Crewel."

"Sir William." Henry considered, thoughtful. "Ah, now I have him. A baron who wed one of my earl's daughters, the lady Elisabeth I believe, yes, daughter of Shefford. But he closed himself up in his estates some six years ago when Elisabeth died. A tragic affair. They were a love match, and he suffered terribly at her death."

"He has closed his daughter up in Pershwick and forgotten her, I am told."

"What do you mean?"

"It seems the man does not wish to be reminded he has a daughter."

Henry shook his head. "I remember her. Not a comely child, but spirited. She had a nervous disorder, I believe her mother said. The poor woman was forever having to run after the child with medicine. You say Sir William is neglecting her? There is no excuse for that. Why, the girl would be around twenty years old. She should have been wed long ago. Even if finding her a husband proved difficult, there is always *some* man who can be bought, isn't there? If she is not for the church, then she must have a husband."

"I agree, my lord." Rolfe leaped at the ideal opening. "And I would be that husband."

There was a shocked silence, and then Henry began to laugh. "You jest, Rolfe. That face of yours sends my loveliest ladies swooning, yet you would settle for a plain girl?"

Rolfe flinched. He supposed it was too much to hope that the ugly duckling had grown into a swan.

"Few marriages are made for preference," Rolfe replied stoically.

"But . . . you are your own man. No one is telling

you you *must* marry this girl, so why would you wish to?"

"Not counting the domestic peace she will bring me, she and I are neighbors. She has lived there for a long time, and can help me in dealings with my other neighbors. Then, too, she has retainers. I have nine knights who follow me, but some are not suited to command and I need men to hold the other seven keeps."

"I can see your reasoning, Rolfe, but I can find you a wife who can accomplish at least half your purpose and is pleasing to look at."

Rolfe shrugged. "There are always women like Amelia."

Henry understood that very well. He was living openly as man and wife with Princess Alice of France. As long as a man had his mistress, what matter his wife's looks? It was true.

"Very well," Henry concurred. "Is it only my permission you require?"

"More than that, Your Majesty. I have offered for the girl and was refused. Without explanation."

"To deny his only daughter a husband?" Henry growled. "By God, you will have her three weeks hence. I will have the banns posted immediately and my messenger will reach Sir William on the morrow." Then, in a less aggrieved tone, he asked, "But you are certain this is what you want, Rolfe? You have no hesitation about this marriage?"

He certainly did, but that need not be mentioned. "I am certain," he declared, and Henry grinned. "Then you will be pleased to know the lady is sole heir to Sir William, and Montwyn is worth five knights' fees, as I recall. She was also her mother's sole heir, and her mother left her a dower of three keeps." Henry chuckled here. "The vassal at Rethel has six sons you might find useful. Lady Leonie is also niece to the earl of Shefford, and there are other uncles and aunts, most of them well placed. It does not hurt a man to be well connected, eh?"

Rolfe was shocked. She was an heiress with a much richer dowry than he'd known about, and highborn relatives as well. He supposed all this ought to please him, but in truth he had believed her a solitary woman, and now he began to wonder if his anger had made him take on more than he wanted to.

Chapter 5

LADY Judith did not know why Rolfe d'Ambert wanted to marry Leonie. If she had known she would have been furious. As it was, Judith was in a state of near hysteria.

She had put off telling William of the king's order in hope that something would come about to stop the wedding. But it was the day before the wedding and she was in a panic.

She sat at the table on the raised dais waiting for William to join her, having sent a servant to rouse him from sleep. It was morning, and much earlier than William usually woke. She prayed his soggy mind would clear long enough for him to understand, but only long enough for that. To have him sober for any great length of time would jeopardize everything she had accomplished over the years. If William ever realized what she had done, he would kill her.

Judith did not dwell long on that thought. She knew that, given the chance to go back in time, she would do nothing different.

William had destroyed all her dreams. He had been in a drunken stupor caused by grief over the loss of Elisabeth, and emerged from it to find that Judith had taken advantage of his drunken state and tricked him into marriage. He beat her nearly to death for this, and the small scar she bore on her left cheek had remained. She would never forgive him for it.

Vanity was her sin and her undoing. She had been so sure William would accept her as his wife and be happy about it. After all, six years ago she'd been a beautiful young woman lacking only a dowry. Her high-boned cheeks, jewellike green eyes, and heavy, dark blond hair set her apart from most other women. Many a man had wanted to marry her for her beauty alone, but none were as well landed as William of Montwyn.

But William, it turned out, did not own all Judith believed he did. Three of his keeps belonged to his daughter. Had she known that, Judith would never have tricked William into marriage.

He was in such a rage over the marriage that Judith had had to lie and say she was with child. It was either that or be cast out immediately. Of course, Judith could never have a child. An abortion the year before had ruined her womb, but William did not know that.

To protect herself from the time when William would ask about her supposed pregnancy, she encouraged his inclination to stay drunk. And she had kept him in a state of drunken forgetfulness since then. She didn't care that she had helped to ruin the man, for she'd hated him from the day he beat her. She hated him still. He was only a drunk now. She could not bear to be near him.

Judith took charge of Montwyn, indulging her every whim, from owning costly gowns and jewels to keeping handsome lovers near her. Everything was in her charge, and she had seen to it right after marrying William that his daughter was not at Montwyn to interfere.

It had been easy at first to tell William that Leonie

was visiting relatives. Later, she found she could make him believe that he saw Leonie regularly, so ill with drunkenness and grief was he. He was, within a short time, permanently disoriented. He could be told anything, be made to believe anything.

Relatives and neighbors stopped inquiring after Leonie, thinking she had gone to Pershwick of her own choice rather than stay with a drunken father. Leonie was told that her father wanted nothing to do with her, and she was forbidden to visit Montwyn. One way or another, Judith managed to keep everyone from learning the truth.

In the meantime Leonie's dowry remained part of Montwyn and Judith spent all the profits. She turned down Leonie's marriage offers, in William's name, for she had no intention of giving up the use of Leonie's land. If killing the girl could have brought that land to Montwyn permanently she might even have killed her, but Elisabeth's acursed will left the land solely to Leonie. If she died without issue, the land would revert to Shefford.

Now, by the king's order, she was being forced to give up the land. Who was Rolfe d'Ambert to be so favored by His Majesty? Judith had dealt with both his offers, first for Pershwick, then for the girl herself, so she knew it was Pershwick the suitor really wanted. Why hadn't he just taken the keep by force if he wanted it so badly? This was infuriating, she told herself for the tenth time as she paced her room. She had managed everything so cleverly, and now this!

"Judith."

She started. She hadn't heard William approach. When she looked at him, she was shocked. He looked horrid, far worse than usual. William was sick every morning until he'd had his first drink, but today he seemed barely able to pick up his goblet. She would have to have her say before he finished even this first drink.

"I have made all the arrangements, William, as you bid me," Judith began quietly. "We can leave for Pershwick as soon as you are ready."

"Pershwick?"

"Where Leonie is, William. We will stay the night there, then go on to Crewel for the wedding."

"Wedding?" He looked at her squarely, the whites of his eyes so heavily veined with red as to be a hideous dark pink. "I do not recall—"

"William, William, you cannot have forgotten your own daughter's wedding," Judith said with feigned exasperation. Of course, she hadn't told him and he hadn't forgotten.

"Nonsense, woman," he said, "Leonie is a child. What wedding?"

"Only a father would still see her as a child. She is nearly twenty, William. You would not see her married. You turned down every offer for her. So the king has taken matters into his hands. You read his order. Shall I bring it so you may read it again? King Henry posted the banns himself. Leonie is to wed Sir Rolfe d'Ambert at Crewel."

William shook his head wearily. This was all too much to grasp. Leonie nearly twenty? What offers had he refused? Henry ordering his child's marriage? By Christ's holy blood, he could not picture his daughter grown up. He saw her still as a child, with those large gray eyes so like her mother's. Married?

"I do not remember signing a wedding contract, Judith. Were Elisabeth's stipulations met?"

Judith frowned. "What stipulations?"

"Leonie's dowry is to remain hers to do with as she

will. It was her mother's wish that she be protected in this way. Elisabeth was protected in our marriage, and she was determined that Leonie have the same advantage."

Judith gasped. Would it make a difference to d'Ambert if he knew? Probably not, for he would realize that once he had Leonie, he could force her to do whatever he wanted. He could even force her to sell the land if that was his wish.

"You need not worry about the stipulations." Judith spoke truthfully for once. "The contracts will be signed on the morrow before the vows are spoken, so you can make them known then. You can even have the contract drawn up now if you wish, before we leave."

"Yes, that would be best. Who is Rolfe d'Ambert?" He was embarrassed to be asking, for he must surely know.

"The new lord of Kempston."

"But Sir Edmond—"

"Dead these many months, William. His son fled before he could be banished. Surely you remember. You never liked him. You suspected his knavery long before others complained of it to the king."

William sighed. What good to say again and again that he could not remember? He felt as if he had been asleep for years. He set his wine goblet aside, but his hand began to shake uncontrollably. A little would steady him, and he reached for the wine again. Only a little. He must see to the marriage contract. And if he was to see Leonie, he wanted her not to see him in this terrible condition.

Chapter 6

LEONIE was told that the large group of travelers nearing Pershwick were from Montwyn. The size of the group gave her pause, but she imagined Lady Judith was paying her another visit and was, this time, traveling with more servants than usual.

She took her usual precautions, sending all her able-bodied men inside to keep to the tower quarters to pose as part of her garrison. She could not argue overmuch if Pershwick servants were recruited for Montwyn, but she protested most vehemently when it came to depleting her men-at-arms.

She sent a servant to the village to warn those who felt the need to take to the woods until it was safe. And she sent Wilda and two other young maids to her chamber, where they would remain safely out of sight. Wilda was brazen enough to protest. She did not wish to miss the excitement of having guests. Leonie snapped, "You wish to be raped in the garden like Ethelinda? Did you see how she looked after Richer was finished with her?"

Wilda was subdued by Leonie's anger and disgust. Richer Calveley treated Lady Judith with the greatest care and deference when he escorted her to Pershwick, making Leonie wonder about their true relationship. When he came to Pershwick without Lady Judith, he showed a different character, as foul as any Leonie had ever known. By Ethelinda's account, he took pleasure in hurting her, and although Leonie had sent a complaint to Montwyn, nothing had come of it.

Aunt Beatrix and Leonie joined Sir Guibert in the hall to greet their visitors. Leonie steeled herself for another unpleasant encounter with Judith, but nothing prepared her for the terrible sight she beheld as an old man approached with Judith. She barely recognized him. Her father—here? She went dizzy with a sudden swirl of fierce emotions: bitterness, hate, sorrow for his pathetic condition and the dissipation in his haggard face. His face proclaimed clearly that he had become a drunkard. But there was love in that face, too, love for Leonie.

"Leonie?"

There was surprise in William's voice, as if he were not sure she was his daughter. It brought Leonie's bitterness surging upward, blocking out all the rest. Indeed, why should he know her? She was a woman now, not a child. He hadn't seen her in six years. Six years!

"You do us honor, my lord," Leonie said coldly. "Seat yourselves by the fire and I will see to refreshment."

William was confused by her icy manner. "What is amiss, dear heart? You are not pleased with your husband?"

The endearment sent a stab through Leonie's heart, but shock followed that. "Husband?"

"You play, Leonie," Judith interjected. "You know your father means the man you will marry on the morrow."

"What?"

"Do not feign innocence, Leonie," Judith replied wearily. "The banns have been posted. The marriage is by the king's order. You know your father sent you notice as soon as the king's messenger came." She turned to her husband. "Is that not so, William?" William played right into the performance by looking thoroughly bewildered. "Do not say you forgot to send word to her! The poor girl has only this day to prepare! Oh, William, how could you forget such a thing!"

Sir Guibert was as shocked as Leonie, but he couldn't allow his mind to whirl, as Leonie's was doing. Guibert's life would change now, just as hers would. Her husband would be her lord and master. Guibert and Leonie's other vassals would be asked to renew their oath to her at the wedding, an act that signified their accepting her husband. There was no question of whether Guibert would renew his oath to Leonie. Whether he approved her husband or not, he could never forsake her. But her other vassals might choose to leave her.

"Who is my lady's husband?" Guibert asked, and Judith smiled, feeling the worst was over. "You will be pleased to know that he is your neighbor, the new lord of Kempston."

In the shocked silence that followed, Guibert looked at Leonie, to see all the color leaving her face. She said not a word. He knew why. She could not refuse the king's will, no matter how she felt about it. And it was time she married, Guibert thought. He had long thought so. She would get used to the match. She would have to.

Leonie wordlessly turned and fled the hall. Closing herself in her room, she threw herself on her bed and sobbed tears of self-pity. Her father felt so little for her that he could wait to tell her of her wedding until the day before it was to happen. Did he care nothing for her? What had become of the loving man who had been a real father once?

She finally remembered that she was not alone and looked around. Her wide-eyed maids had never seen her cry before. Roughly, she wiped her face, angry that she had given in to emotions so childishly. Anger was a boon, bringing her spirit back.

She sent the maids to the kitchen with orders about dinner, then sat by her hearth, glad to be alone to think. She knew why the king was interfering in her life. He wasn't concerned over her unmarried state. His interference had been requested by the Black Wolf. She was certain of that, but she could not guess what the man wanted of her.

It had been nearly a month since the burning of the woodcutter's hut, and Leonie had ordered that no more of her people venture onto Crewel land. The man's troubles had ceased, hadn't they? If they had not, she might think that he wanted to marry her in order to end those troubles. But since there had been peace for a month, that could not be his reason. It was true she had a handsome dowry, but most alliances were made for the aid they would bring as well as for money, and her father's aid could not be counted on. So that was not the Black Wolf's reason. And the lord of Kempston had never seen her, so there was no reason to be found there either. Why did he want her . . .?

Leonie gasped as Alain Montigny's words came back to her. "I must leave. I have heard enough about the Black Wolf to know I cannot stay and resist his taking possession of my land. He would kill me. He would not care that I am innocent of the crimes he believes me guilty of."

"What crimes?" Leonie had asked, frantic.

"What matter the crimes!" Alain cried. "The king

has killed my father and dispossessed me so that he may give Kempston to his French mercenary, Rolfe d'Ambert, that black wolf of the devil's. No wonder he is called that! He is a ravaging beast. I was not even allowed a trial!" Alain wailed.

Leonie was fired by Alain's rage. She had known him all her life. They had played together as children, and she had even thought of marrying him. But the weakness of his character showed itself as he grew older, and she knew he would not make a good husband. But they were friends, and the king's injustice was appalling—worse because Alain did not have the courage to fight for himself, and there was no one to help him.

"If you want to make a stand, Alain, you know I would call up my men."

"No," he stopped her nervously, "I know you would aid me, Leonie, but I cannot ask it of you. The Black Wolf is too powerful. He comes even now with his army to take Kempston. If the king were not behind him—" He let the thought linger, as if the king were the only thing that kept him from fighting.

"Where will you go, Alain?"

"I have a cousin in Ireland."

"So far?"

"I must. If I stay in England, the Wolf will find me and kill me. It is true, Leonie," he insisted. "It is not enough that Henry has given my home to the Black Wolf. The bastard wants me dead so that I can never claim Kempston. I cannot tell you the stories I have heard of him, for they would make you fear your new neighbor. But you should know he is like Henry in that he never forgets an ill, nor relaxes a hatred. Step carefully with him, Leonie. Be warned."

She should have heeded Alain's warning and tried

to be a peaceful neighbor. It was too late now. *He never forgets an ill, nor relaxes a hatred.*

A feeling of dread crept over Leonie. She had caused Rolfe d'Ambert trouble, and he had reason to hate her.

"You have nothing to do, Leonie?"

Leonie swung around to find Judith in her room. "There is naught that needs my attention, madame."

"I am glad to hear it. I was afeared you would balk."

Leonie smiled tightly. "As to that, madame, I can say only that the king's choice is not acceptable."

"I do not blame you, my dear. If I knew my future husband was interested only in controlling my land, I would not like it either."

So that was it! "You know that?"

"D'Ambert tried to buy Pershwick, you see. Of course William had to tell him he could not sell it, that it was part of your dowry. Then he asked for you, but your dear father would not give you to a man interested only in your land."

"My father refused his offer?"

"Of course he did. But you see what came of that. The man went straight to the king, and now d'Ambert will have you, will you nill you."

"No, he will not. I said he is unacceptable. I mean it. I will not marry Rolfe d'Ambert."

Judith's eyes gleamed for a moment. "But you will. In truth, I wish you had a choice, Leonie, but with the king involving himself in this matter, you must see you do not. It would break your father's heart to have to force you, but force you he would. He cannot ignore the king's order."

"I can."

"Do not be a silly chit!" Judith snapped, visualizing a scene between father and daughter that might reveal too much and ruin everything. "Henry cares nothing for any wishes but his own, and it is his wish that you marry d'Ambert. Your father will not defy the king, nor will you."

Leonie jumped to her feet, her temper flaring. "Leave me, Judith. We have no more to say to each other."

"But we do," Judith replied grimly. "You will swear to me by all that is holy that you will wed the present lord of Kempston."

"I swear I will not!"

"Fool!" Judith spat. "You bring this on yourself. Richer!" Judith shouted, and the man Leonie feared stepped into the room. "You know what must be done," she told him. "Do not leave her until she has sworn."

With that Judith left the room. She went to make certain the hall was deserted and would remain so for a while. No one must hear.

Leonie tried to calm the wild beating of her heart, prepared to withstand the worst from this large brute. Long shaggy hair and a thick beard suited his rough manner. Murky blue eyes impaled her with a strange light, unnerving her badly. But it was Richer's slow grin that made her stomach turn over in terror.

Chapter 7

IN Crewel that night, a different kind of fear was taking its toll on Lady Amelia. She did not want to be sent back to court where she had been just another of Princess Alice's ladies-in-waiting, just another pretty face among so many. She had no power there, no control over her own life. She must forever dance attendance on the princess, do her bidding, suffer her moods.

A landless widow without relatives could expect few prospects. More important, Amelia had found being a wife not nearly as desirable as being a mistress. She had been her husband's mistress before they wed and her circumstances changed so drastically afterward that she was not at all displeased when he died. A man will not strive to please his wife as he does his mistress, for a wife cannot leave him, while a mistress can.

She knew, too, that the quality of lovemaking from a husband could not be compared with that of a lover. Perhaps the church had much to do with that, preaching that lovemaking was solely for procreation and not to be enjoyed. Amelia's husband had been an attentive lover until they wed, and then he looked on their joining as a duty and, like other duties, best done quickly.

No, Amelia was not fool enough to want another marriage, not even marriage with her current lover, who was the most handsome of all the men she had taken to her bed. But she also did not want to leave him. He might be abrupt, even prone to rages, but her position as Rolfe d'Ambert's mistress had turned out to be so much better than she could have hoped for. She was treated with respect, almost as if she were the lady of Crewel Keep. She had power here, as much as any wife would have, and she loved it. There was no other woman of rank here, only servants, no other woman she must answer to. Here there was only Rolfe, and he asked nothing of her that she wasn't willing to do.

But Amelia did not deceive herself over the situation. She had all that she wanted here, but it was only by Rolfe's will that she had it. When he finished with her and sent her back to court, there would be nothing she could do about it. All she could do was delay that time and wheedle as many trinkets and gifts from him as she could so that, when the time came for parting, she might be able to buy a house in London where she could sell her favors.

If Rolfe put her aside now, she would have to return to the princess or look for a new lover. She knew she would never find another one like Rolfe, a man willing to take her into his home. It was only because he was unmarried that she had managed that.

It was late when Rolfe entered his chamber and found Amelia ensconced in his large bed. She was not sleeping. She watched him as he crossed to the fire, now burning low. He had not looked her way, and the frown creasing his brow kept her from speaking. Was he thinking how he would tell her they must part?

"Come help me with this armor, Amelia. I have already dismissed that incompetent squire of mine."

So he did know she was there, and awake. The simple request told her so many things that she wanted to laugh. He had not forgotten her! He meant to join her in the bed. That he expected to do so on the night before he was to wed told her what he felt about his intended bride.

Amelia slipped from the bed. She did not reach for her bedrobe. She was a tall, statuesque woman, twenty-three, with a sleek body of which she was proud. She did not need to resort to hidden bindings to attain a stunning effect, even in the form-fitting clothes of the day. Naked, she carried herself proudly, her chestnut hair flowing down her back, her green eyes sleepily seductive.

Rolfe watched her approaching slowly. She saw the immediate effect she was having on him.

"Sit, my lord," she purred. "I am not tall enough to lift your heavy mail from you."

Bemused, Rolfe moved to a stool by the hearth. Amelia caught the hem of his chain mail and lifted it, then brought it over his head as he sat down. Some men remained in their armor for days when they were doing battle, and stank worse than an untended stable, but she had never known Rolfe to do so. He had an odor of sweat about him now that was a clean smell, his own smell. It was pleasant.

"You have been away several days, Rolfe," she said, adding a little pout as she bent down to untie his cross-garters. "I began to wonder if I would see you again before your wedding."

He grunted and Amelia smiled to herself. How much did she risk saying about the wedding? "Sir Evarard has been busy hunting for the feast," Amelia continued. "I myself saw to the cleaning of the hall, for your steward was too busy."

This was a lie. She never bothered with supervising servants, but Rolfe didn't know this. She wanted him to think she didn't mind that he was marrying, that she intended to help.

Amelia next removed his tunic and undershirt, but with such slow deliberation that Rolfe yanked her onto his lap before she could put the clothing aside. She feigned a squeal of protest, and he fastened his lips to hers in a heated kiss.

She felt his urgency, but was unmoved except to feel satisfaction in knowing he wanted her so badly. She leaned back from him, bracing her hands against his chest so he could not capture her lips again. "Then you do still want me?" she asked him.

"What fool question is this?" He frowned. "Does it seem I do not?"

"I was not sure you would, my lord, when I heard of your marriage." She spoke very quietly, as though wounded.

"You need not concern yourself with that," Rolfe replied gruffly.

"But I must, my lord. I have been so afeared you would send me away." The tears sprang to her eyes, just as she'd expected they would.

"Why should I?"

Amelia nearly lost her whole campaign by showing surprise, but she quickly recovered.

"It is my wish to stay, Rolfe, but . . . your wife may have something to say about it."

"She will not."

"You must not be accustomed to women's jealousies if you can say that. If she knows that you favor me in any way, she will demand that I leave."

"She will demand nothing here," he stated flatly. "My will shall be her will."

"But you are not always here, Rolfe." Amelia pouted. "What if she is cruel? What if she beats me?"

He scowled. "Then she will be beaten. I will not have my people living in fear of their mistress."

That was not the answer she was looking for.

"But how can I protect myself from her wrath when you are not here?" Amelia persisted.

"You concern yourself without reason, Amelia. She will not abide here. I marry her for her land, no more."

"Truly?" She could not hide her surprise, and he laughed. "My dear, if I desired her, then I would have no need of you."

Amelia grinned, relief making her almost giddy. "On the morrow, there will be many guests here for the wedding. What do you tell them—"

"That you are my ward."

She put her arms around his neck, rubbing her firm breasts against his chest. "Then my position here will not change, Rolfe? The servants must still do my bidding and—"

"You talk overmuch, woman."

Rolfe fastened his lips over hers. He knew her game and was amused by it. But had he not needed this distraction, he would not have been amused, for he was not a man to be manipulated. If he had not been willing to grant what she asked, the time of asking would have made no difference. He refused to be enslaved by his own desire.

As far as Rolfe was concerned, ladies were silly creatures, good only for sewing and gossiping and making trouble. His mother and her ladies had taught him that. All women used sex to get what they wanted. He had watched his mother work her wiles on his father for years. He had seen the same in every court he had been to. He made it a rule, usually, never to grant a woman anything she asked if she asked it in the bedchamber.

When Rolfe finished with Amelia, she was forgotten. Without the distraction of Amelia, his mind returned to what was troubling him so badly. In a rage, he had decided he wanted Leonie of Montwyn. Another rage had taken him to the king to secure her. Now that the rages were past, he was filled with dread.

He did not want a wife he could feel no pride in and would never love. He planned to confine her to Pershwick, and he told himself it was because of the ills she had caused him, but it was really her reputed ugliness that worried him. Already he was feeling guilty over that. It was not her fault she was ugly. Perhaps her appearance was what caused her to be such a spiteful woman.

Rolfe was sick at heart for what his fool temper had gotten him into. His honor would not let him try to squirm out of the situation, and his guilt mounted each day, thinking of the girl and her expectations. The poor creature was more than likely overjoyed to finally have a suitor, even one she had been doing battle with. Why shouldn't she be pleased? What prospects had she ever had before this one?

His guilt rose to choke him. Perhaps he wouldn't send her away. There was an old tower at Crewel. She could have that for herself. He would not have to see her, and she would not have to bear the disgrace of being sent from her husband's home. Still, her expectations for a child, for a normal married life, would be crushed. He came back to wondering again if he could bed her, whether the sight of her would turn him cold. Every man wanted an heir and he was no different in that. But if the sight of her made it impossible...

For a man whose nerves were usually like steel, these were very uncomfortable feelings. On the morrow, he would have to bed her, at least for that one time, for her parents and the other guests would inspect the wedding sheets the morning after, as was customary. He might choose to forgo some of the customs, such as the bedding ceremony, but there was no way he could avoid the inspecting of the sheets which confirmed the girl's virginity. There was no way to escape it. He would have to bed her or face more jesting taunts than his temper would stand for.

Chapter 8

LEONIE came to at the sound of Wilda's startled cry. She could have cursed the girl for rousing her to the pain.

"What they did to you, my lady!" Wilda wailed. "Your face is black and swollen. May they roast in the fires of hell! May the hand that dared touch you rot and fall off! May—"

"Oh, hush, Wilda!" Leonie snapped, trying to move her jaw as little as possible. "You know how easily I bruise. I am sure I look worse than I feel."

"Truly, my lady?"

"Bring me my mirror."

Leonie tried to grin to ease the girl's anxiety, but her jaw and her cracked and bloodied lips hurt too much to manage it. The polished steel mirror handed her confirmed that she looked like something trampled under the hooves of a great war-horse.

One of her eyes was swollen tightly shut, the other was a mere slit. Blood had dried on her lips and chin and beneath her nose, but it was hardly noticeable against the deep blue-black bruises surrounding the whole of her face. She was loath to imagine what her chest and arms looked like, for Richer had not confined his blows to her head.

She was clothed as fully as she had been when Richer left her. And someone had kept Wilda from coming to her last evening, so she had not disrobed at all. She had, she guessed, lapsed into unconsciousness soon after Richer left, and not wakened since.

"I think I have looked better," Leonie said, setting the mirror down. "I thought he had broken my nose, but now I think it will mend—along with the rest of me."

"How can you jest, my lady?"

"Because it is better than crying, and that is what I will do if I think of what this beating accomplished."

"You will marry him then?"

"You know about it?"

"My lady, the horses are saddled and waiting. Everything is prepared and ready . . . except you."

Leonie would have given anything to stop this, but now that she had given her word, sworn on all that was holy as well as her mother's grave, she would have to marry Rolfe d'Ambert. It did not matter that the vow had been beaten out of her—she had said the words and she would have to abide by them.

Oh, how she wanted to cry. She had been so sure she could withstand Richer's hands, but she was wrong. He had slapped her again and again, and when, her cheeks scarlet, she did not cower or beg, he began using his fists. She had borne as much as she could, believing that the beating could not be worse than whatever the Black Wolf planned for her. But when she realized that Richer would kill her if he was not stopped, and that there was no one to stop him, she had given up. If her father could let this happen, he would not save her.

No one interfered. No one came, even when she screamed. She knew then that there would be no help, and so she did what she had to do.

Sir Guibert would kill Richer for her, but what good

was that? The scum was only following her father's orders. And although she was choking in sorrow and hatred for her father, she did not wish for more violence. Therefore, she would have to conceal what had been done to her.

"Bring me my medicines, Wilda, then find me a suitable gown to be married in. I care not if my husband knows I was forced to wed him, but no one else is to know. Do you understand? Find me a veil, a dark one, and gloves, I think. I have had a recurrence of my childhood rashes, and there is no time to make the ointment to relieve it. Do you hear? That is what you will go and tell my aunt and Sir Guibert."

"But you outgrew those rashes."

"I know, but it is not impossible that I became so nervous about meeting my future husband that the rash reappeared. And it is also understandable that I would wish to hide it. Just make sure Sir Guibert believes the story. Do that now, then return and help me dress. And carry my medicines along to Crewel. I will have more need of them later."

Alone, Leonie put her head in her hands and sobbed. This day was going to be one horror after another.

For the swelling and bruises she applied a mixture of the marsh mallow root and oil of roses. For her nerves and the overall aching she drank a sedating syrup made from chamomile flowers. She would have taken a mixture of white poppy, but she didn't think she should fall asleep during the wedding ceremony.

By the time Wilda returned, Leonie was already feeling the effects of the sedative.

"You told Sir Guibert what I bid you?"

"Aye. He was most sympathetic and said he would himself explain to your husband the reason why you will be veiled. And your aunt began to cry. She wanted to come to you now but Lady Judith has kept her busy through the night and all morning. Why, I don't believe she has had any sleep."

"It is just as well. I do not want her to see me like this." Looking at her young maid squarely, she said, "Tell me something, Wilda. Have you ever had a man?"

"My lady! I—"

"I will not scold you, Wilda," Leonie quickly assured her. "My mother died without preparing me, thinking she would have time for it later. And I could not ask Aunt Beatrix about these things. I want to know what I will face today. Tell me."

Wilda lowered her eyes, speaking softly. "It will be painful the first time, my lady. It is the tearing of your maidenhead that causes the pain and the bleeding that will be displayed on your sheets the next morning. But it is not a great pain and is quickly over. Afterward—is most enjoyable."

"Truly? The other girls at court said it was horrible."

"They lied. Or they repeated what their mothers told them." She shrugged. "For some women it is always painful because they believe it is a sin to enjoy it. But as long as you have some feeling for your husband—" Wilda gasped, realizing her blunder. "Oh, my lady, I am sorry. I know you have no liking for the man."

"So I am doomed always to feel pain? But he has no liking for me, either, so perhaps he will not bother me often. I thank you for telling me, Wilda."

Leonie told herself to stay calm. She could not go to Crewel trembling in dread. If he hoped to see her cower, he had much to learn about Leonie of Montwyn.

Chapter 9

LEONIE instantly recognized the woman who waited in the large hall of Crewel to greet the wedding party. She introduced herself as Lady Amelia, ward of Rolfe d'Ambert, but Leonie knew her as the woman who had given the Black Wolf her favor on the tourney field and accepted his passionate kiss. Ward? Mistress, without a doubt. But Leonie wasn't sorry. The Black Wolf could have a hundred mistresses, as long as he left her alone.

"Sir William, Lady Judith, do you make yourselves comfortable and my lord Rolfe will greet you in a moment," Amelia said in a most agreeable tone. She turned to Leonie then. "My lady, if you will come with me, I will show you to a chamber where you may wait until the ceremony begins."

Leonie said not a word. She followed the older woman, glad to be gone from her father and Judith's company. She had said not a word to either of them during the journey to Crewel. Her father had tried to talk to her, but she had turned away from him.

Leonie knew Crewel well. She knew that Amelia was taking her to the small room next to the chapel in the forebuilding. Crewel was not like Pershwick at all. Sir Edmond had looked to his comfort in all things, and Leonie remembered that one of the reasons she enjoyed coming to Crewel as a child was the fascination of always finding something changed. Once it was a new room added above the raised dais at the lord's end of the hall. Later that space was enclosed to become the lord's chamber. Then a room was added at the opposite end of the hall above the servants' smaller hearth, when Alain was knighted. Soon after that the space between the two large chambers was filled in, and now there was a whole second floor with many stairways circling up to it from the hall. The original ceiling had been so high that, even with the second floor, the ceiling was still high above everything.

It was a place of comfort, and it offered privacy where Pershwick did not, but Leonie's nervousness was mounting. It struck her suddenly that the Black Wolf's mistress had greeted them in the hall. What peculiar behavior. He was treating her contemptuously even before the wedding.

The small room that Amelia brought her to contained two stools and a table with a bottle of wine and glasses on it. "It may be a while before they are ready for you, Lady Leonie. The marriage contract must be agreed upon first."

"I am in no hurry," Leonie replied without feeling, leaving Amelia wondering what to think of her. She had been ready to hate her rival, eager to spite her in any way possible. But the girl before her was no bigger than a child. She even sounded like a child. With her cloak drawn tightly about her and a long veil covering her head and face, there was no telling what she looked like. Girls were married at thirteen and fourteen, or even younger, so she could be very young. *That* would certainly change Amelia's thinking, for she could hardly see a child as a rival.

"Is there something I can do for you?" Amelia asked. "Would you like to remove your veil or . . . ?"

Leonie shook her head. "If you would send me my maid Wilda, I would be grateful."

"As you will," Amelia replied with a heavy sigh. In that instant, she determined she would come back soon and catch Leonie unawares. Surely the girl would remove the veil after she sat in that tiny room a while. It was hot in there.

She found the maid and sent her to Lady Leonie and then, hearing Rolfe's angry voice in the hall, hurried in the other direction, toward the kitchens, to make sure preparations were running smoothly.

That was not something Amelia would ordinarily concern herself with, having customarily left the running of Rolfe's household to the Crewel steward, but she most particularly did not wish to return to the chamber she had moved her belongings into just that morning. That room was a reminder that, at least for the present, she was not first lady at Crewel Keep.

In the tiny room next to the chapel, Leonie heard a voice raised in anger. She recognized it from that day in the woods. The Black Wolf. But it was the first time Wilda had heard him, and even though they could not make out his words, the poor girl's eyes went wide with fright. Leonie could not reassure her, not without lying, so she kept quiet, adding more sedative to her wine.

She could not begin to guess the reason for the Black Wolf's anger. It was he who had insisted on this marriage. She didn't think it had to do with the marriage contract. Her lands were supposed to be hers to do with as she wished. That was her mother's desire. But she didn't think her father, with so little concern for her, would insist on including that in the marriage contract. Even if he did, what would the contract matter to the Black Wolf? He'd showed himself plainly as a man who would dispossess another for his land whenever he wished.

The thought chilled her, even in the stuffy little room. Marriage would make her his property. He could do whatever he liked with her. He could imprison her for the rest of her life, even kill her.

Impulsively Leonie took a small blade which she kept in her medicine basket to cut bandages, and tucked it into her leather girdle, where it would be covered soon again by her veil. She was damned if she would find herself at a man's mercy ever again, as she'd been with Richer.

"Lady Leonie, I have these fresh from the kitchen."

Leonie jumped and swung around on the stool. Amelia had entered the room without knocking, holding a tray of small cakes. She froze, her green eyes wide with shock, at the sight of Leonie's unveiled face.

"Do you always come into a room unbidden?" Leonie demanded, surprised to find that she still had the spirit to be angry.

"I—I am sorry, my lady. I thought you might like . . ." Amazed by her rival's condition, she was suddenly emboldened enough to ask, "You—you did not want to marry Rolfe?"

Leonie noted the ease with which Amelia used the Christian name.

"I did not want him for my husband, no, but as you can see, I was not given a choice." Why not tell her the truth?

"Then perhaps I can relieve your mind, my lady," Amelia offered. "If you will give me a few moments alone."

Leonie nodded to Wilda, and the girl slipped out

of the room and closed the door. Amelia set her tray down on the table, but did not sit down.

"You have not met Rolfe d'Ambert, have you?" she began.

"No."

"Have you heard he is very handsome?"

Leonie almost laughed. "A man can be an Adonis, but have the heart of the devil."

"You do not want him?" Amelia pressed.

"I have said I do not," Leonie replied impatiently.

"Then you will be relieved to know he will not trouble you. He . . . marries you for your land only. You see, he has me to see to his . . . other needs."

"Oh?"

Amelia frowned at the sarcastic tone. "We do not have to be enemies, you and I. If you do not want him, then you can hardly object if I have him."

"I do not object. You are welcome to him. But you have not relieved my mind. Why does he wish to marry me when there are any number of women with more land than I?"

"It is Pershwick he wants, because of the trouble there, which you must know more about than I. I can only tell you what his friend Thorpe told me only this morning. Rolfe is a man of temper, and a man of the moment. If he wanted grander estates, he would have gone after them. If he wants them in the future, he will go after them. He always gets what he wants, and he wanted the troubles with Pershwick ended so he offered for you. When he was refused he went to see the king. Now he has what he wants."

"So he does." Leonie's voice was subdued, for all her fears had been confirmed. "Tell me only this," she asked quickly. "Do you know what he plans for me?"

"He said he would send you away after the wedding."

"Away? Where?"

"I do not know, but—"

A knock interrupted them, and Judith entered. Even that lady was shocked to see what Richer had done. She shivered, remembering her beating at William's hands.

The girl's stunning beauty had vanished beneath her swollen and blackened face. The silver-blond hair flowed softly about her shoulders. The well-rounded little figure was clad in a tightly laced long-sleeved dark gray chemise with a pale gray overtunic embroidered in silver thread. The tunic had full sleeves to the elbow and was slit up the sides to reveal more of the chemise. A silver corded girdle emphasized the tiny waist. But the lovely body did not distract from the horror of her face.

"You are here for a reason, Judith?" Leonie asked coldly as Judith continued staring at her face.

"You will not appear like that," Judith stated.

"Why? Am I not properly attired for a wedding?"

"It is time." At those words, Amelia left the room. Judith remarked distastefully, "I am surprised you would talk to that woman, Leonie. Do you not know she is his mistress?"

"If I did not know, then I have you to thank for telling me."

Judith chose not to react to the sarcasm. "Come. Your father is waiting to escort you. And your husband is already at the altar. He knows you had to be forced, so if you wish to appear as you are, you shame only yourself. I thought that story about the rash was rather clever for your aunt's benefit."

"It was for Sir Guibert's benefit, to keep him from

killing my father's man. And no, I will not appear like this, for the same reason."

With slow deliberation, Leonie put her veil back on and smoothed its folds. Sight through the thick material was distorted at best, but Leonie could see through only one eye anyway. She had to tilt her head back to see at all, and this gave the mistaken impression that she was looking down her nose at people. Under the circumstances, the mistake suited her very well.

"I am ready," she said bravely, and Judith was a little taken aback by her courage.

At the entrance to the small chapel, Sir William took his daughter's hand and placed it on his arm, though she refused to give him a single glance. In the chapel she saw benches filled with guests and, at the altar, the large blurred form of a man. All her terror surged upward as her father began to walk her down the aisle.

"Leonie, if you ever have need of me—"

"You have shown how I may depend on you, Father," she hissed. "You give me to this black rogue. Show me no more of your love and concern, I beg you."

"Leonie!"

There was terrible pain in the exclamation, and the realization ripped through Leonie. But how dared he show his love now? How dared he make her remember the father he had once been? He had drink to make him forget their happy past, but what did she have? She could never forget.

She would have said as much, but the words could not get past the knot choking her throat. And then, in a moment, it was too late and she was left to stand beside the Black Wolf. She would wonder later how she'd managed to say the words that bound her to him.

Was it only the fear she felt from the moment she heard his deep growling voice beside her?

Neither was Rolfe paying much attention to the priest's words. He was fighting the bitter gall that had risen the moment he saw his bride. She was no bigger than a child, stood no higher than his chest. Had this little girl caused him so much trouble? And what made him ill was that she was covered from head to foot like a leper. Her vassal claimed she was concealing a rash. Did he believe that? Dared he hope it was something that would go away as Sir Guibert suggested?

To make this as awful a situation as possible, the girl's stepmother had taken him aside to confess that it had been necessary to force the girl to comply with the king's order. What had they done to her? Denied her a few meals, most likely. That mattered nothing to him. What mattered was her reluctance. He had riddled himself with guilt over his bride's high expectations, and now it seemed she didn't want him! He, who could have chosen a wife from all the beauties at court, was stuck with a reluctant bride!

He should have sent them all packing. He had a perfect excuse, having been outraged when the marriage contract was read. Whoever heard of a woman's dowry being left in her hands after she was wed? But Sir William had remained adamant. It must be done according to his late wife's wishes, and she had left the lands to the girl. He had signed that absurd contract, which was as binding as the marriage itself, and look what it had gained him—a girl no bigger than a child who'd had to be forced to marry him! By Christ's holy blood, he was beginning to wonder if he was cursed.

Leonie felt the ring shoved none too gently over her white-gloved finger. Next the priest bade her husband bestow on her the kiss of peace that ended the ceremony. Rolfe did not try to lift her veil, but brushed his lips over the general area of her forehead. A short mass followed, and then she was led from the chapel by her husband.

Leonie wanted only to leave the hall and his presence, but the wedding feast began immediately and she was forced to sit next to him at the lord's table. Her father was there, silently drowning himself in drink. Her husband began to do the same, and she wished she could follow his example. The mood was gloomy at best, Judith the only one who seemed pleased with events. She was also the only one who kept the lord's table from being completely silent, carrying on conversations and subtle flirtations with two of the Black Wolf's knights.

Leonie's husband said not a single word to her. To queries from his men, he simply grunted. A trencher of food had been set before the newlyweds to share, but neither of them touched the food, Leonie because she would not raise her veil in public, and Rolfe because he preferred wine.

There were other knights in the hall, a few with their ladies, and there were even some children. But no one behaved as such an occasion usually warranted. Leonie knew it was her presence that put a damper on everyone's mood, and she could hardly blame people for feeling uncomfortable around her. They must surely wonder at her pitiful condition, enshrouded and silent.

She tried to leave once, but her husband's heavy hand on her arm stayed her. She did not try again. There was dancing, but she hardly noticed. She dared not look directly at Rolfe, but she watched his large hands gripping his wine cup.

Never in all her young life had Leonie thought she

would fail to enjoy her own wedding feast, but such was the case as she sat rigid trying not to weep, hoping no one would speak to her.

She saw none of the elaborate feast Rolfe's servants and her own from Pershwick had managed to prepare. There were soups with bacon, and two roasted pigs with truffles, three swans served with their feathers, a large honeyed ham, capons and ducks, and as many varieties of mustard sauces and relishes as she had ever seen assembled at one table. The roasted meats had been done by Rolfe's kitchen staff who were not capable of subtlety in preparing food. But because the Pershwick staff had vied to outshine the Crewel servants, there was a great variety of turnip dishes and beans, and peas done half a dozen ways.

Cherries and apples had been stewed, made into pastries, and served fresh, garnished with flowers from the Pershwick garden so lovingly tended by its mistress. There were a dozen cheeses and wines, and a huge wedding cake with almonds and sugared figures decorating the top and sides.

Leonie tasted none of it.

The hour was late when Judith finally rose to do her duty by escorting Leonie to her chamber. By this time Rolfe was so drunk he did not notice her leaving. Leonie sent up a silent prayer that he would be in no condition to visit her. It was customary for the wedding guests to help in the disrobing for the bedding ceremony, and several women Leonie did not know came into the room with Judith and Amelia. Enough was enough, and she sent them all away.

When she was alone, Leonie quickly hid her knife beneath her pillow, hoping she would not need it. But she knew that, while Rolfe might not come to her on his own, his guests would see that he did. That might happen at any time, so she undressed quickly and climbed into the large bed. She had to give up her veil, but with the bedcurtains drawn, she would still be hidden from the guests who would enter the room with Rolfe. And with her long hair unbound, she might be able to hide her face from him, too.

She waited, shivering with tension, until at last the door crashed open and a group of men stumbled into the room bearing Rolfe d'Ambert to his marriage bed. They were all drunk, and there was much ribald jesting until Rolfe's deep angry bellow ordered everyone out. She buried herself under the covers, attuned to the slightest noise, bracing herself for the sound of the bedcurtains opening. After several agonizing moments she heard the curtain open and gave a muffled squeak of fear as his heavy weight dropped onto the bed.

Leonie held her breath until her chest ached. She cringed, imagining every horror she could, until his voice rumbled next to her. "Go to sleep. I do not rape children."

Leonie didn't try to understand what he meant. Something or other had saved her. She was so relieved that she was asleep only moments after she heard her husband's snoring.

Chapter 10

THROUGH the thick haze enveloping Rolfe's mind, he felt a soft form pressed against his chest and thighs. Amelia was not one to snuggle close to him in bed, not even for warmth, and he had been with her long enough to have that awareness deep in his mind.

Yet here was a soft form warming him in sleep, and he threw his arm around her, thrusting his hand between her breasts to rest there. She whimpered in protest, and the sound registered. With a sigh, Rolfe took his arm back and started to turn away. But her warm body snuggled even closer. Fleetingly he wondered what could have brought about this change, and again he put his arm around her. When she did not protest, he began to caress her, gently so as not to wake her. He was in no hurry and still half asleep.

His hand was discovering things that confused him. Amelia's skin seemed softer, like fine satin, and he touched no bony protrusions. Her curves were firm, yet full fleshed, her breasts fuller, too, more of a handful. He did not recall noticing all these changes . . .

Rolfe was instantly awake. It was his wife he was caressing, his wife who had managed to arouse him. He had thought her a child, but those curves belonged to no child.

The girl stirred, moving her backside against him

provocatively, almost as if she sought . . . did she? Was she still asleep, or had he awakened her and now she was telling him to continue? He was shocked that a virgin should be so forward, but his body was reacting far more positively, blood rushing to his manhood, making him crave release despite his bewilderment and hesitation.

She had done it. She had made him want her, even though he didn't know what she looked like, but suspected the worst. It was the opportunity he had prayed for. As long as it was dark and he didn't have to look at her, he could do his duty.

Next to him, Leonie was having an extraordinary erotic dream. She had not known such feelings were possible. She clung to the dream, wanting it never to end, but she was slowly coming awake. She knew, vaguely, that she lay pressed against a man, and that his hand was touching her as no one had ever touched her before. She could not fit the man who was her husband to the man who was beside her because of the pleasure he was causing. She was set to expect pain from her husband, not these sweet sensations.

When her face began to hurt, and pain intruded, she came instantly awake. Scared, she reached under her pillow for the knife.

Rolfe was unaware that he had hurt his wife when his knuckles flicked against her bruised cheek. He meant only to move the great mass of her hair away from her face before turning her onto her back, for he was ready for her and he knew by the sounds coming from her that she was ready too. An annoying pain pricked his side, throwing him off balance. It was several moments before he reacted to the pain, touching his side, and his fingers came away wet and sticky. He roared in anger.

Leonie, first paralyzed with fear over what she had done, scrambled from the bed when he bellowed.

Rolfe did not know she had left the bed, for he left it from his side in the same moment, making his way to the door of the antechamber where his young squire slept. He threw the door open, calling, "Get light in here, Damian! Then wake a servant. I need a change of bedlinen, and the fire needs to be built up."

Leonie dashed for the area containing her chests. A hasty search produced the bedrobe. When a light appeared outside the door, she quickly turned around to finish tying it.

This was what Rolfe saw when Damian entered the chamber with a candlestick. The sight made him catch his breath, for it was his first intimate look at his wife. She was no more than an inch or two over five feet, but what there was to her was perfectly formed. The curves were beautiful, the slim back narrowing to a tiny waist, then rounding to gently swelling hips. She lifted her hair out from beneath the robe and tossed it back like a silver cloud. Lord, she was exquisite from that view.

She went to the bed and bent to pick up the knife she had dropped, but he drew closer, saw what she was reaching for, and shouted, "Leave it, madame!"

Leonie jumped back, frightened, and nearly flew to the shadowed part of the room. It was stupid, so stupid to have hurt him, for now her hurt would be doubled. She had only made things worse for herself.

Rolfe stared furiously at her huddled form, wondering what she had hoped to accomplish with the tiny knife. The blade was not big enough to do him great damage. The cut in his side was no more than a pin prick compared to the wounds he had suffered in all his battles. Perhaps she hadn't meant to hurt him.

Perhaps the stabbing was an accident. Yet she'd had the blade in bed with her. Why?

Rolfe stiffened as the thought intruded. Had she meant to prick herself with the blade and smear blood on the sheets because she had no other blood to give up? How foolish to try that old trick. He didn't care that she had come to him without being a virgin, but he did not like it at all that she'd meant to deceive him.

He liked it even less when two maids that came in to change the bedlinen looked first at him and then at his wife in surprise. He could see by their expressions that they'd drawn the same conclusion he had. The story would no doubt be well laughed-over within a day.

"Damian," Rolfe said while the maids saw to the fire, "get me the thickest bandage you can find and bind up this cut. I want no blood on the sheets except my wife's."

He heard the gasp that came from the shadows, but he did not look at her. Let her begin to feel the shame she deserved to feel. If, in the morning, there was no blood on the sheets to attest to her purity, she would have to live with shame.

Leonie turned cold as she heard him speak and considered what the man meant to do to her. She was amazed that he would admit before others that he meant to harm her. All of a sudden she had a desire to take a good look at this man who was so utterly despicable. She raised her head just enough for her one good eye to focus on him. He was not looking her way, but he was illuminated by the firelight, so she allowed herself a bold appraisal, the very first she'd had.

He had seated himself on a stool by the hearth, with a sheet draped over his loins. The bright flames cast enough light for her to see him clearly. Her husband? Please, no. It would be too cruel to be married to this beautiful young man, knowing that he could inspire only hate in her.

She knew why he was called the Black Wolf, when it was actually a silver wolf on a black field sewn on his banner. The name was for his dark coloring, his black hair and eyes. The hair that covered the rest of his body was just as black, especially the thick mat on his chest.

She did not find his darkness unpleasant. Far from it—too far in fact. God help her, the sight of him was enough to take her breath away. His body was overwhelmingly masculine, rock-hard and muscular, big, frightening. But it was his rugged face that was so arresting, framed by the shaggy cut of his black hair, hair that curled on neck, temple, and forehead. His lips were drawn tight just then, but that did not detract from their sensual fullness. His brow was wide, the nose straight and bold, the square jaw smooth and finely defined and aggressive.

It was a beautifully handsome face. How awful that the man behind it was a monster, cold, heartless, vindictive. For a man to have the face of an angel and the heart of a devil was worth crying over.

While Damian tended his wound, Rolfe sensed the girl's eyes on him. When he looked toward her, all he could see was a small huddled form cloaked in its mass of silver hair. He recalled her response to him in bed, recalled the soft sounds of pleasure that had come from her. She had wanted him, and knowing that had aroused him. Knowing that she was watching him now had the same effect. His desire to have her was becoming painful.

Rolfe snapped at Damian to hurry and be gone, and

Leonie's trembling worsened as the door closed, leaving them alone again.

"Return to bed, Lady Leonie."

It was the utter quiet of the room that made it seem he had shouted at her. In fact, his voice had been husky.

Rolfe grinned as she hurried toward the bed, her back to him.

"Remove your robe, my lady."

Leonie froze, her body stiff with mortification. "My lord, I—"

"Behind the curtains, if you wish," he said impatiently. "I did not mean I wished to inspect you."

Leonie climbed into bed, drawing the bedcurtains tightly closed. A moment later Rolfe grinned again as her robe dropped onto the floor. He wasted no time in putting out the candles, and a few moments later he had joined her in the bed.

He had to reach to touch her, for she was lying on the far edge of the bed, her back to him. He pulled her to the center of the bed, and felt her trembling.

"You are cold?"

She would rather have died than admit her fear. "Yes, my lord."

His fingers moved gently over her breasts, down her belly, then slipped between her legs. "You will not be cold for long," he whispered.

Leonie could not stop trembling. She couldn't understand why he was being gentle with her. When was her punishment to begin? He continued to play with her, to tempt her, but there was no room in her emotions for anything except fear. She was certain there would be awful retribution for stabbing him, but what did he have in mind?

So it was a complete surprise when Leonie found herself mounted and penetrated before she realized what was happening. She cried out as he entered her, but that pain was short and soon became only a dull throb. She lay there dazed, amazed that she was being bedded instead of beaten.

Rolfe was amazed as well. She was a virgin after all. That meant his conclusions were wholly untrue. She had stabbed him on purpose, had meant to stab him. That realization made him finish with her quickly. Having done so, he promptly fell asleep.

He did not snore this time, but Leonie knew her husband was asleep. Well, she was no longer a maiden. Because she lacked desire for him, his taking her had been painful. But it was a pain she could bear if she had to—though she would not have to if she were sent away. Holding that hope close to her, willing it to be so, she fell asleep.

Chapter 11

LEONIE was awakened rudely when a troop of women barged into her room early the next morning. She had barely awakened before the bedcurtains were thrown aside and she was whisked out of bed.

The sheets were removed and taken out of the room to be displayed, as was the custom. But the ritual was forgotten when one of the ladies caught sight of Leonie's face and gave a startled exclamation.

Leonie turned her back and hid her face in her hands, giving the unfortunate appearance that she was crying. Questions rose loudly. The women wanted to know what was wrong with her, but Leonie would neither speak nor turn around.

It was Amelia who took charge, ushering the ladies out. Someone draped Leonie's bedrobe over her shoulders, making her aware for the first time that she had been standing there naked, with only her long hair to cover her. She put the robe on, and then her veil was thrust at her.

Leonie looked up to nod curtly at Judith before she donned the veil. Only her stepmother and Lady Amelia were left in the room with her. Of her husband, there was no sign.

"Who were those women?" Leonie asked.

"It was remiss of your husband that you did not meet them at the feast," Judith replied, "but you will no doubt come to know them soon enough. They are the wives and daughters of knights who serve your husband. I understand they were even allowed to follow the army when Sir Rolfe was but a mercenary. Most unusual circumstance. It could not have been easy to find quarters for them in each town. Is that not so, Lady Amelia?"

"I know nothing of that."

"No, of course you would not," Judith purred. "I forget that you have not been with Sir Rolfe very long."

This bit of hostility wasn't the only thing that displeased Amelia. She had been thoroughly put out to see the virgin blood on the sheets, positive as she was that Rolfe would not touch his wife.

"You missed mass, Leonie," Judith remarked disapprovingly. "But you were not the only one. Your father is still sound asleep. And since your husband has gone about his business without a word to his guests, I must assume the wedding celebration is over. There is no point in our staying."

"You have my leave to go, madame, if that is what is required," Leonie replied stiffly.

"You do not need us?" Judith asked only because it was expected.

Leonie shook her head.

"Then, if I can stir your father, we will go. You wish to say farewell to him? I can't guarantee he will remember, but . . ."

"Again, no."

"Well, we wish you the best, my dear."

"Of course you do," Leonie answered tonelessly before turning her back. Dismissed, Judith left.

"I do not blame you for disliking your stepmother," Amelia remarked. "She is not a pleasant woman."

Leonie was in no mood for conversation with this

one either. "If you will be good enough to have my maid sent to me, I need not trouble you further, Lady Amelia. I would have a bath and tray of food brought here, as I do not mean to leave this room today."

Amelia's lips tightened. "As you will, my lady," she said curtly, hoping she would soon be rid of the arrogant girl.

Leonie had only just finished her bath when Lady Amelia returned to inform her that her escort was ready to return her to Pershwick. This was so unexpected that Leonie was compelled to question it.

"You are sure I am to go to Pershwick? So soon?"

"It is the keep my lord mentioned, as you are familiar with it. No doubt he will supply you with what money you need, and perhaps he will appoint his own steward, but you should not be troubled by him there as long as you do not bring yourself to his attention. I assume that is as you would have it?"

"Indeed! Oh, indeed, yes!"

Leonie was stunned by this turn of luck, and hurried through her preparations as quickly as possible.

Sir Guibert and Leonie's men-at-arms were to be her escort. Guibert was alarmed when told what his first duty for the newly married Leonie would be. But seeing how eager she was to be gone from Crewel, he kept his doubts to himself. Then, too, he had heard that Rolfe d'Ambert was seldom in residence at Crewel, so he assumed the man wished to spare his wife being alone there. At Pershwick, she could be with people she knew.

Guibert had also learned what Rolfe was about—a monumental feat, the taking of seven hostile keeps with only a small army. He wished him luck, but knew the job would not be finished quickly. He doubted his lady would see much of her husband the rest of this year.

It was with some self-disgust that Rolfe found himself riding through the gate of Crewel at sunset, spurred on by a foolish eagerness to be with Leonie again.

All of last night was not clear to him. His wound wasn't bad, but he was hardly flattered to have received it. He did know that it had been a long time since he'd been so intrigued by a woman. No doubt the tension had had much to do with it, but it would do no harm to find out, would it?

Disgust with his own boyish eagerness had much to do with his reaction when he found his wife was not there waiting for him. He simply turned around and returned to the siege of Wrothe Keep. Relief was partly why he did so. He did not chastise Amelia for overstepping her bounds. He had told her only that he would send his wife away, not instructed her to see to it for him. But Leonie's absence was a good thing, for eventually he would have been disgusted with himself over his foolish desire to be with her. He certainly did not want the woman to know he desired her. He was not forgetting how spiteful she was.

Several miles away, in Axeford Keep, where Sir Warren was temporary castellan for Rolfe, his wife, Lady Roese, was telling him how shocked she had been that morning when she saw Leonie d'Ambert's face. Warren, who knew of his lord's troubles with Pershwick, assumed correctly that the lady had resisted the marriage. It was a natural conclusion that if she had been beaten, it was her father who had done it.

But Warren's wife, who had been away visiting her family for several months, knew nothing of the Pershwick troubles. She knew little of Rolfe d'Ambert, either. Her husband liked him, but that spoke only of Sir Rolfe's being a good overlord. It said nothing about his character. She knew only that Sir Rolfe had a hot temper, and she concluded that he had beaten his new wife. In her opinion, Lady Leonie had been married to a cruel man.

Unfortunately, Sir Warren did not clear up the misunderstanding. He did no more than grunt when he was told Lady Leonie's condition. In truth, he wasn't really listening. His wife told the story the next day to Lady Bertha, who was staying in Axeford Town, and from there the story spread quickly.

It did not take long for a firm debate to ensue, and many husbands and wives, as well as the serfs of Axeford, Kenil, Blythe, and Crewel argued the issue in the following weeks. The men knew their lord, and sided with him. The women did not know him, and they felt that men will always defend each other blindly and against all evidence, so they held to their opinions and sorely pitied the lady in question.

The serfs, who loved gossip, simply divided sides, man for man and woman for woman. And unbeknownst to anyone, the issue went a long way toward winning the loyalty of the people of Kempston for their new lord and lady.

Lady Amelia was furious when she heard the gossip, not because her lover was being maligned, but because the woman being pitied was Lady Leonie, and this would not help Rolfe to forget about her. He might even bring her back to Crewel just to still the wagging tongues.

Rolfe was in fact unaware of what was being said about him in the weeks after the wedding. The gossip was not something his men wanted him made aware of. Even Thorpe took pains to keep it from him, knowing his temper very well.

Briefly Rolfe wondered why his men acted strangely, hushing conversations when he drew near, shouting abuse at their womenfolk in his presence. And, damn him, he had never seen so many disgruntled females. Every woman he encountered was in a pique.

But Rolfe had too many other things on his mind to ponder the peculiarities of women and serfs. He kept to the camp outside Wrothe Keep for several weeks, conducting the terms of surrender.

Yes, he had much to occupy his mind. Yet drifting into his thoughts with alarming frequency were images of a petite form with soft curves and whispering sighs. Lady Leonie, his recent bride, was not forgotten whether or not he wished her to be.

Chapter 12

LEONIE's every prayer had been answered. Her husband was forgotten. Her life was her own again. No steward had been sent to Pershwick to tell her that a man ruled her life now. She had taken great pains to prepare for a steward, abandoning all her hiding places so that the steward could never accuse her of trying to keep anything from her lord. Everything was in order. But no one arrived and she stopped expecting anyone.

No longer did she have to worry that Judith's steward would come raiding either. She had freedom, independence, and peace.

But good things do not last forever. One afternoon, working in her garden, she heard the call to halt from the gate, but gave it little thought. Sir Guibert was away, leaving her master-at-arms in charge of defending the keep. The man took his responsibilities very seriously, ordering the gatekeeper to question anyone who wished to enter the keep, familiar face or not.

Leonie continued to fill her basket with parts from her elderberry tree. The gatherings would make dyes for the weaving room, black from the bark and root, green from the leaves. Shades from blue-lilac to purple would have to wait until the berries ripened in the fall.

A second basket, filled earlier, contained herbs and flowers for medicines and cooking: chicory and endive, lovage, sweet marjoram, spearmint and catsmint, white poppy, rosemary, and the petals of marigolds and violets. Leonie trusted no one else to gather these cuttings, for it was too easy for a servant to mistake one herb for another and pick something poisonous for a salad.

The sound of horses entering the bailey made her wonder who could be visiting Pershwick, for Sir Guibert was not expected back until that evening. Horses heralded either guests or a rich merchant, and few of either came to such a small keep as hers.

She leaned over the low garden wall to investigate, and spied a man bearing the Black Wolf's colors over full armor. He was dismounting from a huge black destrier. There were two men-at-arms attending him.

She jumped back away from the wall before he could see her. In a panic, she wondered why her husband was there. She was trapped there in the garden, for she would be in plain view if she left it.

With that thought, she decided to hide in the garden until he left, all day if necessary, so she moved to the far end of the garden and knelt behind some laurel bushes, praying that Rolfe would leave and she would be spared a meeting with him. But apparently no one above was inclined to grant such a petty request, for it was only moments before she heard someone walking into the garden. Rather than face the embarrassment of being caught hiding, she gathered her courage and stood up.

She was lucky. She saw him first. Her old green bliaut blended well with the surroundings, and he was facing the other end of the garden anyway. She even had a moment to compose herself before he turned around.

She cringed. Besides being afraid, she knew she

looked terrible. She was wearing working clothes, and her long braids were wrapped tightly in a hair veil to keep them from trailing in the dirt when she bent over. Even the circlet holding the veil across her forehead was only a strip of worn leather. She looked her worst, and she was facing a man who terrified her.

When Rolfe did not see his wife immediately, he told himself to turn around and go. He had no good reason for coming. It had been impulse that brought him, and he could only blame mental and physical tiredness for causing him to act without thinking. He had slept poorly all the last week. But could he tell his wife that he yearned for her company? That he missed her? That he wanted to see how she fared? It was better she think he didn't care. Yet there he was, ignoring that, and looking for her.

The best thing for them both would be for him to find her uncloaked and revealed at last. It was not unreasonable to hope that might happen. She was among her own people here, and would probably not hide herself. That would end the mystery, and end, too, the yearning he had for her.

With that hope, he turned around, making one last effort to find his wife here where her servant had said she would be found. This time he saw a girl he must have missed before because her clothing was so nearly the color of the foliage. The lady was not his wife. Dear God, would that she were! For as he moved close enough to see her well, he was stunned by how remarkably lovely she was.

Never had he seen such fair skin, such delicate rosy lips, straight little nose, and sweetly oval chin. She had, not the rosy cheeks of English maids or the dark beauty of the French, but ivory skin, pearllike, without a blemish to disturb its smooth surface. Long silvery lashes hid her lowered eyes, and he longed to see their color.

He seemed unable to speak, to say something to make her look up at him. He could only stand there, staring at her like a fool.

Who was she, this exquisite girl? She did not carry herself like a servant. She was surely old enough to be married. Was she a companion to his wife? How terrible for his hideous wife to be near such a beauty every day!

The girl began to fidget, twisting her fingers together nervously, and Rolfe realized he was making her uncomfortable. Did she know who he was? If so, then she realized she was subject to his will because his wife was her liegelady. Everything he was feeling for her sharpened with that thought, and he knew how much he wanted her. Lord, this girl was making him forget his scruples!

"Be at ease, little flower," Rolfe said gently. "I mean you no harm."

"Do you not?"

He liked the sound of her voice, soft and whispery. "Have I given you reason to fear me?"

She raised her eyes to him at last, then quickly lowered them. Leonie had forgotten how beautiful he was. With his helmet clasped in his hand, his black unruly hair curling around his head gave him a boyish appearance contrasting with the rest of his powerful body. His silence had unnerved her, but his gentle voice was just as frightening somehow.

"Your overlong silence was disconcerting."

"Forgive me, my lady. I deliberated too long, wondering what name to call you."

"I have a name, but if you wish to choose another, that is your prerogative."

"You misunderstand, my lady. It is your own name I would call you by—if you will tell me what it is."

Leonie's eyes widened and she looked up at him. "You want me to tell you my name?"

Patiently, he said, "That would be helpful, yes."

She frowned. Was this some game he found amusing? No, she didn't think he would amuse himself that way. But that left only one other possibility. She was so insignificant to him that he truly had forgotten her name!

She drew herself up as tall as she could. "What does a name matter?"

Rolfe was amazed to see those lovely silver-gray eyes become stormy. He had riled her somehow. Well, if she wanted to keep her identity a secret, that was her affair.

"Indeed, 'little flower' will do just as well," he said agreeably, taking a step closer.

"I wish to discuss something with you, in a more private place," he said softly.

"Private?" She stepped back and looked around, wondering how much more private he wanted to be. "Where—did you wish to go?"

"Where you sleep, little flower."

There was no need to be more explicit. She was mortified by the telltale blush spreading over her face. She had never expected him to come to her home for *that* reason. Amelia had said he wouldn't bother her in that way, and she had believed her. The dreadful thing was, she could not refuse her husband.

"If—if you will follow me, my lord."

She had trouble saying the words, and even more trouble walking. Her legs felt leaden, and tears threatened. For all his gentle manner, she suspected an angry motive for his wanting to take her to bed. On their wedding night he had been drunk, perhaps too drunk to recall the revenge he'd wanted to exact from her. Had he come now to punish her? She would not beg for mercy. She *would* not.

Rolfe was so surprised he almost didn't follow her. Her acquiescence had been too easy. Did that mean she did this often? Who was her husband that she cared for him so little? An older man, or one she despised? Still, Rolfe wanted her, so he followed.

As they crossed the bailey to the forebuilding leading into the great hall, Rolfe suddenly remembered where he was. His wife was there somewhere. Did she know he was there? Even if she did, how could he give up this opportunity? The girl leading him to her bedroom was exquisite.

He barely noticed the room she brought him to, so intent was he on the girl as she closed the door and turned slowly to face him.

"I do not suppose there actually was something you wanted to discuss?" she asked him.

Rolfe mistook the hopeful note in her voice for teasing and smiled, shaking his head. "Come here, little flower."

Leonie detested the ridiculous name he had chosen for her and wished she could tell him so. She detested, as well, the fact that she feared him.

She approached, miserably, eyes downcast, and waited in front of him. She didn't quite know what she expected—a slap, an announcement regarding the wretchedness that would be the rest of her life, a beating.

What she didn't expect was to be drawn gently into his arms and held. They stayed that way, and then he picked her up and carried her to her bed. He settled her carefully, then sat down beside her, running his finger along her smooth cheek.

His eyes, like dark brown velvet, moved over her disturbingly. There was a look in those eyes that made her body go rigid, and when he bent his head toward hers, she gasped. His lips touched hers and she imagined a thousand gasps trapped inside her, trying to escape through her belly, for that area came suddenly alive with the strangest sensations.

The pressure of his lips increased steadily and then her mouth was opened and their tongues entwined, and Leonie was bemused to realize who was giving her this first kiss.

Rolfe might have guessed her inexperience if she hadn't followed his lead so well, but deep in her lived the knowledge that this was one man she didn't dare resist, so she followed his every move. It caused him to think she wanted him as much as he wanted her.

He sat up, his breathing irregular, and pushed aside her leather girdle. The laces on the sides of her bliaut were not so easily shed and, impatient, Rolfe drew the dagger at his waist and slit the sides open.

Her small shriek drew his eyes back to hers. "Do not begrudge me my impatience, dearling, for you have caused it. Your laces will be replaced, I promise."

Leonie bit her lip. It was his methods she objected to, not her ruined laces. She was reminded of Ethelinda's rape, for Ethelinda had been cut from her clothes too. Rape was no more than her husband was offering her, for he quickly took his knife to the laces of her chemise as well.

She began crying silent tears of shame and misery, and she hated him for that. She had sworn she would never cry in front of him, and now . . .

"Did the laces mean so much to you, little flower?"

he whispered, his face a study in contrition. He truly thought she mourned her silly laces, and he was sorry for it. What was she to make of this?

"I—I have a hundred laces to replace them, my lord, but I have never had my clothes cut from me."

"Ah, then I am indeed at fault. Will it appease you to do the same to me?"

Leonie stared wide-eyed at the sharp blade he placed in her hand. "You jest, my lord. I could not cut through your mail."

"You will have to help me remove that, but the rest you can shred to rags if it will stop your tears."

The idea of taking the knife to his clothing with his permission was so ridiculous that a very slight grin curled Leonie's mouth.

"If I could find clothes to replace yours I would do it, but we have no one here quite as large as you are, and I wouldn't like to send you away with only your mail covering you. Though I *would* be interested to hear how you explained that to your men," she said with a laugh.

Rolfe laughed with her. Tears in bed were not something he was accustomed to, but neither was humor, and he found it delightful, especially from this shy girl.

"As to that," Rolfe said, grinning, "I would have told the truth—that a saucy wench was so hot for me that—"

"Lies!" Leonie gasped, a giggle escaping. "Would you really say such an awful thing?"

"My men would believe me after seeing my bony knees poking out from beneath this heavy armor," he said.

"Then it is just as well I decline the use of your dagger."

"Well, indeed. And now, if you would help me remove these trappings?"

Leonie nodded, grateful for the opportunity to move behind him, to where he couldn't see her. He had almost made her forget that she was naked, but her vulnerable state made her feel even more embarrassed when she realized that he would soon be naked too.

What had Leonie confused was a strange feeling of acceptance. Her fear of him was gone, dispelled by kind words and lighthearted banter. She spared a moment to silently beseech God not to let this be a cruel trick.

"Wouldn't it be easier for you to stand before me, dearling?" Rolfe asked as he removed his belt and sword and set them on the floor. He lifted the heavy chain-mail hauberk to his waist.

"No, my lord." Leonie gripped hold of the armor. "I am not so tall that I could manage this even with you sitting."

It was the truth, for she had helped Sir Guibert often enough, and each time he was forced to kneel while she stood on a stool to raise his armor over his head. But even on her knees behind Rolfe's back she was having trouble, and at last had to stand up on the bed to finish the task.

At last he was naked, and Leonie moved slowly to stand in front of him. She wondered if she could unbraid her hair for the mantle it would make, but doubted he would have the patience to wait for that. He was thoroughly enjoying her bashfulness and he reached for her, putting his hands on her waist, then moving them slowly up and down her sides, over her gently curving hips, over the full swell of her breasts.

She was biting her lower lip in an endearing way, a little frown puckering her brow. She was trying to keep her head down, too mortified to meet his eyes. His head bent and his lips fastened on the high pointing perfection of a nipple, his tongue grazing over skin like silk. He heard her gasp, and just at that moment there was a single knock.

The door opened and Beatrix stepped into the room. "Leonie, I—oh! Oh, my lord, forgive me!" Beatrix turned scarlet. "Leonie, I—I did not—oh, it can wait—" Beatrix backed out of the room as fast as she could.

Leonie's first impulse was to laugh, and she would have except for the look on her husband's face. He wore such a perplexed frown.

"You must not mind my aunt," she said. "She shares this room with me and . . ."

He did not take his eyes from her face. Nor did his expression change.

"Lady Leonie?" It was a question.

She jerked away from him.

"So now you remember my name," she said bitterly. "It is not consoling that you had to be reminded before—"

His face went tight, but whether or not it was anger she couldn't tell.

"*You* are my wife?" This, too, was a question.

"Of course I am. Who else—"

The Black Wolf fell back on the bed laughing, laughing so hard he writhed with it. Leonie stared at him incredulously until everything came together in her mind. Who else had he thought she was? It didn't matter to him.

Oh, the shame of it, the shame! He had not been making love to his wife, but to some stranger he'd chanced upon in the garden. No wonder he hadn't known her name, he thought he'd never met her before. But for him to do such a thing in her keep, where he knew his wife would hear of it, where her people would see how little respect he bore her!

Leonie moved away from the bed and opened her clothes chest, taking out the first thing she touched, a short linen shift. Attired, she returned to the bed where her husband was still convulsed with laughter. Calmly, she picked up a pillow and began hitting him with it until she finally gained his attention.

"Cease, my lady. You have made your point," he said, chuckling.

"Then will you kindly take your amusement somewhere else? Quickly, before I lose what little patience I have left."

Rolfe sat up and reached for her, sobering when she stepped away from him.

"Come, Leonie, you cannot blame me if I am delighted to learn I have a beautiful wife."

"Sweet Mary, help me," Leonie said to herself. Eyes of frozen silver flashed at him. "My lord, I see I was not clear enough. I want you to leave—now!"

Rolfe made no move. "You are angry."

"Yes."

"I cannot blame you."

"How good of you."

He grinned at her. "Do not spend your fury so, dearling. No harm was done. Thanks to your aunt, a misunderstanding was avoided."

"Let me understand you correctly, Sir Rolfe," Leonie said furiously. "You are saying that if you had made love to me, believing I was a stranger, that would have been merely a *misunderstanding?*"

"But you are my wife, not a stranger. You see my reasoning?"

"What I see, my lord, is that you are a lecher of

the worst kind!" His eyes narrowed, but Leonie was so furious she couldn't stop. "I am told everything that happens here. I would have known of your transgression before you were finished with the girl. Do not mistake me. I care not how many women you have, but if you take one from Pershwick, then I and everyone here will know of it. I will not have my people pity me for my terrible husband."

"Are you finished, madame?"

Leonie swallowed hard, knowing she had gone too far.

"Yes," she murmured, looking at the floor.

"The only thing that matters here is that you are my wife. That means you belong to me, to do with as I will. Do you deny the truth of that?"

Miserably. "No."

"Then do not forget again that you are answerable to me, not I to you."

He gathered his things and left. With the closing of the door, she let out the breath she had been holding. No beating for her audacity, only a warning. But a despicable warning . . . from a despicable man.

Chapter 13

WILDA hesitated outside her lady's door, dreading the news she must give her. She knew Sir Rolfe had been there yesterday, and that he had left in a very ugly mood. Her lady was downcast all the rest of the day and, indeed, now the very worst had come of the encounter.

The sky was still a hazy predawn violet when the troop of men rode up to the gate demanding entrance. Not even the kitchen servants had risen yet, it was so early. The commotion caused a call to arms, which turned out to be unnecessary. The belligerent shouting was the result of a mistake. The night guard was a Pershwick man recruited from the village, and he spoke only English. The men-at-arms outside the gates were fresh from France and understood no English. The knights waited far behind them, and did not hear the exchange. All was chaos until Sir Guibert arrived and unraveled the situation.

The mounted men-at-arms now waited in the bailey, and the four knights with them had been brought into the hall. Wilda was sent to wake her lady. Sir Guibert frowned at her for hesitating outside the door, but, oh dear, she did not want to be the one to bring this news.

"Wilda!"

She sent Sir Guibert an aggrieved look before opening the door and stepping into the dark room. She lit a candle, stalling for time.

"I am not ready to rise, Wilda," Leonie murmured sleepily as the light woke her.

"Sir Guibert sent me, my lady, to tell you there are men here, your husband's men, waiting. They—they say you must go with them to Crewel."

Silence from the bed. Then a tiny whisper. "Why?"

"They would not say," Wilda admitted.

"Give me my bedrobe. Hurry."

Wilda did as asked, not realizing that Leonie meant to rush out of the room wearing only that.

"My lady!"

Leonie didn't stop until she saw the four knights gathered by the hearth with Sir Guibert, and then she wanted to run back before they saw her. She had expected only men-at-arms, servants she could demand answers from. But knights of the Black Wolf would not be intimidated. Why were there four of them? Was trouble expected—trouble from her?

It was not easy to carry herself forward into the room, but she forced herself.

"You are here by Rolfe d'Ambert's order?"

Her question was met with silence. Three of the knights actually turned away. The fourth, the man she knew to be Sir Thorpe, scowled at her. She turned frightened eyes toward Sir Guibert, who lost his temper.

"You will answer my lady or she will not leave Pershwick!"

"Your *lady?*" Sir Thorpe echoed, and the four knights looked at her with a mixture of surprise and embarrassment. But Leonie was more embarrassed, realizing that they hadn't guessed who she was. It was her own fault, dressed as she was, her hair not even covered.

"Your pardon, Lady Leonie," one of the younger men began. "But we did not realize—"

She waved a hand. "I know. You must forgive me for not greeting you in proper attire. You are . . ."

"Richard Amyas."

He hastily introduced the others to her. Amyas was a handsome young man with dark brown hair and green eyes that admired her frankly. Sir Reinald was even younger, with a devastating smile, golden hair, and brown eyes. His skin was a contrasting olive hue, and he was so handsome as to be almost angelic looking.

Sir Piers was the complete opposite. His face was so battle scarred that he aroused pity, but he had the loveliest violet eyes. He eyed her coldly, and she wondered why.

Thorpe de la Mare was the oldest of the four, and near Guibert's age. He had the same dark coloring as Rolfe, and he seemed to find something amusing. His dark brown eyes fairly danced with laughter, and it was all Leonie could manage not to ask him what amused him so.

Sir Richard told her that her husband had charged them with seeing her safely to Crewel. She waited breathlessly for him to say more, but there was no more.

"Did he say nothing else?" she asked, perplexed and afraid.

"Only that you are to bring with you all that belongs to you by way of clothes and personal effects, so it is assumed you are to reside at Crewel."

She nearly fainted. She had once been resigned to living at Crewel, resigned to suffering there, but then she was sent back to Pershwick and everything was all right again. Now, it seemed, all was lost.

"It will take time to pack everything," Leonie heard herself saying in a dead voice.

"That is why we are here so early," Sir Thorpe supplied cheerfully. "But do hurry as best you can, my lady."

Hurry to what awaited her? *Do not linger or you will begin to cry.*

She said to Guibert, "See to their comfort and then send to me all the servants you can gather." With a nod to the four knights, Leonie returned to her room. For the rest of the morning, if she did not allow herself to think, she was able to give crisp orders about the packing. If she did think, she became a mass of trembling nerves, and was overset by tears she could not stifle.

Confusion tormented her. Despite herself, she had begun to relax with Rolfe, and to enjoy him. That was why she was so devastated when his callousness returned. He did not need to be charming and he knew it, did not have to win his wife to his bed. He needed only to order her there. She had thought she could bear that if she must, but could she, loathing the man? She especially despised his handsomeness, which was like a devil's beacon, attracting her despite herself.

What hope did she have not to be torn apart by the warring emotions he caused in her?

Chapter 14

IT was late that night when Rolfe returned to Crewel from the siege at Wroth. He had been at Crewel briefly yesterday, after leaving Pershwick, but had stayed only long enough to speak with Lady Amelia.

Now Rolfe did not even want to think about that meeting, which had gone from bad to worse. He had told Amelia that she must return to court and why, but she burst into tears and begged him not to send her away.

Her tears had only annoyed him. After all, there had never been any love professed between them. But he understood her emotional state well enough when she confessed she was pregnant. It was not pleasant news, but Rolfe could do no less than allow her to stay until the child was born. She had agreed she would leave the child with him and go her own way, agreed most happily in fact. She'd promised to stay out of his way, to cause no trouble for him and his wife.

He had wanted her cared for elsewhere during her pregnancy. "It would be better for you to stay at another of my keeps," he told her. "Axeford is well settled."

"But why, my lord? Your wife knows nothing about us. She thinks I am your ward."

"Regardless—"

"Please, do not." Amelia began to cry again. "I could not bear to be thrust on strangers now. And your wife will be glad to have me, I swear. Sir Evarard has no wife. There is no other lady here to keep Lady Leonie company. Please, my lord."

He should have refused, but he did not. He owed it to the woman to see to her comfort during her confinement, and since he could not foresee any real harm in it, he agreed.

Now as he entered the keep, a vague unsettled feeling nagged at him that he could not explain. But it was forgotten when he spied Thorpe sitting alone by the large hearth at the far end of the hall. He had known he would wait up for him.

Not many others were still awake. The male servants had their pallets spread along the walls and most were fast asleep. A few men-at-arms were at the smaller hearth laughing softly. The only sconces still lit were those by the stairways leading to the floor above, and the hall was so big they provided little light. Nor did the two fires offer much light. They were not fed often on warm nights.

Thorpe did not greet Rolfe until he'd settled into the high-backed chair beside him. The eyes the older man fixed on Rolfe might have been staring at a speck of dust for all the interest they revealed. So it was to be that way, was it? Thorpe was never more annoying than when he was savoring a triumph. He did not brag or gloat, but forced comments by his silence.

"I will assume from your silence that you had no trouble following my orders. She is here?"

"She is."

Rolfe had not realized how tense he'd been until now. "You had no trouble at all?"

"There was a moment when her vassal was ready to draw his sword on us, but—" Thorpe chuckled at Rolfe's expression.

"Did she—"

"By no means," Thorpe said quickly. "Her man took exception to the lack of respect we showed his lady. It was a natural mistake. We did not know who she was when she came to us—something I am sure you can appreciate."

There it was, a not-too-subtle chiding for Rolfe's not warning them about what they would find. He imagined Thorpe's surprise on first seeing Lady Leonie. No doubt it had been as great as his own.

"What was her reaction?"

"She did not smile or seem pleased to see us, if that is what you mean. She wanted only confirmation that it was by your order she was to come here. After that, she did not delay at all in readying herself."

"And here?"

"Be more specific," Thorpe replied innocently.

"Why? You know my every thought, sometimes even before I have it," Rolfe countered. "Do not make me hunt for what I wish to know."

Thorpe chuckled again. "There is very little to tell. I think she expected you to be here when she arrived. When she saw that you were not, she retired to your chamber and has not shown herself since. The two maids she brought with her are also there. So what of Damian? Is he to share your antechamber with her two maids?"

"I left him at Wroth. And no," Rolfe answered thoughtfully. "I think henceforth I will want no one sleeping so close. There are many places to sleep in this keep."

Thorpe grinned. "Of course."

After they had joked for half an hour more, Rolfe started up the narrow curving stairway to his chamber on the second floor. He did indeed find the two maids sleeping in the antechamber. One in fact had put her pallet directly in front of the door, and when he opened it she awoke with a shriek. That woke the other maid as well, and a moment later the inner door to his room was thrown open by his wife, who stood there clutching a hastily donned bedrobe.

The dim light from a single candle did lovely things to the planes of Leonie's face. Rolfe was held by her spell for several moments before he recollected himself and brusquely ordered the two maids out.

"When I am away you may sleep here if that is my lady's wish, but not when I am in residence. You may return here in the morning to assist her, but you will not enter here unless you are bid. I need no one to wake me. If I have not yet risen, no matter the hour, I do not wish to be disturbed. Is that understood?"

Wilda and the older Mary both looked to Leonie first. At her nod, they nodded to her husband. His temper might have exploded over that, but in fact he was amused, although he kept his expression carefully blank.

"Go below. Sir Thorpe will show you to the women's quarters."

As he entered the inner chamber, he said, "It was good of you to return to Crewel so quickly."

"Did I have a choice, my lord?"

"No, but you might have thought of a hundred things to delay your arrival. I am pleased you did not." She had not moved from the door. "Close the door, Leonie, and come in."

She did not like his using her name so easily, nor did she trust his calm. She closed the door slowly and moved reluctantly back into the room, going directly to a chest by the bed where she found a belt for the robe.

Rolfe sighed when she finished tying the belt but made no move toward him. "Is this to be the way of it?" he said as he unbelted his sword and laid it aside. "Must I always ask for your help?"

Leonie reddened. He was right of course. He should not have to ask her for anything. A wife's duty was to anticipate all of her husband's needs.

Yet she did not come forward, for the situation reminded her that she was not a normal wife. Why should only some things apply to her as wife, when the most important things did not?

"I am not a squire, my lord."

He stiffened, looking at her carefully. "You refuse to help me?"

Leonie shivered. Actual defiance she did not dare, but . . .

"There are servants here."

"And you would prefer to expend yourself simply to wake one, rather than come near me? It is late, woman. All are abed but you and I."

"I . . . as you wish, my lord."

She forced her feet to move, telling herself that at least she had made her reluctance known to him, whether it angered him or not.

Rolfe began to lower himself to a stool, but she said, "I will need that to stand on."

The stool was only two feet high. Rolfe looked at it skeptically anyway. "It was not made for standing."

"I have done this for Sir Guibert," she insisted, climbing onto the stool.

"You will fall," he warned her, and she scoffed, "I will not."

"I forget how tiny you really are," he said as he knelt.

How husky his voice was, a caress. He was looking

up at her, and Leonie refused to meet his eyes. She quickly bent to grasp the hem of his hauberk. The sooner done...

She had the last of the heavy armor over his head, but she'd forgotten how much weightier his chain mail was than Sir Guibert's. Her last hard tug sent her backward, the hauberk still in her hands, its weight throwing her off balance.

"Drop it."

She dropped it, and he grabbed her.

"I think you are not suited for this task," he said.

"Put me down."

The dismay she felt in being held in his arms made her voice overly harsh. He touched her feet to the floor, then he released her altogether, whereupon she ran to the bed and drew the curtains around her.

Rolfe picked up the stool and sat down on it, gazing thoughtfully at the bed. His little wife was not going to unbend. He had thought his warning of the day before had given her new incentive, but apparently he had only made matters worse. He ran his hands through his thick hair, exasperated. He had not known what to do yesterday besides give her a show of his temper, but it hadn't warmed things up, had it? No, anger did not inspire her. The trouble was, he wasn't sure he could control his temper.

He'd been stung more than he cared to admit when she professed not to care how many women he had as long as they were not Pershwick women. Jealousy he could understand, but not to care at all?

How could he reach this lovely girl, show her he wanted to start anew? Had she not guessed his intention in bringing her here?

Rolfe quickly divested himself of the rest of his clothing. He did not blow out the candle, nor did he close the heavy curtain on his side of the bed, for that would trap the bed in darkness.

Leonie had her back to him. She had not disrobed, and she was buried deep beneath the covers. He threw them aside and lifted her off the bed to set her down on his lap. She made no sound. He held her thus, cradled like a child, stiff and unyielding though she remained.

He held her for a long while, thinking. Finally he asked, "How old are you, Leonie?"

The voice was soft, yet startling in the quiet room. Leonie actually had to think before she could answer.

"I have lived nineteen years."

"And I ten more than that. Do you think I am too old for you?"

"I—suppose not."

Rolfe nearly laughed at the grudging reply. "Do you abhor my blackness then?"

"Blackness? You are not so hairy that your golden skin is—"

Leonie clamped her mouth shut, appalled. Next she would be telling him how handsome he was!

"Will you tell me, then, what displeases you so about my appearance?"

There it was. He really did want to hear it. She would rather cut out her tongue than flatter his vanity. If he wanted praise, he could find it elsewhere—as no doubt he did, often.

"You would be bored to hear it, my lord, the list is so long."

Leonie was delighted to hear him chuckle at her jibe.

"Dearling, there is nothing about you that displeases me. You are a mite small, but I think I like even that."

Oh, cruel lies! You do not send away what pleases you.

"You did not want a wife."

"Why do you say so?"

"Is it a sign of a happy groom to drink himself into forgetfulness?"

"In truth," he said uncomfortably, "I was reluctant to force myself on you after being told why you were hiding beneath your veil."

Leonie was surprised, not surprised that he knew she had been beaten—her father would have been forced to admit that—but surprised to know he'd been acting out of consideration for her. Rolfe destroyed that illusion in a moment, however. "And what little I knew about you before the wedding was not flattering."

"I see," she said coldly. "Then I assume it was not my person you were interested in."

"Few marriages begin differently."

"True. But few progress as ours did. You did not want a wife."

"What I found distasteful, Leonie," he said in a burst of honesty, "were my reasons for marrying you. Anger led me to offer for you, and soon there was no way out. But it was time I took a wife."

She did not reply, and Rolfe was mystified. He'd told her the whole truth. What was there left to say?

He moved her chin upward gently, coaxing her to look at him. "Is it not enough that, whatever the reason we married, I am now well pleased?"

"You sent me away," she said after all, in a small voice, surprising herself.

"A mistake," he said huskily, and began to bring his head toward hers.

"But—" She was so confused! "Do you tell me—is this why you brought me back here? To begin anew?"

"Yes. Oh, yes, dearling."

He breathed the declaration against her mouth, and then he kissed her. He had never been so completely attuned to a woman before, nor experienced such relief when she yielded. The moment he felt her relax against him, he began his assault in earnest. But he did not forget her inexperience, knowing he must go slowly.

Leonie was kissed a dozen different ways in the long minutes that followed, from soft nibbles to deep probing that played havoc with her insides, spinning her up and down. In a second she would be giddy, then there was only sweet lassitude, and then she was soaring dizzily again.

She did not know when her robe melted away, but she was acutely aware of the first touch of Rolfe's hand on her bared breasts. It seemed right for his hand to be there, resting on her with only the slightest pressure. When his hand began to move softly over her, the hand seemed to grow hotter. Her nipples hardened against gentle kneading.

She turned, one hand slipping behind Rolfe's back, the other stroking his shoulder. Her fingers splayed out, wanting to touch, thrilling to the play of muscle beneath skin, the hardness of him. She returned his kisses, exerting her own pressure now, daring him.

Gently he laid her on the bed beside him, and before her head even touched the pillow, his mouth had fastened on one rosy-peaked breast, his tongue doing what his fingers had done before.

He began a thorough exploration of the soft planes of her belly and thighs, coming closer and closer to the core of her womanhood until such a terrible yearning was built in her that she arched upward to meet his exploring hand. When he slipped his long fingers into her warmth, she moaned, her head thrust back. Her fingers closed in his hair, pressing him closer to her.

Few men had ever treated a woman with such reverence. The hands that touched her were worshipful, soothing, and exciting all at once.

Rolfe's tongue slid down the valley of her breasts and over her belly to mount her pubic mound and pay it equal homage. His hands gently nudged her legs apart and then his arms slipped beneath her lower back to pull her up.

Her head fell farther back and a gasp caught in her throat as his lips pressed deeply into her belly. Then he rested his cheek on her thighs for several wrenching moments. She was nearly mindless, ready to beg him to take her.

Rolfe, fully aware of her peaking desire, began a slow ascent, his body gliding over hers, the hair on his chest playing erotically over her sensitive breasts, making her tremble. His tongue slipped again into her mouth and at the same moment, with nerve-shattering slowness, his velvety hardness slid into her warmth, all the way, until he was completely sheathed.

For an eternity, only his mouth moved, tasting deeply of her sweetness. But nothing could distract her from that other warmth filling her, and when it began to slip out of her, she could not help the whimper that escaped her. But that changed to a gasp of pleasure as the warmth returned. That was his gift to her, making each deliberate stroke so exquisitely prolonged.

After her ecstasy had mounted feverishly, Rolfe withdrew until she held only the throbbing tip of him in her. She cried out, suspended on a precipice, and then he plunged deep within her a final time and she exploded with trembling ecstasy that pulsed through her, each shock more extraordinary than the last, until she fainted. She barely felt the last gentle kiss placed on her lips.

Chapter 15

"MY lady?"

Leonie opened her eyes to find herself lying on her belly, clutching her pillow, an unusual position, as she never slept like that. Then she remembered last night and warmth rushed through her.

"My lady?"

Wilda was standing at the side of the bed, holding out her bedrobe. Leonie sighed. She would rather have lain there and savored her memories, or found her husband there instead of Wilda. But a quick glance around told her that he was gone.

"Have I overslept?" Leonie asked.

"No. Now that *he* is below, I thought it safe to come and wake you for mass," she said sharply.

Leonie grinned. She knew why Wilda was angry. "If I share the room, I must share his habits." She changed the subject. "Did you sleep well?"

"I fear I did not. The fleas!" Wilda's voice rose. "I was nearly eaten alive!"

Leonie sympathized, for she had a few bites herself. "This place is—" She recalled the shock she had felt yesterday when she'd had her first good look at the hall.

"Dreadful," Wilda finished for her. "The kitchens and servants' quarters are even worse than the hall, and I fear to go near the garderobe. Only this room is fairly clean."

Leonie frowned as Wilda began combing her hair. "Why, do you suppose? True, Crewel has not had a lady to supervise since Alain's mother died, but there was the Montigny steward in charge. And Lady Amelia is here now." She shuddered recalling the vermin she had seen in the rushes in the hall, vermin mixed with bones, rotten food, even dog excrement!

"That one obviously does not bother herself," Wilda said. "And the servants, from what I have already seen, do nothing they are not told to do. They have no will even to improve their own quarters."

"How can my husband . . . I would not have thought him a man to live this way."

"But he is rarely here, my lady."

"What?"

"That is what I learned from Mildred," Wilda confided. "A man of war, living in army camps and the like—the conditions here cannot be much different."

"But, Wilda, what do you mean about his rarely being here?"

"Since he took possession of Crewel, Mildred says, he has been away a great deal."

"What else did Mildred tell you?" Leonie asked, knowing that Wilda kept very little to herself.

"It seems, my lady," Wilda began eagerly, "that for all his being given the whole of Kempston by the king, only the gates of Crewel opened to him without a battle, and that was only because Lord Alain had fled and all was confusion here anyway. Do you recall the tourney we heard about?"

"Vaguely," Leonie replied uneasily.

"Well, that was an excuse to gather the Kempston

vassals and castellans in one place so they could swear allegiance to their new lord."

"I see," Leonie mused aloud. "Instead of being summoned one by one. A lone man might refuse and simply lock himself in his keep."

"Indeed, that is what Mildred said," Wilda said, proud of her lady. "And they did all come, but not to swear! All seven attacked Sir Rolfe, then fled."

Now Leonie understood what she had witnessed that day. She was disgusted that Sir Edmond's vassals would behave so despicably, even if motivated by fear. They hadn't even given Rolfe a chance to prove himself.

"What did my husband do after the attack?"

"He besieged all seven keeps."

"How . . . seven? Does he have enough men for that?"

Wilda shrugged. "How many men does it take to besiege a keep? Pershwick has never—"

"I know, I know," Leonie interrupted impatiently, her mind elsewhere. She was amazed. It was an impossible task, for one must close up all seven keeps at once, in order to keep one from helping another. That would surely take thousands of men. But such a large force so near Pershwick would have been reported to her. Yet she had heard of nothing like that.

"Are you sure you heard correctly, Wilda? Could it not be that my husband is just making war on *one* of the Kempston keeps?"

"No, my lady. Four of the keeps are already won. Wroth is now under siege, and the others are closed, awaiting his orders."

Leonie was realizing what all this fighting would mean. "I will not see much of my husband for many months, then, will I?"

"That should ease your mind."

Leonie smiled to herself as Wilda went to fetch her

a bliaut. The maid believed she still detested this marriage.

"Wilda," she called, "I want to wear my best today, the blue silk we got from the French merchant."

"But you only wear that for very special occasions. You even refused—"

"I know. I did not think my wedding was special enough, but now I want to wear it."

Wilda did not argue, and Leonie was strangely silent as the maid laced her into the long-sleeved dark blue chemise. Over this was placed the wine-colored bliaut of Spanish wool. It was slit up the sides to reveal the dark blue chemise beneath, and its bell-like sleeves were heavily embroidered. The bliaut was lovely, molded to her body in the current fashion, with silver embroidery around the high neckline. The girdle, worn loose around the waist, was made from strands of silver cord, and it trailed to her knees.

Leonie left her silver hair loose, and thick locks of it fell over her breasts as her braids usually did. A silver cord circled her head, holding in place a small square of white linen. She completed the costume with soft leather shoes over blue woolen stockings.

"Do I look like a lady befitting my lord's station?" Leonie ventured with a little smile.

"You do indeed." Wilda smiled back, delighted that she had played a part in making her lady so beautiful.

"Then let us hide in here no longer. We will have much to do in the next few weeks, so we must begin our work."

Wilda's eyes lit up as she understood. "Give me leave, my lady, and I will have these lazy wretches—"

"All in good time," Leonie interrupted. "First I must have my lord's permission."

Wilda did not like that at all. Her lady no longer had the final say, and she didn't even try to keep her displeasure from showing as she and Leonie left the room.

Chapter 16

BUT Leonie had a surprise waiting for her. After she left the small chapel, where the Crewel priest held several masses every morning, Amelia stepped directly into her path.

Leonie quickly masked her surprise, but Amelia couldn't manage to conceal hers. She had expected Leonie to be comely, now that her bruises would have healed. Why would Rolfe have brought her back unless he found her to his liking? But this radiant girl with her finely molded aristocratic features and opalescent skin was far too beautiful. What man would want a mistress when he had this for a wife?

Amelia panicked. Her lie about the baby had convinced Rolfe, and she'd planned that, in a month or two, when Leonie was gone again, she could say she had lost the child. All would then be as it had been before.

But *this* wife would not be gone in so short a time. Why, this woman might never be sent away again. And with her there, Amelia couldn't say she'd lost the child, for she would find herself packing immediately. Her only chance now was to get herself pregnant, quickly. But what if Rolfe couldn't be tempted now? Faugh, anyone with dark looks like Rolfe's would do; Sir Evarard, or even that beautiful boy knight, what was his name? It didn't matter who fathered the child.

Once pregnant, she could stall for time, even convince Rolfe to support her and "his" child indefinitely.

"Lady Leonie, I must confess I did not recognize you."

"There has been much of that happening of late," Leonie said smoothly.

Amelia was delighted. Good. The wife did not like it that the mistress was still in residence. With a little help, she would like it even less.

"I must apologize for not greeting you when you arrived yesterday," Amelia improvised quickly, "but I had so much to do, settling my belongings. Rolfe gave me very little warning, and I had to move everything quickly. But you must have had the same inconvenience."

Leonie was astounded by the woman. To brazenly tell her that she had only just moved out of Rolfe's room, that she had continued to share that room after Rolfe's wedding! And of course all the servants knew. If that were not enough, the woman was insinuating that she would not be leaving Crewel keep even though Leonie was in residence. Coldness settled over Leonie.

"Will you still live here?" Leonie demanded.

"But, my lady, where else would I live?" Amelia said innocently. "I am Rolfe's ward—"

"I know what you are."

"Oh." Amelia shrugged. "I tried to tell Rolfe you might object, but he insisted there was nothing to object to. It might be best if you . . . didn't mention to him that you know of our, well, do you understand? Rolfe doesn't like jealousies."

"Jealousies!" Leonie choked.

"Have you seen Rolfe's temper? It is terrible to behold." Amelia's shudder was real enough. "I try to stay out of his way when he's in a rage. You will, too.

But that is neither here nor there. No, I know you won't be jealous. Did you not tell me you didn't want Rolfe?"

"And did you not tell me he wouldn't trouble me?" Leonie countered.

Amelia sighed. "Now you see how changeable he is. But take heart, he will doubtless change his mind again."

Leonie refused the bait. "Tell me, who sees to this household?"

"Rolfe had put me in charge, but it is a task I would give up gladly."

"Would?"

Amelia lowered her eyes. "I told Rolfe I would be glad of your help, but, ah, he told me not to bother you about it. He said he did not want you making things like Pershwick. He did not like the way you ran Pershwick. He must still be angry over—"

"Do you know where my husband is right now?" Leonie cut her off.

"Of course. He always tells me where he is going. He was called to the stable. Some fool put his warhorse next to your palfrey and—"

Leonie turned her back on Amelia before she finished and stepped out into the bailey. There she stood for a moment, letting the warm sun wash over her and tried to pretend that the whole conversation had not happened. She might as well have tried to pretend she was not here.

Chapter 17

IT was a lazy day, sun kissing velvet flowers, a chorus of birds singing. A glorious summer day of warm fragrant breezes.

Leonie waited in the bailey after leaving Amelia, hidden, until she saw her husband return to the hall. Once he was gone, she stopped by the stable and saw for herself that her gentle mare had not been harmed by Rolfe's horse. Relieved, she walked along the path until she came to the woods. She lingered there, hoping to find solitude in the forest.

She found solitude, but it was not welcome. She wept, which led to disgust with herself. She decided to go on to the village, needing the distraction, but that proved equally upsetting, for while she had forgotten the mischief her people had caused there, the Crewel serfs had not forgotten. The women spared her only a shy word or two, and the men shied away. She did not stay.

By midafternoon she was back inside the walls of Crewel Keep, but she still could not bear seeing her husband yet. She located the kitchen garden, seeking further distraction. The garden amazed her, the vegetables and herbs so overgrown with weeds they couldn't be seen.

It was bad enough that Crewel was filthy, but a garden was a source of food. A garden gave spices that made moldy dishes at the end of winter palatable. A garden gave herbs that healed and comforted. It was intolerable to find the garden in this condition.

"You are being searched for, my lady."

Leonie whirled around at the sound of the tiny voice. A girl seven or eight years old was kneeling on the ground pulling up weeds. At least *someone* was making an effort.

"What is your name, child?"

"Idelle."

Leonie smiled encouragingly, for she could see the little girl was nervous. "You should have help with all this weeding."

"Oh, no, my lady. Cook would not like it if I couldn't manage this task alone. I am only to pick a few greens for the salad."

"Greens? And did cook tell you which greens to pick?"

The young face crumbled. "I asked him, but—but he said any greens. Have I done wrong? I did not mean to do wrong, my lady."

Leonie said gently, "No, you did as you were told. How long have you helped in the kitchens, Idelle?"

"Not long. I was learning to weave, but Lady Amelia doesn't like children within the keep, so my sister sent me to the kitchens."

"Then someone should have shown you what to pick and what to throw away in this overgrown mess. What you have there I call 'good-for-nothings.'"

Idelle grinned. "Truly?"

"Truly." Leonie smiled back. "Now let me see." She bent down and parted a heavy clump of foliage. "Ah! There *is* something edible here, after all. These will do for a salad." And she began filling the girl's basket with as many dandelion leaves as she could find.

"Once again I find you in a garden."

Leonie's hands froze. Even her breathing stopped.

"I told you they were looking for you," Idelle whispered.

Leonie tried to smile and failed. "So you did. Go back to the kitchen, Idelle. The cook will have to make do with what you have."

They both rose at the same time, Idelle to move quickly past the awe-inspiring lord of Kempston, and Leonie to face him.

Once again she was struck by the handsomeness of the man, and for a fleeting moment all else was forgotten as she looked him over slowly. From the thickly muscled legs in fine hose to the brown tunic shot with gold thread, everything he wore emphasized the power of his body.

Meeting those velvety brown eyes brought back Amelia's words. She decided she would not demean herself by asking him questions about Amelia, or about his bringing her there. His wanting to start anew, as he'd said, was obviously a lie. And more lies would only confuse her. Also, she did not want him thinking she was upset over Amelia.

"You call this a garden, my lord?" That was a safe enough subject.

Rolfe spared the briefest look around before his gaze returned to the lovely vision before him. "What would I know of gardens?"

"You saw mine at Pershwick."

"Did I?" He moved closer, grinning. "No, little flower, I saw only you."

She felt a fluttering in her belly and her face flushed hot as fire. This would not do, this complexity of emotions he was able to stir in her. She had to stop his effect on her.

"Do you call me 'little flower' to remind me of how you might have shamed me before my people?"

Rolfe's spirits sank. She was angry. Her eyes shone like polished silver, her dark brows were slashed together, and her lips were set in a hard line. Once again, her anger caused his own to rise.

"Damn me, I thought that was settled!"

Leonie flinched, but she didn't move. Virile strength exuded from the powerful body so close to her, but she held her ground.

"I merely questioned your motive in reminding me of the incident."

Rolfe frowned. How cleverly she made him feel like a cloddish bore for attacking her. Dealing with this particular woman was not going to be easy.

He smoothed the tight line of her lips. "Do you realize the effect you have on me, dearling?" he asked gently. "I see you and my thoughts fly away. If I reminded you of something unpleasant, it was unintentional and I apologize."

Leonie was stunned. Could she believe him? Was he toying with her, trying only to placate her? If so, he was succeeding, and her anger was quickly giving way to nervousness.

She lowered her eyes, utterly confused and helpless. "You—you sought me out, my lord. Was there something you wanted of me?"

He chuckled softly, wickedly, and she drew back.

"My lord—"

"Rolfe."

"I—"

"Rolfe," he insisted. "You are my wife and formality is uncalled for when we are alone."

The reminder was uncalled for! As if she could forget she was his wife! And now he was waiting for her to say his name and, in saying it, acknowledge his ownership of her.

"Leonie?" His voice was husky. "Are you still so shy?"

She could use that excuse . . . but she decided not to hide her feelings just to keep him in a good mood.

"It is more than shyness, my lord," she said frankly. "Perhaps in time . . ."

Rolfe sighed and Leonie felt a certain triumph over not giving in.

"Time I do not have," he told her. "I leave here on the morrow. I do not know when I will return, but when I do, I shall expect you to be more at ease with me. We have been married more than a month."

"But we have not been together that long," she reminded him coldly.

"Even so, you have had time to adjust," he declared.

"I beg to explain," she said stiffly. "You sent me away from here and I thought I would not see you again. *That* is what I adjusted to, my lord."

"So!" he said as if he had learned something important. Leonie grew uncomfortable when he said nothing further.

"My lord, you still have not said why you sought me out."

"I had the ridiculous notion that spending the day with you would be pleasant. Where were you, my lady?"

She began to despair. Everything was getting worse. This quiet anger was worse than shouting.

"I—I walked to the village."

"Who accompanied you?"

Sweet Mary, he was going to make an issue of even that!

"You must know I went alone."

"If I knew, madame, I would not ask. Alone? This is not Pershwick where you may do as you please."

"I am most aware of the truth of *that,* my lord," she said bitterly.

His eyes narrowed. "Perhaps you care nothing for your safety, but you are mine now and I protect what is mine. Must I place a constant guard on you?"

"Do not!" She gasped. "I—I know I was wrong to leave the keep without escort, but I was not thinking. I needed—some time. It will not happen again, my lord," she finished quickly, embarrassed by her stammering.

She looked away from his penetrating eyes, and he gripped her chin. "I am not asking more than I should, Leonie. Do not begrudge me my concern."

She hated herself for being so nervous with him. She hated his reasonable tone. But most of all she hated what he was doing to her, this up and down of churning emotions. She was angry one moment, intimidated the next—and worse was this strange feeling that intruded whenever he touched her.

His fingers moved from her chin up across her cheek. Leonie held her breath, waiting for him to kiss her, but he only gazed into her eyes. His eyes were dark and unfathomable.

"Anger is beneficial at times," Rolfe said. "It clears the air, stimulates the blood. Do not hide your anger from me, Leonie. I may not like it, but I will like it less if you let your anger fester. Do not sulk with me, wife. And never, never bring anger to my bed."

A quick, feather-light brush of his lips against hers and then he let her go and walked away.

Leonie stared after him, bemused, her fingertips on her face where he had touched it. Her heart was racing.

Chapter 18

THE hall had filled quickly and servants were bringing in large platters of food. A maid lost her balance and her huge cauldron of soup tipped a little, spilling soup onto the rushes. Five dogs instantly converged on the spot, but the hot liquid was not tempting enough. After a few sniffs, they went back to following the platters of meat, hoping for another accident.

Erneis, the Crewel steward, had seen the accident, but he went on filling his plate, giving it no more thought. The maid would think no more of it either. She would not return later to clean up the mess, because no one would tell her to do so.

Common occurrences in Crewel Keep, gone on so long that those conditions were taken for granted. The men-at-arms might deplore the filth, but it was not their place to order these servants. Sir Evarard had lived under worse conditions and took little notice. The servants never did anything on their own initiative and had, in fact, grown lazy.

Sir Thorpe had long ago given up trying to get anything done. He never stayed long enough in Crewel to oversee a thorough cleaning, anyway. And Rolfe had too many other things on his mind. Amelia seemed to have no knack for handling servants. It was enough that she had kept Rolfe's room reasonably clean.

Rolfe had mused aloud about having a wife in residence, hoping the problem would be solved. But it was not to be. Amelia told him that she had had words with his wife and that Leonie said she could not be bothered with the running of Crewel. Rolfe was furious, especially after the scene in the garden. She could see to Pershwick, which was hers, but she would not see to Crewel?

But Amelia pointed out that ladies of Leonie's stature were accustomed to spending their days in needlework and gossip. Rolfe knew that to be true, for his own mother had never lifted a hand to run her household. No doubt Leonie had an able steward at Pershwick. Ah well, Rolfe thought, let things stand as they were.

Unfortunately, his anger over that difficulty did not have a chance to abate before Leonie came in. She was wearing the same unhappy expression she had worn in the garden, and he almost sent her away, but too many eyes were on them.

Neither one spoke, and his anger mounted. She was going to nurse her anger, and that infuriated him. He wanted her to be the way she had been the night before, when she talked with him, accepted him. He had believed they were making a new start.

Damian had returned to Crewel in the afternoon with Rolfe's newly polished armor. Cleaning armor was the only thing the boy did well. Rolfe was not used to having so young a squire, nor did he have enough time at present for the boy's training. It was Damian's duty to attend him, to select his clothes in the morning, help dress him, and to serve him at table. Strict rules governed all a squire did, even the carving of meat and presenting of his lord's wine cup. Damian knew all that was required of him, but nothing was ever done smoothly.

Today, having used all his patience on his wife, Rolfe had none left for the boy. When his wine was spilled a second time, he dismissed the boy with harsh words that rose above the din in the hall. Silence followed, and then everyone resumed eating. Rolfe's losing his temper was a common enough occurrence, after all.

Leonie was already on edge, having watched Lady Amelia direct the serving of the meal with Rolfe's apparent approval.

"Are you always so hard on the boy?"

Rolfe's dark eyes impaled her. "So. You have a voice after all."

Leonie looked down at the table. "I did not know I was required to speak. There is nothing I wish to say."

"Common courtesy is alien to you?"

"No, my lord," she replied softly. "It is returned when it is received."

He grunted, dismissing the fact that he had said not a word to her, either. "So now you have found something you wish to say—and it turns out to be criticism. You would have done better to keep silent."

"I know my opinion means nothing to you, my lord, but you would be better served by your squire if you showed a little patience. The boy is only nervous."

"You have trained many squires, have you?"

"No."

"Surely at least one? How else would you know how I should treat mine?"

Leonie held firm under his assault. "Common sense, my lord."

"Patience cures clumsiness?"

"He would not be so clumsy if you did not scowl at him so," she replied.

"I see. So when Damian faces his enemy on the field, he will do well if his enemy smiles at him? But let that enemy scowl at him even once and what have you? A sword dropped through nervous fingers instead of spilled wine. Your common sense would be the death of Damian."

Leonie blushed furiously. Everything he said was true. If Damian did not learn to control his nervousness now, he would not live to be a knight. Serfs and women could be clumsy, fighting men could not.

"I concede," she offered. "Yet I still say you were overly harsh with the boy. A small measure of patience once in a while would benefit you *both*."

"You recommend patience for the boy—what do you recommend for yourself?"

Leonie raised her eyes to his slowly and asked in a sweetly innocent tone, "Have I raised your displeasure, too, my lord?"

Rolfe was not amused. He was in fact infuriated by her attempt to make light of his anger.

"What do you recommend?" he repeated darkly.

"Retreat."

"Unacceptable."

"Then another measure of patience, my lord."

"Patience without reward is not worth the effort," he shot back.

A warning. He expected too much. If he was not willing to give, neither was she.

"Reward comes only to the deserving."

"You mean I am not deserving?"

"That is a matter for your conscience, my lord."

"Damn me, what has conscience to do with this?" he demanded. "My conscience is clear!"

"No doubt," she returned.

To say any more now was dangerous. Rolfe drained the last of his wine and bellowed for more.

Leonie let out a sigh. She should never have spoken to begin with. There was no reasoning with such a man.

Most men lived by a double standard and her husband was no different. You could not tell him he was wrong, and you could not question his integrity as he saw it. And as he saw it, there was nothing wrong with his keeping a mistress in the same household as his wife. Or with letting his mistress direct the household. A man's adultery was always winked at, but woe betide the wife with inclinations to stray. Hypocrites all! She might have to live with it for there was very little she could do about it, but she would not condone the hypocrisy of it.

The meal was ruined, but she had no appetite anyhow. It was bad enough having to eat with her belly knotted with tension, but the food was awful, tasteless, without benefit of spices. Even the minced meat paste made with milk and bread crumbs to spread on bread was lacking herbs. There was cheese made from ewes' milk, but the butter that would have enhanced the vegetables was rancid. It vied with the stench from the rushes.

"Do you give me leave to retire, my lord?"

Rolfe looked at her for a long time before he nodded curtly. But he stopped her just as she turned away.

"Leave your spite behind, Leonie. I will join you soon."

It was still early, and the last place Leonie wanted to await her husband was in his bed. The memories it aroused warred with her embitterment, causing a frustration that had her pacing the floor. It was not fair to be placed in this limbo. She could not have Rolfe d'Ambert for a real husband, nor would he leave her alone. All that was left was a frustration that she would have to tolerate until he no longer found his newest possession amusing.

After a while, when Rolfe still had not come, Leonie searched through her chests in the anteroom until she found the Pershwick accounts. She took them with her to one of the chairs by the cold hearth and settled herself there. She had brought the accounts with her so she could put them in order before turning them over to Sir Guibert.

All the long hours she had spent learning to read and write so she could keep her own records, and now her skill would go to waste—for a while anyway. How long would he keep her there? If only she knew.

Hours later, Rolfe found Leonie curled up in the chair, the parchments spread over her lap, an inkwell on the low table beside her. He had not expected this. The church, which dispensed all learning, frowned on imparting any at all to women. Very few men outside the church could read and write. Rolfe could write, but it was a skill he did not make use of, relying on clerks to see to such things.

Rolfe picked up one of the parchments and examined it. But her eyes opened, and he dropped it back on her lap.

"Do you make sense of those scratches, my lady?"

Leonie sat up, startled. "Of course. They are my records."

"Who taught you to write?"

"A young priest at Pershwick."

"Why would he?"

Leonie was wary, but his tone was agreeable. He seemed merely curious.

"I threatened to dismiss him if he would not."

Rolfe had to stop himself from laughing. "Did you? I take it he succumbed to your threats. But why would you want to learn? Did he not keep accurate records for you?"

"Accurate, yes, but he balked at certain changes I wanted made. It is a long story, my lord. Rather than involve the priest in what I wanted done, I decided to do it myself, so I insisted he teach me."

"I am pleased, then. Here is one thing you cannot object to doing for me," Rolfe said. "You will serve as my clerk."

"Me?" she cried. "You mean you do not write?"

"I spent my youth on the training field, not cloistered with a tutor."

He felt no embarrassment over the half lie. It was true that he had not given up any training time for learning, nor was he ever cloistered with a tutor. His tutor had had to follow him onto the training field, an inconvenience the old priest did not appreciate.

"But surely you have a clerk?"

"I am not asking you to take over the Crewel accounts," he said. "But you can deal with simple correspondence."

She bristled. "I suppose I can, if you do not think it will overtax my intelligence."

Her sarcasm amused him. "Not at all."

Leonie rose stiffly. "Very well, my lord."

She put her accounts away, and when she came back into the room, Rolfe was sitting in the chair she had vacated. His eyes fastened on her, hooded, unreadable. She raised a hand to hold her linen bedrobe closer together, acutely aware of how thin the cream-colored robe was.

"Come here, Leonie."

It was a soft command, but it was a command.

Nervously she glanced at the big bed. As abhorrent as it was to her, it did offer an excuse.

"It is late, my lord, and—"

"You have had a nap, so do not say you are overtired."

She met his steady gaze, but it was a moment before she could get her feet to move. Finally she stood near him.

"Closer."

She took another step, and then Rolfe reached out and pulled her down onto his lap. His hands locked around her, resting on her hip. Hesitantly, her eyes met his.

"I am glad you took my warning seriously, dearling, for I do not give warnings more than once."

Leonie closed her eyes. He assumed she was acquiescent because he had ordered it. He was going to find she was not a servant.

"What happens, my lord, when your warnings are not heeded?" she asked.

His lips nuzzled her neck. "You do not want to know."

"But I do, my lord."

"Rolfe," he corrected, his lips moving to the center of her throat.

Leonie groaned. "I am sorry, my lord, but I cannot."

"Cannot what?"

"Call you by name."

He leaned back. His hands came up to clasp her face. "Just say it. It is a short name, easy to say. Say it."

He was smiling and his tone was husky, persuasive. But as she gazed into his eyes, she saw Lady Amelia. That lady sat firmly between them.

"I cannot."

"You mean you *will not*."

"Very well, I will not."

Instantly, Rolfe was on his feet, Leonie held firmly in his arms. He carried her to the bed and dropped her there, glaring down at her.

"Woman, if I did not think you had more sense, I would swear you do this purposely, just to rile me. If you wish to sulk, do so, but do so alone. If you are wise, you will be done sulking when I come to you again."

He strode angrily from the room, slamming the door.

Leonie lay back, slowly relaxing. She sighed. She guessed she would not see him again before he left in the morning. That suited her fine. But then she realized where he would spend the night and she tensed.

Surely someone would see him going to his mistress, and no doubt everyone would know of it by the next day, for things like that were kept secret only from the wife. *This* wife already knew, however, and her husband did not care whether she knew or not. That was the vilest insult, that he made no attempt to spare his wife's feelings.

Chapter 19

ROLFE had indeed left Crewel by the time Leonie ventured into the hall the next morning. Thorpe de la Mare had gone with him, leaving Sir Evarard as castellan of Crewel, in charge.

Leonie was in a foul mood after losing so much sleep trying to convince herself that what her husband did did not matter to her personally, only the shame of it disturbed her. Her mood was not lightened when she found Lady Amelia breaking her fast at the high table with Sir Evarard, the two of them laughing together.

They presented a tableau illustrating that the mistress was accepted there and the wife was not. It was also stabbingly clear that Amelia was in an excellent humor.

The two fell silent as they saw Leonie. She did not greet them or even glance their way again, but continued on toward the chapel as if that had been her destination all along. She knew she was too late for mass, so she didn't even glance inside the chapel, but left the forebuilding and stepped outside into the bright morning light.

She had a decision to make, one that might get her into even worse trouble with her husband, but one that was worth considering for her own sake.

It was simply not her way to be idle. That only

encouraged the kind of mood she found herself in. She needed to be occupied.

Of course, Amelia must surely be gratified to find herself placed above Rolfe's wife in his household. But if Amelia knew the art of maintaining a household, she was surely keeping her knowledge to herself.

The problem was, no one at Crewel seemed to care about the conditions they lived in. For Rolfe to sacrifice his own comfort in order to honor his mistress showed great depth of feeling. Leonie could do nothing about Rolfe's feelings, but she would not live in a pigsty or be mistress of one.

If she was to order certain tasks done, who was to deny her? Rolfe might, when he returned, but by then she would have accomplished much and the improvements might assuage his wrath. Would Lady Amelia dare complain? Leonie was willing to risk an argument with that one.

The decision made, she went to find Wilda and Mary. She found the stairs that led to the servants' quarters above the first floor. At the top of those stairs she found, not one large room, but a narrow hall. The servants' quarters were on the left side, and there were many small rooms on the right side of the hall.

Wilda came when Leonie called her name softly. "My lady."

Leonie's curiosity was aroused. "Are stores kept up here?" she asked, looking at the row of rooms.

Wilda understood and shook her head. "My lady, I never heard of such as this. It was Sir Edmond's idea to offer his guests privacy, so he ordered those small chambers built, each with a bed and other conveniences."

"Each one of these is a small bedchamber?"

Wilda nodded. "Mildred said Crewel was never without guests. Sir Edmond liked to impress his guests."

Leonie was not surprised that the maid knew so much. Servants gossiped. "Private chambers instead of a pallet in the hall is impressive indeed. I did not realize the Montignys were so wealthy."

Wilda frowned. "There are rumors—"

"For shame, Wilda. You know I do not countenance rumors," Leonie said automatically, and because Wilda knew her lady disliked gossip, she fell silent. It was just as well, for Wilda did not want to be the one to tell her lady about the rumors concerning her and her husband.

It suited Wilda to have the servants at Crewel think Rolfe d'Ambert had beaten his wife on their wedding night. She disliked him because of the insult he was dealing Leonie by keeping his mistress in their home. Wilda had no desire to correct the women servants' opinions, or to argue with the men who took their lord's side. She was going to stay well out of the battle and had warned Mary to do the same. Rolfe d'Ambert was not a man to be patient with servants.

She said only, "Well, Sir Edmond did serve the best foods and wines."

"He must have had a different cook," Leonie said dryly and Wilda giggled.

"Indeed, I understand the cook fled with the coming of the new lord. The one who rules the kitchen now was enlisted from the stable."

Leonie was appalled. "Surely there must be some assistants of the old cook who are still here?"

"Yes. They could improve the fare, but they will not." Wilda lowered her voice. "There was much resentment here against your husband, and there still is."

"Was Sir Edmond loved?"

"No. He had a heavy hand. But with him there were no surprises and the servants always benefited from the abundance of food left over from his entertaining. But Sir Rolfe is here so little that they have not had any chance to know him, so they don't trust him. And his temper frightens everyone. No one is willing to draw his master's attention to himself."

Leonie nodded. She had half guessed as much. She glanced once more at the row of closed doors. "Are these rooms all empty?"

Wilda knew her lady well. "She sleeps in the large room that was Sir Alain's," she whispered.

"But where does Sir Evarard—"

"That one is a soldier through and through. He sleeps with the men-at-arms. Mildred says he would be happiest rolled in a blanket under the stars."

"And how would Mildred know that?"

Wilda grinned. "One thing Sir Evarard does not dislike about his being settled instead of marching from one campaign to the next is the women here. He is a handsome young man, my lady."

Leonie controlled an urge to grin. "And you are thinking of trying him out yourself?"

Before Leonie's marriage, Wilda would never have admitted such a thing, but now she answered loftily, "I have thought of it."

Leonie shook her head. How could she scold Wilda for wanting pleasure? It never did any good to point out the sinfulness in a union without marriage.

"In the next few days," Leonie said, changing the subject, "you will have little time to think of such things. You wanted a chance to put the Crewel servants to work, and now you will have it."

Wilda was delighted. "You have his permission then? We may begin—"

"Not his permission, but we will begin anyway."

"But—"

Leonie cut her short. "I cannot live like this. And he is not here to stop me."

"Are you sure, my lady?"

"Most sure."

Amelia was shocked when every woman servant in the keep descended on the hall with brooms and soap and water. She pulled Leonie aside.

"Rolfe will not like it."

Leonie smiled tightly. "Then you must put the blame on me, for this place offends me and I will not stay here another day under these conditions. Of course, if my husband is pleased, then you must take the credit yourself. I am sure you intended to clean the house, but have been unable to find the time."

The sarcasm was heavy, yet it went right over Amelia's head. "To do anything here, you must constantly supervise. The serfs are too simple to carry a task through on their own. Do you not think I have tried?"

Leonie kept her doubts to herself. It was an effort just to talk to this woman.

"I have my own methods of doing things."

"If Rolfe is satisfied..." Amelia grumbled.

"But I am not satisfied, Lady Amelia. I am not asking you to volunteer your help, however."

She would not ask for permission either. See if the woman dared overrule her.

Amelia was wise enough to back down. She had gained too much to risk a confrontation with Rolfe's wife over such a trifling matter as this.

"Suit yourself, my lady," Amelia said before moving away.

Leonie nodded to Wilda, whose eyes twinkled as

she began shouting orders to the women gathered around her. And so it began. There was some grumbling once the task was explained, but Wilda's sharp tongue quickly took care of complaints.

Leonie would have pitched in to help, as she had always done at Pershwick, but to do that here would lower her position. As it was, too many of the servants looked first to Lady Amelia for approval.

With Wilda in firm control in the hall, Leonie gathered some men servants and directed them to follow her outside. She sent four men to gather new rushes, and another to summon Sir Evarard. Then she took three men to the kitchen.

The staff were instantly resentful of her presence, having gone so long without any interference. Besides the cook, a lean man of middle age, there were five male assistants and three children, who were allotted the easiest tasks. Little Idelle was one, and Leonie had to stop herself from smiling at the girl until after she dealt with the rest of the staff.

The condition of the long shed that served as the kitchen was appalling. Smoke and grease were so thick on everything that it was a wonder the building hadn't burned down. The pantry, larder, and buttery were in no better condition.

She took no pity on the cook, for he was solely responsible. "You may return to the stable where your talents will be better used," she told him, daring him by the severity of her expression to object.

He seemed relieved. After he left, she ordered the three men with her to begin removing everything from the kitchen. The five male assistants and Idelle were told to follow Leonie to the garden. There she looked at each man in turn, judging their attitudes and knowing that if her plan didn't work, she would end up being the cook herself.

She turned her attention to the little girl and allowed herself to drop her severe manner for a moment. "Idelle, do you remember the 'good-for-naughts' you were picking from the garden?"

Idelle's eyes widened. "I did not pick them again, my lady, I swear."

"I know, but now I want you to pick them again, every one of them."

"But there is so much!"

"Exactly. And since they serve no purpose, they do not belong in the garden. Do you see?"

Idelle saw only that it would take forever to do what her lady was asking, yet she wanted desperately to please Leonie. "I will do it."

Leonie grinned at the forlorn face. "I did not mean you should pick them yourself. No, these men here will do the picking, roots and all—especially the roots. You will stand by to watch and see they do not miss any, and to see that they do not rest until the task is done."

"You mean they must do as *I* say?" Idelle gasped.

"That is correct."

"My lady, I protest!" One of the men spoke up. "It is not—"

"You question my will?"

"No, my lady, but—"

"Is it the task you object to? Or that you must follow the orders of a child? But I have seen with my own eyes that you know nothing about keeping a kitchen clean, and I have tasted what fare has come out of that kitchen, so I assume you also know nothing about cooking. What good are any of you, except to pull weeds?"

One of the others stepped forward. "I can produce meals that would tempt any palate, my lady."

Leonie raised a brow. "Can you? Well, I will not ask you why you have kept that knowledge to yourself until now, but I will give you this day to prove your words. If you do not lie, you will be cook henceforth, and the kitchen will be yours to rule. But if you are not telling the truth . . ."

She left the threat up in the air. It was best for them to guess how harsh she might be. If she threatened a beating, some might think they could withstand it or that she wouldn't follow through. The same with banishment. But if they had no idea what she would do, they were not likely to risk incurring her wrath.

"I—I will need help, my lady." The new cook indicated his fellows.

"What is your name?"

"John."

Leonie smiled at him, surprising and enrapturing him. "You will have all you need, John, help and supplies. I ask only that you do not order more than you need, or find yourself short. Report daily all purchases to Master Erneis for the accounts. Can you guess what else I want done?"

He could not meet her eyes but he answered, "A thorough scrubbing from top to bottom."

"Yes. All utensils, pots—everything. There is no excuse for an accumulation of filth in the kitchen and I will not tolerate it again. See that the cleaning is done before the next meal is started. You may make use of the three men who have already begun the work, the men I brought with me. Eight men should be quite enough."

"Thank you, my lady."

Idelle looked miserable again as the five men followed their new leader to the kitchens. "Does this mean I will have to pick all the 'good-for-naughts' by myself?"

"Indeed, no." Leonie grinned. "But this is an important task, important to me. Can you think of anyone who would do a good job of it?"

"My friends in the kitchen," Idelle suggested eagerly.

"The other two children?"

"Yes."

"Then you may get them to be your helpers. And there is no rush, Idelle. The point is to do a good job the first time. When you finish, there will be much planting here that you can help me with."

"I would like that, my lady."

"Good. Now run and get your friends. Sir Evarard is coming to speak with me."

Leonie moved across the bailey to meet him. He did not look at all agreeable.

"Sir Evarard—"

He cut her short rudely. "Do not think, my lady, that this will please Sir Rolfe. You wait until he is gone and then you turn this place upside down. He will see that you are set on causing trouble."

"You dare take that tone with me?" Leonie said icily. She glared up at the man, her eyes hot. "If you will not give me the respect due me as your lord's wife, then I will not abide in the same keep with you. You can tell *that* to my husband when you bring him tales of what you *think* I have done!"

The man squared his jaw stubbornly. "You think to talk circles around me, my lady, but no one can even enter the hall because you have caused such a mess. What excuse do you have for tearing everything apart?"

"You idiot! Do you not recognize the process of

cleaning when you see it? But how could you, since there has been no cleaning done here since you came?" She added icily, "The hall will be in proper order by the end of the day. And the food you eat tonight will be wholesome. What I have done, Sir Evarard, is save myself from having to treat you for food poisoning, which would have struck you and everyone else here soon enough if the conditions in the kitchen were allowed to go unchecked. Now you tell me—who is inconvenienced by what I am doing except the servants who are now paying for what they have neglected all this time?"

Sir Evarard was no longer as belligerent. "Perhaps I did not understand."

"Is that all?" she demanded stiffly, and he reddened. "Forgive me, my lady. I saw only the upheaval. I thought you still meant my lord ill. It—it is known that you were forced to marry him, and a woman forced is discontent, so I believed that you . . ."

Leonie relaxed completely, all her anger flowing out of her. "You are very loyal to my husband."

"There is no other lord I would serve," he declared staunchly.

"Then let me put your mind at ease, Sir Evarard. I will tell you something if you swear you will not repeat it." She waited for him to nod, then told him, "I ask you not to repeat it, because I have not told Sir Rolfe this. I want him to think I accept the blame for the trouble my people caused him. I accept all the blame. But the truth is this: my people did *not* act on my orders. There were no orders. But my people are loyal to me, overzealously so. They acted on their own after they heard me curse Sir Rolfe."

"You only cursed him?"

It was her turn to blush. "It was a—rather heated

curse. But if I had known what events it would set in motion, I wouldn't have lost my temper that day."

His eyes lit with unexpected humor. "It is a good thing your men-at-arms are not as loyal as the others."

"They are," Leonie said with a grin. "They just didn't hear me cursing the Black Wolf that day."

"He does not like that name," Sir Evarard said hastily.

"What?"

"My lord does not like to be called the Black Wolf," Evarard repeated.

"Oh. I thank you for the warning."

He smiled at her. "I thank you, my lady, for telling me what you have."

"Do not mistake me, Sir Evarard. You were correct in thinking I am not content here. But that is between my husband and myself. I wanted you only to know that you need not fear I will ruin anything that is his. It is my lord who will know what I feel, not his possessions or his people."

She could see it in his eyes. Their truce was over. She should have left well enough.

Leonie sighed. "I am sorry, Sir Evarard, but we differ in our opinions of Rolfe d'Ambert. He has offended me too grievously for my opinion to change, but I will say no more to you against him."

Sir Evarard held his tongue. He was drawing his own conclusions, and they were the wrong ones. He assumed the lady had been offended by being sent away from her husband directly after the wedding. But she was back now, and she ought to have forgiven that slight. He did not guess that she was referring to Lady Amelia's presence at Crewel Keep. He knew she had been told Amelia was Rolfe's ward, and he saw no reason for her to suspect the truth.

Too, if anyone knew how thoroughly Rolfe's affair with Amelia was over, Evarard did. Amelia was now sharing Evarard's bed. More exactly, he was sharing hers. He would never have trifled with his lord's former mistress, but she had convinced him that Rolfe had relinquished all claims to her. Proof was, the lady said, that Rolfe did not even care if she stayed in his household, so completely had he dismissed her from his mind.

Sir Evarard brought himself to the present situation. "You sent for me, my lady?"

Leonie stepped back into her role as mistress of Crewel, however empty that role often seemed. To display her authority, she would give orders, not make requests.

"I want one of your men to ride to Pershwick. He is to speak to Sir Guibert, or if he is not there, then to my aunt Beatrix. He is to say he comes from me, that I need wormwood and chamomile from my supplies. They will know why I need those herbs."

"We have supplies here, my lady. I do not think Sir Rolfe will like you taking from Pershwick."

"My husband has no say in what I take from Pershwick, for Pershwick is mine," Leonie stated firmly. "And since those herbs have not been in use here, I doubt that you have them in supply. I want the herbs today. The wormwood will help combat the fleas here. It must be strewn before the new rushes are brought into the hall, and afterward as well. The chamomile will curb the odors in the rest of the keep until all the rushes can be changed. I will not tolerate filth, Sir Evarard, and please do not question my motives when I give orders."

"As you will, my lady," he replied brusquely and turned away.

"I am not finished," she said sharply.

He turned back reluctantly. "My lady?"

"How often do you hunt, Sir Evarard?"

"Every day. For sport as well as for the table."

"You use the dogs or do you have hawks?"

"Hawks are too tedious to carry with us and we did naught but move from place to place before we settled here. My lord has not yet purchased good hawks. The few we have here bring down an occasional bird. I do not use them. I prefer the dogs."

"Then I can assume the hunting dogs get enough exercise, and if not, that can be seen to outside the walls of the keep. Inside, they will no longer have free rein. And I do not mean just inside the hall. Their habits are too foul."

"But they are fed in the hall."

"No longer," she replied, shaking her head with distaste. "Is there no master of the hounds?"

"Yes."

"Then tell him to keep the animals penned at all times when they are not in use. If Crewel has no dog pens, he is to build some—adequately, so the pens can easily be cleaned daily."

"The man will balk, my lady," he warned her.

"Then you will replace him," she replied smoothly. "And if there is no one else who qualifies, then deal with him harshly until he stops balking. Otherwise I will have to bring my own man here from Pershwick."

"I will see the matter settled, my lady."

He said it so quickly that it was comical. She supposed she could use that threat again if she had any more trouble. He wouldn't be the only one at Crewel who would resent outside help. She'd do well to keep that threat in her arsenal, she told herself.

Chapter 20

HE could not stay away even for a week, was Rolfe's thought about himself as he rode into the bailey at Crewel in time for dinner, five days later. He felt as much disgust with himself as he had when he'd found himself drawn back to Leonie the day after his wedding, when he hadn't even known what she looked like. Still, there were reasons other than his wife for his early return.

The campaign at Wroth had come to a standstill. For the fifth time the tunnel they were working to get under the walls had collapsed. Rolfe could not afford this new delay. Time was working against him now. The remaining keeps that he had yet to win had been closed up for nearly seven months. They would be getting desperate, reaching a point where they would be forced to open up and fight. And if Rolfe was not there with the bulk of his force when one did open up...

He had a decision to make about Wroth Keep, but it was a decision he could make at home as easily as he could camp outside of Wroth—easier here, in fact, for once he took his wife to bed he could at last put her from his mind long enough to devote his thoughts to Wroth.

Rolfe had not looked forward to eating at Crewel, so he had eaten when he stopped at Kenil to check on the repairs in progress there. The food there was good, and he was considering moving the Kenil cook to Crewel. But on entering the hall at Crewel with Damian and two men-at-arms, he was greeted with a very pleasant aroma.

He had only a moment to wonder about it before his eyes fell on Leonie, and his sense of smell gave way to other senses. She was sitting at the high table, an ethereal vision in an ice-blue bliaut, her silver hair in two thick braids resting one on each breast. A short blue square of lace was her only head covering. Evarard and Amelia were dining with her, but seemed to be talking only to each other.

The hall was full and noisy, yet it seemed to Rolfe that there was only himself and Leonie. He gazed at her to his heart's content, willing her to look at him. At last, sensing something, she did. Their eyes locked, and his desire for her rose hot and strong, stunning him with its force.

When she saw Rolfe, Leonie's heart jumped into her throat. She took a deep breath to steady herself as, his expression intense, he moved toward her. A tight knot formed in her belly.

She was about to learn what he thought of the changes she had made in his home, and she found she wasn't feeling at all brave. The rushing of her blood roared in her ears.

But Rolfe, whose eyes did not leave hers for a second, was paying no attention to his surroundings, and sudden hot color flooded her face as she realized what made him look at her so intently. She quickly bent her head and turned a little away from him as he approached the table. She was not going to acknowledge him—she couldn't find her voice.

Many eyes watched Rolfe crossing the hall so purposefully, but he was blind to everything except Leonie. Wilda and Mary held their breath, fearing for their mistress, while Rolfe's men grinned at one another. Amelia failed to keep the resentment from her eyes, though no one noticed her because the meeting between lord and lady held everyone's attention.

Leonie gasped as her chair was pulled away from the table, and shrieked as Rolfe scooped her up and, without a word, started toward the stairs. Behind them, laughter erupted in the hall, and cheers, as the assembled company watched them disappear up the stairs.

Leonie was so mortified that she hid her face against Rolfe's chest. Shame paralyzed her, and it was not until their door closed on the noise below that her voice returned. "How *could* you?" she cried, struggling against him.

Gripping her firmly, he answered innocently, "What have I done except to bring you where I want you to be?"

"Everyone knows exactly what you intend!" she stormed, mindless of all but her shame.

Rolfe chuckled, his eyes velvety brown with warmth. "You make too much of it, dearling. They might think I brought you up here to beat you. Would you be appeased if you returned to the hall with a blackened eye?"

"You make light of it," she told him furiously, "but even animals show their mates some respect. I would be appeased only if I returned below immediately."

He kissed her so forcefully that her thoughts disappeared like silken threads on the wind. When he finished, his kissing fired by passion, she was so bemused that she hardly knew he had set her on her feet.

"There," he said. "With your lips swollen, everyone

will think I only wanted to steal a kiss. So you may go below and be appeased now, Leonie."

"You mean it?" She gasped.

"I want you, but if my keeping you here is going to upset you . . . Go quickly now, before I change my mind."

Leonie lowered her eyes, her voice tremulous. "Thank you, my lord."

"My lord," he repeated disgustedly, sighing. "Finish your dinner. And please order me a bath and send my squire to me. Also, Leonie, have your maids come and take their things away now if they moved back here while I was away. But you must return here within the hour or you will again have reason to call me an animal."

Leonie hurried out of the room. The tasks Rolfe had set her to made her feel almost like a real wife and she saw to them with a measure of pride. It was enough to obviate her embarrassment, and she even relaxed enough to finish her meal.

But as the time neared for her to return to Rolfe, her calm fled. Rather than delay and let her nervousness get the best of her, she mounted the stairs in a rush before she could succumb to the urge to find a hiding place.

He had finished his bath and was sitting in a chair by the hearth. He had moved the chair to face the door, and was staring at her as she entered. He wore a bedrobe of fine yellow silk. It made his eyes a lighter brown. He wore it loosely, falling open to reveal the thick black hair of his chest. It was to this mat of hair that her eyes kept returning, and she blushed furiously when he caught her staring.

On the table beside him was her own soap and a thick woolen towel that she had told Wilda to give to

Damian for Rolfe. The soap had been put back in its little wooden box to dry, and the wet towel folded.

Rolfe's eyes followed Leonie's. "Was there a subtlety in your offering me that sweet-smelling soap?" he inquired.

"No, my lord. For as long as I have known you, you have not smelled unpleasant to me." He grinned at the unintended compliment. "The soap is made with oil of rosemary. I thought you might prefer it to the abrasive soaps I found here."

"Is it costly?"

"Costly only in time, my lord. I make it myself."

"Then I am pleased you offered it." His voice deepened when he added, "But I would have been more pleased if you had found your way back here sooner."

"I am not late."

"You quibble with me when you know what it cost me to let you go?"

"I—I don't understand."

"Perhaps," he replied softly, "but I think it more likely you do."

Leonie had no answer for that. He was looking at her in a way that increased her nervousness so much that she darted over to the bed, praying that preparing it for sleep would distract them both. But the bedlinens were already turned down, and there was nothing for her to do.

She sat down on the far side of the bed, away from him, refusing to look at him any more. The picture he presented was all too masculine, corded muscle, virile strength, compelling handsomeness, all wrapped up in self-assurance. She would wager that *he* was never afraid, while she sat there feeling her belly churn with dread.

She closed her eyes, but that didn't stop him from coming to stand before her. "Let me help you disrobe."

"I can manage," she whispered, and Rolfe tensed.

"Are you still sulking, Leonie?"

"I do not sulk. I never sulk. Children sulk! I am not a child."

She rasped out each word, fighting with the laces at her side. He stood there patiently, watching her whip her bliaut off, then vengefully attack the laces of her chemise. Finally it was discarded, leaving only her knee-length cream-colored sleeveless shift. The garment was so thin that he could see her nipples. Rolfe caught his breath.

She was so incredibly lovely, this wife of his, even when she was bristling with anger. He had thought about her too much while they were separated, her image a living dream, seeing her eyes flash with silver fire, or soft with innocent confusion. Her hair was a glorious beacon, haunting him as he imagined running his fingers through the silver softness. Her body, the sweetly curving ripeness, was before him now in all its beauty—no longer a dream. This exquisite girl had yielded to him once. Would she again?

Leonie bent over to remove her slippers and stockings. Then, knowing she could not remove her shift, not with him standing there watching her, she folded her hands and was still, head bent, averting her gaze.

Rolfe gently removed the lace square from her head, lifting the braids and unbraiding them. Swiftly, he removed her shift and tossed it aside. Before she could protest, he took her face in his large hands and made her look up at him.

"Leonie, I did not ask your forgiveness for what happened at Pershwick. I ask it now. Do not be angry with me over that anymore."

She was so surprised she couldn't speak. But Rolfe wanted no answer, he wanted an end to her anger. And he desperately wanted her to want him.

He bent and kissed her, gently at first and then, as she began to respond to him, his kisses became more passionate. At last she moaned and he carried her to the center of the bed and lay down beside her, wrapping her hard against him. She forgot everything else and melted into him, enraptured, gloriously happy in his love.

Chapter 21

A SILVER moon peeked through swiftly passing clouds, and wind whipped over the parapets, foretelling a summer storm. The hounds howled in their confinement, and the horses moved restlessly in the stable.

Rolfe paced back and forth before the hearth, the single candle burning on the table near him casting his shadow against the walls. There were three hours yet before dawn, hours in which he must decide . . .

"My lord?"

Rolfe turned toward the bed. Leonie hadn't closed the bedcurtains, and he saw her curled on her side, eyes wide with concern.

"I did not mean to disturb you, Leonie. Go back to sleep."

It was the sound of his footsteps that had awakened her. A large man did not move quietly.

"I have much on my mind," he offered with a tired sigh. "It does not concern you."

Leonie lay quietly watching him, then spoke. "Perhaps if you speak of what troubles you, my lord, it will not seem so terrible."

His eyes fixed on her and he shook his head impatiently. How like a woman to think there was an easy solution to everything.

Leonie was chagrined. A husband should confide

in his wife. "There is nothing a man cannot tell his wife, unless he does not trust—"

"Very well." Rolfe cut her off, her persistence irritating him. "If you wish to hear of war and death, then I will tell you. On the morrow many of my men can die, for I can no longer think of a way to take Wroth Keep without attacking. Talk of terms ended long ago." He sat down and began elaborating. "The walls are thick and the tunnel it has taken so long to make collapsed once again. They are well supplied, it seems, for they taunt us from the walls and swear they can outlast us. My men are angry and impatient to fight, and in truth I can see no other way."

"You will move war machines against the walls?" she asked.

"I dealt with Kenil Keep that way and now the repairs there are costing more than my army. I am not making war on an enemy, Leonie. I am only securing what is mine. I don't want to take the keep by rendering it useless."

"Can you scale the walls?" she asked, feeling silly for asking naïve questions. But it seemed she was not far off the mark.

"I am left with no other choice. I have three other keeps to win yet, and they are becoming desperate because they have been closed off so long ago. Any day now one or more could open their gates and try to escape. If so, they will find they have been tricked, because they are being held at bay by only a handful of men—not an entire army, which is what it looks like from inside the keeps."

"Is *that* what you have done?" Leonie gasped.

He frowned. "I came here with only two hundred men. I hired more from the king's army, but that's still not enough to divide among seven keeps. Each keep believed I moved on it first. They each thought they had only to stay within their walls and wait, and help would come from one of the others. I let each keep see the whole of my army so they would think the odds were against their fighting before they had help. Later, I moved my men around to continue giving that impression. But if one of the remaining keeps should discover the ruse, they will be so enraged that every man I have camped there will be slaughtered."

Leonie was shocked. "Would you yourself have to fight in the attack on Wroth Keep?"

Rolfe glowered. "I do not send my men where I would not fight. I lead all movements, as I have always done."

"You have scaled the walls of many keeps?"

His expression became remote. "I have fought the wars of many men—including your king, who is now my king. I fought wherever I had to, in whatever manner was necessary. It is only recently, in this effort to secure what is mine, that I have used so much restraint. It is usually my way to see a thing done quickly, yet I have tried to destroy as little as possible."

"But you say you must attack Wroth."

"I must take the risk and I may lose men, but I can waste no more time on Wroth Keep."

"Then leave it," Leonie suggested in all seriousness. "Move on to the next keep and return to Wroth last."

"And have my men feel they are retreating? I told you, they have been angered by the taunts thrown down from the walls. They plead to attack."

"How many of those men will die before you even breach the walls and begin the actual fighting? How many will break their necks when the scaling ladders are pushed away from the walls? How many will be roasted by hot oil and sand?"

Rolfe gazed skyward. "Why do I speak of war with a woman?" he asked in exasperation.

"Have you no answer for me, my lord?"

"The risks are known to us all," he replied harshly. "War is not a game."

"Oho," she scoffed. "I have my doubts about *that*, my lord, for you men surely love war as children do their games!"

He scowled. "War does not concern you, wife, unless it comes to your own gate. Go back to sleep. You are not helping me."

She let him sulk for a few moments, then went on. "Would the risk be less if there were fewer men manning the walls of Wroth?" she asked.

She thought he would not condescend to answer, for he had turned his back to her. Stubborn man, she was thinking when he finally said, "Wroth has been in constant readiness. They have not grown lax in their vigilance, and the vassal there is no fool. I regret he could not be won over." There was real regret in his voice.

"But if there were only a few men to throw off the ladders?"

"A fool question, madame," he replied curtly. "The risk would be less, naturally."

"Could one man manage to get inside Wroth undetected?"

"That has been considered, but it would take more than one man just to open the gates, and the likelihood—"

"Not to reach the gates, my lord, to reach the water supply."

Rolfe swung around, his face contorted with amazement. "You would poison them all? Even the servants! Damn me, I did not think you were cold-blooded!"

"Not poison!" she hissed indignantly. "You are surely quick to condemn me! I suggest that you put hazelwort in the water. It is a strong purgative. It will kill no one."

Rolfe's laughter began slowly and turned into loud guffaws. "It would have them fighting each other to get into the garderobes."

"And those without relief, overcome by strong cramps and vomiting, will be a good deal less vigilant on the walls," she added.

"Damn me! I would never have thought of such a wicked ploy." Rolfe was astonished.

"Not wicked if it saves lives, my lord," she said sharply.

"Agreed. Where can I get hazelwort?"

"I—I have some in my medicine basket, but not nearly enough."

"You keep a medicine basket?" He seemed truly surprised. "You really are learned in the healing arts?"

His tone implied that he had heard as much, but hadn't believed it. "There is much of me you do not know, my lord," she answered honestly. He nodded, but did not want to stray from the subject.

"How is this done?"

"It takes the juice of five to seven leaves to mix in just one drink, but the result is not a gentle purgative, so less might do per portion. You will need many plants, at any rate, and we can surely find them in the woods. I have done so easily. Another way is to steep both leaves and roots in wine. This you should do as well, for if a man can reach the water supply, he can probably also get to the wine vats and contaminate them. It would be safer to dose both wine and water."

"How long will the preparations take?"

"It is not an easy process."

"You will have all of tomorrow, and you can make use of every servant here if need be. Will that do?"

His autocratic manner grated on her and she nodded without speaking.

He approached the bed and took hold of her hand. "If this works, Leonie, I will be much in your debt." He smiled. "After all the trouble you caused me in the past, I am glad to have you on my side. You are not an easy enemy."

Just when she had begun to warm to him, he had to bring up the past. Still, this was her chance to explain everything to him, and she knew she ought to take it. But his superior manner had caused her to retreat again, and she decided to leave well enough alone. There would be time to explain later, wouldn't there?

Chapter 22

ROLFE woke Leonie with a long kiss, then inadvertently spoiled the moment by reminding her to begin the work of gathering hazelwort. He failed to note her stiffly set features as he left their room.

After spending such a lovely night, he was in a magnanimous mood. He doubted he could find fault with anything today, he was so happy. Leonie was no longer sulking, and had accepted his apology. The proof of her forgiveness was the offer of help, and he was delighted by her idea.

Help was far from what he'd expected from Leonie. Had their marriage made such a difference to her then? He regretted having married her for the reasons he'd had, because the truth was that if he'd met her before the wedding, he would have wanted her for the right reasons.

He sighed. Could Leonie be feeling the same happiness he felt?

On his way to the chapel, Rolfe stopped and took a good look at the hall. The whole look of the place surprised him, but there was even more.

"Damn me, this room actually smells . . . pleasant," he muttered.

"Summer flowers, my lord." He whirled around. "If only they bloomed in winter, so we could be graced by their fragrance all year round."

Had Amelia been lying in wait for him? She had, and she spoke without really knowing what Leonie had ordered strewn on the new rushes. But she wanted him to believe the changes had something to do with the seasons, for then he couldn't blame Amelia for not having done what Leonie had done.

Rolfe smiled. "You have been busy while I was away, Amelia. I heartily approve."

Amelia lowered her eyes to hide her amazement. Hadn't Leonie taken proper credit? Had she meant it when she told Amelia the credit would go to her?

"I did little, my lord," Amelia said sweetly.

"You are too modest," Rolfe replied. "If only my wife had the same ambition you have. What did she do while I was away?"

"She has spent much time in the garden," Amelia said evasively, in not quite the same sweet voice.

Rolfe grunted. "I think me she loves gardens too much." He looked around. "Where are the hounds?"

"They—have been penned."

He considered that. "An unusual idea, but I can see the merit in it."

Amelia was gaining courage under Rolfe's continuing praise. As long as he thought she was responsible for all the improvements, she would not deny it.

"I think you will enjoy your meals more, too, my lord," she said smoothly. "The cook has been dismissed, and the new one is considerably talented."

Rolfe and Amelia moved away together, and as they did, they passed Wilda, whose face was livid. She had heard all she needed to. Walking as fast as she could, she found Leonie in a storage pantry near the kitchen, looking over baskets and jars.

"She did it!" Wilda hissed at her mistress. "That terrible woman is taking credit for all you have done.

The gall! My lord has only to ask anyone here if he desires to learn the truth."

Leonie was rigidly still for a moment, and then she shrugged as comprehension dawned.

"Surely you will tell him the truth, my lady?" Wilda urged.

"And let him think I seek praise? No. And he didn't want me making changes here. He may like what I have done, but if he realizes I went against his wishes, he may not be so pleased."

"I cannot—"

"We will not argue over this." Leonie cut her off firmly. "You must help me, Wilda, for there is a task he *has* asked me to do and it will require much work."

As the day wore on, Leonie gave a good deal of thought to Amelia and Rolfe. Since their night of love, she had begun seeing her husband in a new light, and come close to forgiving him for their terrible start.

Yet certain truths remained to trouble her, things that went beyond his keeping a mistress in residence. Alain Montigny's assessment of Rolfe seemed exaggerated now. Hadn't Rolfe shown consideration for her last night? Wasn't he trying to win a battle with the least possible bloodshed? Rolfe didn't seem like a man who would want to hunt down poor Alain and kill him, as Alain claimed. But despite the good things she knew about Rolfe, it wasn't right that Alain had lost Kempston when he was innocent of any crimes.

Oh, it was all so unreasonable—and the king had forced all of it on her. She had a good mind to write him and tell him what she thought of this interference. But no one questioned the king's will, certainly not a woman.

Leonie was busy gathering and steeping herbs all day, and when Rolfe came in that evening he was pleased to know that all was ready. He told her that everything was arranged at Wroth, and that he had a volunteer ready to be secreted inside Wroth Keep that night with her concoctions.

What Rolfe didn't tell her was the initial reaction of his men to her idea. Not a single man had trusted her, and Thorpe was especially vocal about it, sure the plan would bring them disaster, not success. Rolfe remained steadfast, however, and eventually one of the soldiers spoke up, telling the others that he knew from experience that hazelwort would do exactly as Leonie claimed. Once he told his story, Rolfe had trouble telling them the details of the plan because of all the laughter.

But he told Leonie none of this, and she saw only her husband's grin. His good humor made hers worse. Why was everything so much easier for him?

"You are unhappy, my lady?"

Leonie turned to Mildred, working beside her, extracting juice from the hazelwort. Four tables had been set up in the bailey for the steeping of leaves, while the kitchen staff worked on the wine mixture.

She hadn't spoken to Mildred in the week she had been at Crewel, though she knew Wilda had made friends with her. Leonie remembered Mildred from her visits to Crewel when the Montignys held the keep. She had even ministered once to Mildred's mother. It was a minor thing that Sir Edmond's stupid leech had been baffled over. But their prior acquaintance didn't give Mildred the right to pry. How dared the woman ask such a personal question?

"Do you have so little to do, Mildred, that—"

"My lady, please, I mean no disrespect," Mildred said hastily. "It is my greatest wish that you not be unhappy here at Crewel—for I fear it is my fault that you are wed."

The declaration was so ludicrous that Leonie's anger fled. "*Your* fault? How is that possible, Mildred?"

The older woman's gaze fell away as she whispered, "I—I was the one who told my lord that you lived at Pershwick." She faltered, then confessed, "It was then he decided to marry you so he could have Pershwick under his control. I am so sorry, my lady. I would never have caused you grief on purpose."

The poor woman looked so miserable. "You blame yourself for no reason, Mildred. My husband would have learned what he wanted to know from someone else, if you hadn't told him. I am the one who caused his attention to be drawn to Pershwick in the first place."

"But he did not know you lived there until I mentioned it. He was terribly angry to learn that a woman was responsible for his troubles."

"No doubt," Leonie said dryly. "But I was responsible, so I have only myself to blame for being here now. Think no more about it, Mildred, you are not to blame."

"As you wish, my lady," Mildred replied reluctantly. "But I will pray for you that my lord Rolfe's temper does not rise again, as it did on your wedding night."

Leonie blushed, assuming Mildred was referring to her stabbing Rolfe. "I hope you told no one what you saw that night, Mildred."

"I would never carry tales, my lady, nor would Edlyn. But everyone knows what he did to you. I did not think my lord was a cruel man—hot-tempered, but not cruel. Why, any man who would beat his wife only a few hours after their wedding—"

"What?"

Mildred looked around quickly, hoping no one was listening, but the others only glanced up, then looked away again.

"My lady, please, I did not mean to upset you," Mildred whispered.

"Who told you my husband beat me?" Leonie hissed.

"Lady Roese saw you the next morning, and she told Lady Bertha, and—"

"Enough! Sweet Mary, does *he* know what is being said about him?"

"I do not think so, my lady. You see, only the women insist my lord Rolfe did it, though none are brave enough to speak to him about it. The men swear beating a woman is not in his nature, and the disagreement has caused many arguments. John blackened the eye of his wife, and Jugge flung a bowl of stew at her husband. Lady Bertha is not speaking to her husband after the tongue-lashing he gave her, so now he brings her gifts to try and sweeten her temper."

Stunned and embarrassed, Leonie said, "Sir Rolfe did not beat me, Mildred. If you recall, I wore a heavy veil when I came here. Do you know why?"

"A rash."

"There was no rash, Mildred. That was a lie, made up . . . never mind why. My father had me beaten because I refused to marry."

"Then—"

"My husband is being blamed for something he did not do! I won't have it. Hear me well, Mildred. I want you to see to it that the truth is known. Can you do that?"

"Yes, my lady," Mildred assured her, considerably surprised by the revelation.

Leonie left her then, too mortified to stay in Mildred's company. She needed a little time alone.

What, she was wondering, would Rolfe say if he knew what was being gossiped about him? Would he find a way to blame his wife for the unfair talk making its rounds among his people?

Chapter 23

AT dawn, the camp outside the walls of Wroth Keep was quiet. Dreams of victory had followed the men into sleep. The watch reported hourly to Thorpe de la Mare, but the news he was expecting had still not been sent. The camp stirred and came to life just after dawn, but there was little to do. Most of the preparations had been made the night before, so the men waited for word, talking among themselves and getting restless.

At midmorning, Thorpe approached Rolfe inside his large tent.

"It appears the plan has worked. There is so little activity on the walls that they seem deserted."

Thorpe said it so grudgingly that Rolfe laughed. "You were hoping for different news?"

"I still do not believe your wife would help you."

"I told you, she wants to spare lives, both ours and those inside Wroth."

"More likely only those inside Wroth." Thorpe grunted.

"You will not stir up my anger this morning, my friend. I'm in good spirits. Leonie's concoctions have worked! Let us go and take Wroth now."

"You will be careful?"

Rolfe chuckled at the large man's concern. "You are acting like an old woman, Thorpe. I am not here to take tea. I'm here to secure this keep. But I promise not to sheathe my sword until you tell me it is safe to do so. Does that satisfy you?"

The taking of Wroth was ridiculously easy. As the ladders were scaled, moans were heard. The foulest stench greeted them when they reached the top of the walls. Everywhere men were bent over with cramps or puking up their food. Some of the men tried to fight Rolfe's men, but they had no strength and resistance was quickly quelled.

In short order, the keep was emptied and the prisoners taken to an area Rolfe had set up away from his main camp. The knight, John Fitzurse, would be held for ransom. The rebellious vassal might have been killed, but Rolfe was feeling a little guilty over the easy conquest, and so was inclined to be lenient.

It was still morning when Rolfe entered his tent and tossed his helmet to Damian. Then he settled down at his improvised desk. It was on his mind to send a message to Leonie, but she might know there was no clerk there, and he didn't want to write the note himself. He didn't want her to know he could read and write with ease. That would give her an excuse to refuse to act as his clerk. The sooner she began doing wifely things, the sooner she would accept him.

Thorpe entered the tent, and Rolfe asked, "All is secure?"

Thorpe nodded. "Will you offer the soldiers here what you offered the others?"

"Are they mostly recruited serfs, or hired men?"

"Serfs I think, since most speak only English," Thorpe replied.

"Then I will offer them what we offered the Axeford and Harwick soldiers. They can stay and fight for me or go. The hired men, too, because the fewer of our own men we have to leave here the better. Who do you suggest I put in charge?"

"Walter Wyclif. He has asked for Wroth, and since Richard and Piers and Reinald want to stay with the army—"

"But I would have given Sir Walter a larger keep, one of those we've yet to win."

"He wants to be settled now. He's tired of riding back and forth from Axeford Town where his wife is staying. He wants Lady Bertha with him, because he says she causes too much mischief when she's left alone."

Rolfe chuckled, but Thorpe frowned. "I would not laugh, my friend. You yourself have a wife who is prone to mischief-making."

"She's caused no trouble since she married me," Rolfe said defensively.

"Not yet," muttered his friend.

Rolfe was in the midst of defending his wife when they heard horses galloping into camp. As they left the tent, a rider dismounted, nearly bursting with news.

"My lord, Nant Keep has surrendered!"

"What terms?" Rolfe demanded.

"No terms. Their food supply ran out, and it seems they had rationed it so long, they were too weak to fight. The vassal simply begs mercy."

"I believe my luck has turned, Thorpe," Rolfe said, grinning.

But as the words left his mouth, another rider skidded to a halt and shouted, "My lord, your mill at Crewel has been set afire!"

Rolfe glowered at Thorpe. "Have five men ready immediately, but you stay to lead the army to Warling Keep."

"Sir Piers can lead the army—"

"I do not need a keeper! I will see to the fire myself. Do as I ask, Thorpe."

Less than ten minutes later Rolfe was riding toward Crewel, five men-at-arms following in his wake. Fifteen miles separated the two properties, and they rode hard, the ancient road leading through forests and open fields.

Rolfe's large destrier was not bred for speed, yet he reached the area of the Crewel mill well ahead of his men. Pausing beside the rapid stream that cut through the woods north of the village, Rolfe saw dozens of village men as well as several of his soldiers. They were moving slowly, so he guessed the fire had been put out.

He urged his horse ahead, but there was no longer any need to race the wind. He was barely within shouting distance when the arrow struck him. It tore through several chain-mail links and then it lodged in his hip. Rolfe caught a fleeting glimpse of forms slithering away into the shadows of the woods before a full measure of pain washed over him.

Chapter 24

LEONIE was accustomed to seeing blood, even as much blood as this. She had treated many wounds, but she became almost hysterical at the thought of treating Rolfe.

Their eyes met as he was carried, conscious now, into the hall. The look in his eyes froze her. There was fury in that look, furious accusation. *Why?*

"My lady?"

Wilda and Mildred were looking at her anxiously.

"Yes?"

Wilda said, "Sir Thorpe wants to move my lord Rolfe to his—your—room. Will you see to him?"

"Has he asked for me?"

Wilda could not meet her eyes. "He asked for the leech."

That hurt more than his accusation. "Then that is that."

"But, my lady," Mildred whispered, "Odo is only a barber! I know many barbers have some knowledge of healing and serve as leech, but Odo is a fool. He would rather let a man die than admit he cannot help him. You remember Odo, my lady. He is the one you chastised when he nearly let my mother die."

Leonie stared hard at Mildred, then turned away. Had she mistaken Rolfe's look, or did he truly believe she had somehow contrived to wound him?

Upstairs, she found a guard in the antechamber, barring her entrance. She tried to pass him and he moved quickly to block her way.

"I am sorry, my lady," was all he would say.

"Did my husband order you to keep me out?" she demanded.

He looked down at his feet without speaking. That was answer enough.

"Is the leech with him now?" she asked.

"I—"

He was interrupted by a bellowed curse and a crash from behind the closed door. Leonie turned stark white, and then the color rushed back into her cheeks as her temper exploded.

"I could have saved him that pain!" Her eyes stabbed the guard with her fury. "Let me pass now before he suffers more."

"I am sorry, my lady, but you must not—"

"You have no more sense than that fool in there who dares to call himself a healer. Do you hear that, Odo?" she shouted at the door. "If you harm him or maim him with your ignorance, I will see you hanged by your thumbs until they fall off! And if he dies, you will wish a thousand times that you had died instead!" Then she whirled at the guard, now staring at her wide-eyed. "And so will you!"

Inside the room, Odo had heard her clearly. He hesitated as he bandaged the gaping wound where he had ripped out the arrow. But it was quiet outside the door now, and as long as the lord was now unconscious, he could bandage him easily.

Leonie had been heard below the stairs, and she received many strange looks when she returned to the hall. She paced, in anger and frustration, striding back and forth before the cold hearth. No one dared speak to her.

Sir Evarard refused to go against Rolfe's orders and admit her to their room, although *he* was allowed inside. Leonie finally sent a messenger to Thorpe de la Mare, hoping that Rolfe's friend, an older and wiser man, would put an end to this foolishness.

But Sir Thorpe arrived early that evening and closed himself in the room with Rolfe, not emerging until late that night. Leonie waited for him in the hall, and attacked him the moment he came down the stairs. "How is he?"

Thorpe eyed her coldly. "Sleeping."

"And the wound?"

"He will mend—no thanks to you."

"You too?" she hissed. Knowing she was too angry to restrain herself, she turned aside, staring at the ceiling, reining herself in. Then she turned back to him. "Sir Thorpe, no matter what you think—no matter what *he* thinks—I was not responsible for what happened. Nor would my people attack him now. He is my husband. *Why* do you believe I caused this?" she demanded.

Thorpe settled into a chair and bellowed for a servant to bring food. Not until food and wine had been given him did he pierce her with his dark eyes . . . eyes so like Rolfe's. "He saw whoever fired the arrow moving off through the woods toward Pershwick. Evarard says that you have returned to Pershwick since coming here."

"That is true. My aunt Beatrix continues to live there. I have every right to visit her. How does that condemn me?"

"You had time to plan your husband's death while you were there. It is well known that you did not want to marry him and are still not reconciled to the marriage. It is equally well known that before you even met him, you caused him much grief. The conclusion is obvious. You want to rid yourself of him."

"If that is so, why did I help him take Wroth Keep? Also, I could have poisoned him myself at any time and blamed it on that filthy kitchen. But I had his kitchens cleaned instead."

"*You* did that?"

"Oho! So another one is quick to believe that the changes were Lady Amelia's doing. After living here in this filth hole for so long, she all of a sudden decided to take his property in hand, is that right? Oh, believe what you like. Believe also that I would leave to a chancy arrow what I could easily have done properly. I do not do things in half measures, Sir Thorpe. If I had wanted my husband dead, he would be dead."

"You have always been against him, Lady Leonie. Can you deny *that?"*

"I shall neither make denials nor offer excuses for what I felt in the past. I was told the Black Wolf was a monster. Alain Montigny was my friend and your lord meant to kill him if he could find him. Yes, I despised him for coming here. Alain, whose home was stolen from him, had to flee for his life. I would even have gathered my people to help Alain keep what was his, but he chose not to fight."

"But *you* chose to do so, Lady Leonie."

"There you are wrong," Leonie said frigidly. "I cursed the Black Wolf for the usurper he was, only that. My people did the rest, taking my anger as theirs. It became their cause. But the only harm I have ever done him was when I wounded him on my wedding night." She added hastily, "And that was an accident—one he doesn't even remember."

Thorpe scowled blackly. "Then it is good that Rolfe doesn't want you near him."

Leonie gasped. "You have not heard a word I've said! I wish to help him. I can ease his suffering. I can—"

"You can stay away from him. Even if he would relent and let you treat him, I do not trust you, Lady Leonie. It is because of my foolish tongue that you are wed. Once I saw you, I was foolish again, thinking it was not so bad that you and he marry. But I was wrong. And he is wise enough now not to trust you again."

"You are a stubborn man, Thorpe de la Mare, and I will pray for my husband's sake that you do not remain so. Odo will do him more harm than good."

"The leech? He is finished now, and Rolfe will heal quickly, as he has always done. Did you think this was his first wound?" Thorpe shook his head.

"I hope you are right."

As he watched her walk away, Thorpe's eyes narrowed. Mildred, who had waited in the shadows, listening, saw his look and made her decision. Stepping forward, she hissed, "You are wrong about her." She received the full impact of those dark eyes, but she steeled herself, adding, "She knows all there is to know about healing and giving comfort. And she would not harm my lord Rolfe. She even threatened Odo, knowing his bumbling ways. Ask Sir Evarard if you do not believe me."

"Women defend each other whether or not there is cause," Thorpe said disdainfully.

"As do men."

"He does not need her help!" he growled. How did this woman have the temerity to challenge him, he wondered. Were the Pershwick serfs even worse?

"She would not harm him!" Mildred insisted. "She was furious when she learned he was being falsely accused of beating her. She has made the truth known, for his sake. Is that the action of a woman who bears him hatred?"

Mildred left then, amazed by her outburst. And like Lady Leonie before her, Mildred was the recipient of Thorpe's narrowed gaze until she was out of sight.

Chapter 25

AFTER four days, Rolfe was worse. Thorpe was at wit's end. It had seemed a simple wound. Rolfe had received worse than that and recovered quickly. This wound actually seemed to be sapping his strength. A fever started the second day and climbed until Rolfe raged in delirium, calling for his wife one moment and cursing her the next. He didn't recognize Thorpe at all.

Odo, that cur, had sneaked out of the keep, escaping before he could be blamed for Rolfe's worsening condition.

Thorpe did not know what to do. No, that was not the truth. There was one thing he could do, and finally he did it, sending a servant to fetch Rolfe's wife. When she came into the room, her servant Wilda with her, he had the grace to look ashamed. He flinched when she let out a stream of curses.

"Why did you not call me sooner?" she demanded of Thorpe. "The dirt within the wound is killing him."

"I did not change his bandages," Thorpe replied defensively. "So I haven't seen the wound."

"You should have! I warned you Odo would do more harm than good."

"Can you help him?" Thorpe asked humbly.

Looking at the pus-infested wound, she said, "I truly do not know. How long has the fever been this bad?"

"Three days."

"God's mercy."

Thorpe lost his color. The hopelessness in her manner said all he needed to hear. Praying, he moved closer to the bed and watched her. First she forced liquid down Rolfe's throat, succeeding in getting him to swallow. Thorpe felt respect well up in him. Then she began crushing leaves to pack onto the wound along with some foul-smelling stuff. Water was set to boil and she began mixing together the contents of several bottles.

When she brought a little knife out of her basket, Thorpe gripped her wrist. "What is that for?" he demanded.

She eyed the large man. "His wound will have to be opened so I can search for what is causing this fever. Would you like to do it?" she asked him pointedly. Thorpe shook his head and let go of her wrist.

Leonie cleaned the knife, then very carefully removed the leaves she had packed against the wound. Using the knife, she started to probe inside the wound, cleaning it. There was complete silence for several long moments, and then she let out a horrified cry.

"Death is too good for that leech." Leonie glared at Thorpe in a way that made him feel wholly to blame for Rolfe's condition. "He removed the arrow, but he left inside a piece of Rolfe's chain mail that the arrow carried with it!"

She extracted it slowly and carefully, then resumed cleaning the wound. When clear blood finally began to ooze from it, she sighed gratefully. With the wound now clean, she covered it with her concoction.

At last she sat back and looked at Thorpe, her expression no longer anxious. "The blood must be allowed to seep from the wound until his fever abates, so we know the illness has left it. I will not sew the wound until then. He will be weakened more by this, but I dare not stop the bleeding until I am certain the wound is clean. I have tonics to aid him in fighting the fever, and to restore his strength." Thorpe nodded and she went on. "I will give him something for the pain too." When he remained silent, she asked, "Will you let me stay and watch his progress and do what needs doing?"

"He is out of danger?" he asked softly.

"I believe so, yes."

"Then stay, my lady."

"If he wakes enough to realize I am here, he may not like it."

"Then he will not like it," Thorpe said stubbornly, too grateful to care what Rolfe would think.

"Very well." She sighed. "But I ask you not to tell him what I've done."

"Why not?"

"I do not want him upset while he recovers. Let him think the leech healed him as he should have done."

"I would not lie to Rolfe."

"You do not have to lie. Just say nothing about it. I will try to leave before he awakes."

Late the next day she was bandaging the wound after pulling its jagged edges together, when Rolfe's eyes opened and locked with hers. The fever had ravaged him, and there was a heavy growth of beard covering his face. He looked terrible, and his eyes grew dark with anger when he saw her.

Leonie said not a word, but finished what she was doing and left the room. Thorpe, sleeping in a chair by the hearth, woke when he heard the door closing. He approached the bed.

"So, you are back with us?"

"Where have I been?" The voice was very weak.

Thorpe smiled at his old friend.

"You came very close to dying."

Rolfe eyed him skeptically. "From a little arrow hole?"

"That little hole was stinking with disease. You had a very bad fever."

"Never mind that. What was she doing in here? Is this how you guard my back, by letting in the very one responsible—"

"Easy, Rolfe." Thorpe cut him short. "I do not think her guilty of this. I am sure she is not."

"I told you what I saw."

"Yes, and that was damning—but not conclusive," Thorpe told him obstinately.

"You defend her now? You wouldn't trust her at all before this. I don't *want* to believe her capable of this, Thorpe. I believed I was making progress with her, and now this."

Thorpe shook his head. "You haven't had time to consider what happened without the pain of your wound clouding your thoughts. Think well before you place the blame on her, because anyone could have fired that arrow. It could have been a man turned out from one of the keeps we won, or even someone from here for that matter. Did Pershwick ever attack with weapons before? Then would they do so now, when you have their lady firmly in your power?" He moved away a bit and eyed Rolfe carefully. "Do you know why she was against you before? Did you ever ask her about it?"

"What difference would it make?"

"*Did* you, Rolfe?"

"No," he said curtly, "but I suppose you have learned why. Else why would you be badgering me like this?"

Thorpe grinned. "I see your mood is improving."

"Do you have something to tell me or not?"

Thorpe shook his head. "We were wrong about her, you know. And she has been misled about you. It is up to the two of you to work together to clear things up, Rolfe."

"Riddles, when I am lying here suffering." Rolfe sighed. "Where is that cursed leech anyway? My hip feels as though there's a fire in there."

"No doubt, after all you've been through. As to Odo, he left two nights ago, fearful of losing his thumbs."

"More riddles?" Rolfe said, exasperated.

"Your wife was very clear about what she would do to Odo if he caused you harm, and as it was Odo's incompetence that nearly killed you . . ."

"You keep telling me I was at death's door. With the leech gone, I suppose I have you to thank?" Thorpe was shaking his head emphatically. Rolfe's eyes widened with sudden understanding. "She used her knowledge to make me well? To help me again? Why did you not tell me that before? Why, Thorpe, I do believe the lady is beginning to care for me."

"I would not make too much of this," Thorpe said hastily. "She may have saved your miserable life, but I believe it is simply her way to help others if she can. Don't see more in it than you should. It will only cause you trouble later."

But Rolfe was not listening. He was delighted. He

was ecstatic. She had come to care for him. Did that mean he would soon be able to make her love him?

That question occupied Rolfe completely, until he fell into an exhausted sleep.

Chapter 26

LEONIE saw Erneis sneak out of the hall just as she entered it. For a long time she had tried to corner the Crewel steward, to talk with him about the accounts, but he was always in a rush to be somewhere, or else he could not be found. Why was he avoiding her?

She followed the little man outside the hall, stopping him just before he could disappear into the stable. "A moment of your time, Master Erneis." He stopped, turning around as slowly as he could, making no effort to hide his reluctance to speak with her.

"Master Erneis, you were steward for Sir Edmond, were you not?"

"For several years, my lady," he said, a little surprised by the question.

"Do you find the new lord of Crewel a hard master in comparison?" Leonie asked agreeably.

"No, indeed, my lady. Of course, Sir Edmond was much more . . . my lord Rolfe is very seldom here . . ."

He was becoming quite flustered, and Leonie took quick advantage of his confusion.

"I want you to give me the Crewel accounts, Master Erneis."

"You?" His eyes narrowed. "What can you want with them?"

"My husband wants to see them." The lie slipped out easily.

"But he cannot read either." The man was no longer simply flustered, but alarmed.

Leonie smiled encouragingly. "He has little to do while he is recovering, Master Erneis. I suppose he wants to know what kind of profits he can expect from Crewel." She shrugged, then added deliberately, "But being a soldier only come into property recently, he probably won't understand the accounts. I suppose he will have his clerk read the accounts to him."

"I can do that," the steward insisted.

"But you are always so busy."

"I will make the time."

"That is unnecessary. His clerk has plenty of time."

"But—"

Leonie lost her patience. "Do you argue with my lord's orders?" she demanded.

"No, no, indeed, my lady," he assured her quickly. "I will get them for you now."

When he handed over to her the pitifully small stack of parchments, Leonie kept her surprise to herself. Household accounts were kept by the year, usually from Michaelmas to Michaelmas, which celebration was only a few months away. These records should contain nearly a year's worth of expenditures and profits, but it looked like no more than a month's worth had been recorded.

She took the accounts up to the small room she had been sleeping in, and looked them over carefully. It was worse than she had imagined. The steward was supposed to confer with the kitchen staff and the stable staff at the end of each day and record all supplies bought and the exact amounts paid. He was also supposed to record supplies used from stock, and all items delivered by the villagers in payment of rent. Any surplus sold from those rents was also to be recorded, as profit. Recorded, too, were sums paid for services, such as for transportation of goods to be sold, or work done by the smithy or other craftsmen beyond what they owed in rents. Every transaction was to be noted.

A daily accounting from Pershwick would list the amount of bread, grain, wine, and beer that had already been reckoned elsewhere in the accounts. Correct amounts would be noted as depleted from stock. Items bought from merchants or Rethel Town, such as pots, cloth, and spices, and all services rendered, were scrupulously recorded. Bought for the kitchen would be special cheeses, fish not stocked—few items, for Pershwick was well stocked and nearly all meat and fowl was provided from the manor. For the stable would be listed hay, oats, grass gathered, mostly all stocked as well, a major expense being the purchase of a horse or two to replace those who had become too old for service. These old horses were given to the poor.

Master Erneis had lists for the kitchen and stable, but only by the week. Worse, there was no listing of items, only notations of sums paid out each week. He recorded the villagers' payment of supplies, but he showed only paltry amounts. No sales of surplus were recorded. But Leonie had seen grain and sheep and oxen and cattle delivered, then transported to Axeford Town for sale. Why was this never recorded?

That was bad enough. Worse were the totals for each week's expenditures, ridiculous sums, thrice what she would spend in a month. These totals did not include supplies for Rolfe's army, of that she was certain. Sir Evarard had told her that Rolfe was paying to have the army supplied directly from the towns nearest each keep.

Leonie had inspected the stores. She knew that while they were not abundant, much would be replenished when the harvesting began in a few weeks, and they were not depleted enough to explain the expenditures claimed.

Master Erneis was not doing his duty. That was plain.

Anger carried her back downstairs to look for the culprit. She enlisted two of the garrison soldiers to stay with her in case they were needed, but didn't tell them why. She tracked the steward to the kitchens. Before she went in, she told the guards to stay outside.

Master Erneis looked surprised as Leonie entered the long narrow shed, the parchments in hand. "You return the accounts to me so soon, my lady?" He reached for them, but she held them away from him.

"Master Erneis," she asked levelly, "where in these accounts are listed the horses you have purchased?"

"Horses?" The man frowned. "What horses?"

"The horses." Her voice rose. "Surely you have bought dozens of horses."

"I have ordered the purchase of not even one horse, my lady. What made you think—"

"No horses? I am mistaken, then. Did you purchase baubles for my lord to give the lady Amelia?"

"My lady, please." Erneis drew himself up indignantly. "I have never bought trinkets for ladies, nor has Sir Rolfe ever bid me do so. What has he said about these accounts to make you question—"

"What might he say?" she interrupted.

"My lady?"

"Where are the monies kept that you use for the household, Master Erneis?"

He frowned. "There is a locked chest in one of the storerooms."

"And my husband replenishes the store of coins when needed?"

"That has not been necessary thus far. He left ample—"

"How much?"

"My lady?"

"How much money did he give you to run this household?" she asked sharply.

"Several . . . hundred marks," he replied uneasily.

"How many hundred?" she asked softly.

"I do not—"

"How many?"

He fidgeted, casting glances over his shoulder at the cook and his helpers, who were looking on curiously. The questioning was sounding more and more like an interrogation.

"Eleven or twelve hundred," Erneis said evasively. "I do not recall exactly. But, my lady, I do not see why this concerns you—unless you wish to buy something. If that is the case, I would be more than happy—"

"I am sure you would," she said curtly. "So I may assume that what you have not spent from the funds my husband gave you is still within the locked chest?"

"Of course, my lady."

"And the rest accounted for in these?" She raised the papers slowly and held them in front of his face.

"Indeed, yes."

"Then you will not object to having your quarters searched before you are turned out of Crewel, will you?"

Erneis blanched. "My lady? You—ah—I misunderstand your meaning, I think."

"I think not," she replied tightly. "You have been able to lie to my husband about the accounts because he is a man of war and not used to running an estate, so he cannot be expected to know the expenditures involved. But you were a fool to think you could hoodwink me. I am not an idle woman. I have been my own steward for several years. I know exactly what it costs to run a household this size, down to the last coin." His eyes widened, and she smiled. "I see the light is dawning for you, Master Erneis."

His lips tightened. "You have no proof, my lady, that I did anything wrong. Crewel is not Pershwick. There was chaos when Sir Rolfe came here. Supplies were low and costs high."

"Were my husband not injured I would let him deal with this, for you try my patience," Leonie said angrily. "You say I have no proof?" She turned to the cook and demanded, "It is stated in these accounts, Master John, that last week you needed supplies costing thirty-five marks. Is that right?"

"My lady, no!" The man gasped. "Not even ten marks were spent."

Leonie's eyes flew back to the steward, whose pale face was now mottled with anger. "Well, Master Erneis?"

"You have no right to question me concerning the accounts, Lady d'Ambert. I will speak with your husband—"

"No, you will not!" she snapped, stepping back toward the entrance and signaling to the guards, who had been listening, amazed. "Take Master Erneis to his quarters and search his belongings. If the money he has stolen can be found, he may leave Crewel with the clothes on his back—no more. If the money is not found"—she looked at the little steward once more—

"you will get your wish to speak to my husband. And I doubt he will be lenient."

Leonie returned to the hall to wait, stewing with anger, wondering if perhaps she should not have handled the matter herself. Should she have told Sir Evarard, or Thorpe de la Mare, and let them take care of the steward?

It was a very short time before she learned that the episode was, for good or ill, finished. The guards approached her sheepishly to say that the steward had flown while they were searching his belongings. Only fifty marks had been found. Out of hundreds, only fifty? How was she going to tell Rolfe?

Chapter 27

ROLFE groaned as he bent over to open the large chest. He knew he should not be out of bed at all, as Thorpe had warned him repeatedly. He was weak and his wound had been stitched together only the day before.

But Rolfe was impatient. Ever since he had learned that Leonie had helped him instead of causing his wound, he had wanted to make amends for his boorish behavior. What must she think of his distrust, especially after she had only just helped him to win Wroth?

He had spent most of the day wondering what he could give Leonie by way of a special gift. He didn't want her to think he was buying her forgiveness, but he wanted to give her something lovely, something she would treasure. He realized that he did not know her likes and dislikes, and that he had no inkling of what she already possessed. A visit to her chests in the anteroom was called for, and he waited eagerly for Thorpe to leave the room so that he could rise from the bed.

The first two chests contained only clothes. The third, smaller chest held Leonie's treasures. He felt a twinge of guilt when he saw how little was there. There was an ivory chess set, and a small wooden box lined with velvet that contained twelve silver spoons. There were pouches holding imported spices. On the bottom of the chest wrapped in soft wool was a jeweled leather girdle, and another of gold cord. In a small box he found three gold brooches. One was set with garnets, another was enameled. Besides these there were two silver hairpins, a gold buckle, and one fine piece, a gold necklace with six large garnets spaced between the links of the chain, a gold cross dangling from the center.

So few fancy jewels for one so beautiful. But Rolfe knew that Leonie had been put aside by her father as a child. Who had there been to gift her with pretty trinkets, to watch her eyes glow with surprise and delight? A flash of hatred washed over Rolfe for the man who had hurt Leonie so badly.

The door opened softly and there she stood. And there Rolfe stood—her chest open to him, and blood soaking through the sheet he had wrapped around himself. Caught red-handed, with no excuse.

She simply stared, her expression unreadable, saying not a word. Rolfe flushed and turned away, making his way slowly back to the bed.

Leonie followed him into the inner chamber. Silence hung in the air until, at last, she spoke.

"If you were looking for my medicines, my lord, de la Mare should have told you my basket is there by the hearth."

Rolfe sighed. "So he should have."

"But I must warn you against trying to treat yourself. You could do more harm than good if you are not familiar with the remedies. I am willing to help you."

"Are you?"

Leonie turned away, unnerved by the suddenly soft tone. "You should have waited until I came."

"But I was not sure you would come."

She met his eyes. It was apparent that he hadn't yet

heard about the steward. But something was troubling him.

"Why would I not come, my lord?" she asked pointedly. "You have made it clear that you must always be obeyed."

"But you do as you please anyway."

They were suddenly speaking of what was wrong between them, and neither had intended that to happen. "I do not allow anyone, my lord, to command my thoughts and feelings. Otherwise, as your wife, I am yours to command."

Rolfe nearly laughed. Of course she was right, he could not control her thoughts or feelings and it was unreasonable for him to have tried. What he needed to do was work on changing her feelings, some of them.

"If you would rather not tend me, Leonie, I will understand."

She found the humility in his voice less than convincing. "The gift I received from my mother to heal and comfort is mine to share. If I cannot use it, it becomes worthless. Now will you let me stop your bleeding?"

He nodded, and she pulled the sheet to the side to remove the stained bandage. As she worked, she glowed with pleasure, proud and glad to be using her skills.

"You find pleasure in helping others?" Rolfe asked suddenly.

"Yes."

He sighed. He had been wrong. As Thorpe said, it was simply her way to help people. He was nothing special to her.

"Something is wrong, my lord?"

"No," he lied glibly. "It has just occurred to me that

I may have hurt you by calling for the leech instead of you."

"I was not hurt," she assured him quickly. "I was angry at the foolishness of it, because I knew Odo was incompetent. But your order to keep me from you was understandable. You were weak and in pain. You were not thinking clearly."

"Why do you make excuses for me?"

She shook her head. "If you had been yourself, my lord, I am sure you would have had me put in irons instead of simply barring me from here."

"Put in irons!" He frowned. "I would never . . . You are my wife."

"That is not the issue," she said angrily. "Someone tried to kill you. That person must be found and punished—no matter who it was. I would expect no less if I had tried to kill you."

Rolfe laughed ruefully. "I admit I thought of you first when the arrow struck and I saw the villain moving off toward Pershwick. I did not *want* to believe you capable of arranging my death, but the thought was there, and not unreasonable, given your past . . . I am truly sorry for doubting you this time, Leonie."

Why wouldn't she look at him? She had finished changing his bandage, and was rummaging in her basket. She held up a small blue bottle. "Will you let me give you this for the pain, my lord?"

Rolfe frowned at the evasion. She wouldn't meet his eyes, and she seemed most uncomfortable suddenly.

"No!" he snarled, regretting it immediately.

"So you still doubt me?" she asked softly.

"I did not say so."

"Yet you refuse my tonic, and I know you are in pain. You fear I mean to poison you, is that it?"

"Damn! Give me that!" He grabbed the bottle from her and took a swallow. "There! Now tell me why you cannot forgive me."

"But I do," she said softly, her gaze steady. "I can only hope that you will be forgiving when I tell you—"

"Do not tell me." He cut her off abruptly. "I want to hear no confessions from you."

"But I want to tell you about—"

"No!"

She stood up and glared at him, all meekness gone. "You would make me wait and dread your anger until someone *else* tells you? Well, I will not do that. My lord, I dismissed your steward and I am not sorry for it."

She waited for the explosion, but Rolfe simply stared at her in amazement.

"Is that all?" he asked.

"Yes," she replied stonily.

"What—what did you expect me to do, Leonie?"

"You have every right to be angry, and it won't hurt your wound if you feel like shouting at me."

"Perhaps," he said quietly, trying not to grin, "if you told me why you dismissed him?"

"I discovered Master Erneis was stealing from you, and not just a little. Hundreds of marks."

"How do you know he was stealing?" he asked sharply.

She quickly explained. "I am only sorry that I handled it badly, for he is gone now and so is your money."

"You still have not said why you are sure he was stealing."

"My lord, I wouldn't know how much you gave the steward to begin with, but he said you gave him eleven or twelve hundred marks. You have been here seven months, and in that time he recorded spending nine hundred marks. That is far, far too much."

"Leonie, how do you *know* that?" Rolfe asked in exasperation.

She flushed and bowed her head. "I—I was my own steward, which I did not tell you. I know that an estate this size should be self-sufficient unless there are frequent guests staying here, and I know what it costs to maintain a household of this size."

Rolfe shook his head. Her own steward, yet she refused to take the reins at Crewel.

"It must be obvious to you that the management of property is not my strength. So I will have to take your word for it that I was cheated by my steward."

"I swear I read his accounts correctly and—"

"I was not doubting you. But this leaves me without a steward. Evarard cannot take over, for he would know even less than I do."

"Indeed."

"So what do you suggest? You dismissed the man. Have you anyone in mind to replace him?"

"I can think of no one."

"Well, I can. You will have to fill the position yourself."

"Me?"

"Is that not just? You are responsible, you realize."

"Yes, of course." Leonie turned away, carrying her basket to the hearth so that he would not see how delighted she was. He thought he was punishing her, when in fact he was ordering her to do what she thrived on. She would have made the suggestion herself, but had feared he would refuse. After all, he had denied her any responsibilities at Crewel—until that moment.

She managed a controlled expression, then turned back to face him. "If there is nothing else you wish to discuss, my lord, I will have your dinner sent to you."

"You will join me?" he asked sleepily. The morphine he had drunk from the blue bottle was affecting him.

"If you wish."

"Good. And, Leonie, where have you been sleeping?"

"I—I moved a few of my things to a room across from the servants' quarters."

"Bring them back." Sleepy though he was, his manner brooked no refusal. "You will sleep here from now on."

"As you will, my lord," she murmured, blushing.

She left the room then, happy and apprehensive all at once.

Chapter 28

A FIRE crackled in the great hearth as servants moved through the hall, setting the tables for dinner under Wilda's careful eye. Amelia worked her stitchery by the fire, deliberately ignoring what was going on around her. Sitting beside her, Sir Evarard was enjoying a mug of ale, his duties finished for the day.

When Leonie came downstairs from the lord's chamber, Amelia's eyes fastened on her. She watched intently as Leonie said a few words to her maid, then left the hall.

Amelia sat back with a smug smile. She had waited for the day when Rolfe would confront his wife with her crimes. Evarard had told her what Rolfe suspected, and whether or not it was true, he would surely send Leonie back to Pershwick now.

Amelia had kept out of the way when Rolfe was wounded, for if he had died and no one could prove that his wife was to blame, Amelia would have been sent packing. She could not have afforded to be enemies with Leonie.

But Rolfe was recovered now, and believed his wife had wanted him dead.

"Do you think he has told her to begin packing?" Amelia asked Evarard, who had also watched Leonie crossing the hall to the servants' stairs.

"Packing? Why?"

"To go back to Pershwick, of course."

"Why would he send her there?"

Amelia stared at her lover angrily. She was always having to explain every little thing to him because their minds did not run the same course. She could never confide everything to Sir Evarard, for he was a man plagued with honor.

"Did you not tell me that he believes her responsible for the fire at the mill and the attack against him?" she whispered, exasperated.

"That was a mistake," Evarard said casually.

"A mistake? Whose mistake?"

Evarard shrugged. "Sir Rolfe knows now that he was wrong."

"How do you know that? Did he tell you so himself?"

"Sir Thorpe said so before he left. He has gone to begin the siege of Warling."

"But he was tending Rolfe."

"The lady Leonie will see to him now, so there is no reason for Sir Thorpe to remain here."

Amelia gritted her teeth. "Do you think she will still be tending him when he hears about poor Erneis?"

"Sir Rolfe will deal with that in his way, but I doubt he will put his wife from him simply because she overstepped her authority. He is most pleased with her in every other way. Why, look at all she has done since she came here."

Amelia suppressed a scream of fury, stabbing her needle into her embroidery instead. Evarard seemed not to notice her agitation.

It was not fair! Just when Amelia had begun to hope that she could drop her pretense of being pregnant, saying that she had miscarried. Now she would have to continue her affair with Evarard, at least until he got her with child. That had to happen immediately. If she had her monthly flow again, she might as well give up, for Rolfe was not a stupid man. As it was, if she did have a child, she would have to pretend it was a delayed birth.

She tried to stop her mind from whirling. Yes, she would have to become pregnant. She might even be forced to allow the pregnancy to run its course, unless . . .

Leonie must be told about the child. Amelia could let it slip as though by accident, then step back and see what that news did to the relationship between the lord and his lady. Leonie's pride might have kept her from speaking to Rolfe about having a mistress living in his house, but it was another thing entirely for the mistress to bear him a child—especially a child conceived *after* the marriage.

It would not matter if Leonie confronted Rolfe, for he could not deny the child. But Leonie might not even ask him about it, but simply leave. Once she was gone, Amelia might still have time to get rid of the child, using the potion she'd learned about at court years ago.

As Amelia dreamed on, her smug smile returned.

Chapter 29

THEY were going to court. Leonie's stomach turned over in dismay when she was told. Much to her chagrin, she had to write the letter accepting the king's invitation.

Rolfe would not hear her excuses, but insisted she accompany him to court.

"Henry wants to meet you," was all he would say. And no one refused the king what he wanted, she reminded herself bitterly.

Rolfe was not well enough to travel, so the day of departure was set for a week hence.

That week flew by. Leonie prayed her nervousness would not bring back her old rash, prayed, too, that she wouldn't make a fool of herself. So many years had passed since she had been at court. Would she remember how to behave?

Rolfe understood and did his best to ease her anxiety. He told her amusing stories about the king and his barons, pointing out that she might even meet some of her relatives there. She wasn't sure whether that made her feel better or worse.

They were sleeping in the same bed, but he wasn't well enough for lovemaking. She spent nearly all her time reading to him, eating with him, being on hand if he wanted to dictate a letter. They talked a great deal, Rolfe telling her about himself, forcing her to talk as well.

In all ways he tried to please her, except in the way that mattered most and always stood between them—Amelia. Every time she attempted to speak to him about his mistress, pride kept the words bottled up. If only he would send Amelia away. If only. But she dared not ask. She feared his refusal, which would tell her only too plainly what she didn't want to know. Did he love Amelia? She tortured herself over the question time and time again.

She reined her feelings in, maintaining a distance that was necessary for her defenses. She could not afford to relax with him, laughing easily and teasing him, as was her nature. She might then find herself hopelessly in love with him, and that she must guard against fiercely.

The morning they were to depart for London would be the first time Rolfe would leave their room. He left all preparations for the journey to Leonie, even his packing. She enjoyed this wifely duty.

Her own packing caused a dilemma, however, for she owned only two fine bliauts. So Wilda labored long and hard to make a third one from a length of Spanish wool Leonie had been saving.

Leonie was an expert needlewoman, and had embroidered many altar cloths and christening robes. She spent little time on her own clothing, however, finding the current style easy to adapt to whatever need arose. The long garment with detached sleeves was easy to wear when she worked in the garden, wearing serge sleeves and overblouse and bliaut. The style was equally easy to adapt to formal wear. The fact was, she didn't have many clothes because she didn't need many.

The note arrived just as they were leaving for London, handed quickly to Leonie by a village serf she did not know. She had no time to read it, so the note was forgotten, stuck into the tight sleeve of her chemise to read later. Catching sight of Rolfe having a private word with Amelia put the note further from her mind—and put her in a bad mood that lasted most of the day.

They broke their journey at a small inn, and Leonie retired early, wanting to be asleep by the time Rolfe joined her. As Wilda was unlacing her, the note fell to the floor. A frown creased Leonie's brow as she read it.

"It is from Alain Montigny."

"Sir Alain? But I thought you said he was in Ireland, my lady."

"Not any longer. He asks me to meet him at the pasture dividing the properties." Leonie's frown deepened. "Whatever is he doing here?"

"Will you meet him?"

"I would have, but he wanted to meet at noon today."

"I thought he was afraid of your husband."

"Yes, he is."

"Then what can he be thinking of, coming back to the Black Wolf's den?"

"Do not call him that," Leonie snapped.

"I—I beg your pardon, my lady."

Leonie's eyes widened. Sweet Mary, what was wrong with her?

"Never mind, Wilda. Get some sleep. It has been a long day."

As Wilda slipped out of the room, Leonie tossed the note into the fire, then crawled into the bed her maid had fitted with the sheets they had brought along. But she could not sleep. She couldn't stop thinking of

Alain. What could he be thinking of, coming back to his home when he had sworn it would be worth his life to do so?

She began to wonder if that had been a lie. Everything Alain had told her that day about her husband had turned out to be either lies or fearful delusions. From all she had come to know, Rolfe d'Ambert was not the man she had cursed that fateful day. He had faults, but harsh vengeance was not in his nature. She herself could attest to that.

"Are you asleep, Leonie?"

How quietly he had come into the room! "No, my lord."

"Will you help me then? I have sent Damian on to bed."

She smiled. Lately he asked for her help so reluctantly, entirely different from his previously arrogant demands. She wondered if he regretted his earlier manner.

"Sit here, my lord."

She got up from the narrow bed that was so much smaller than their own and began to unlace his chausses. His heavy hauberk had been removed by Damian.

"I would like to check your wound," Leonie said. "To see if the ride today has opened it."

"That is unnecessary."

How tired he sounded. "Humor me, my lord."

"'Humor me, my lord,'" he repeated wearily. "You ask for much, but give so little. Humor *me*, my lady. Tell me why you will not give us a chance?"

She stiffened, then looked away. "You know why."

"Of course." He sighed. "I had thought your feelings might have changed."

She was genuinely puzzled. Why would he ask her that when it was he who was not allowing them a chance? She was then struck by the incredible thought that he might be keeping his mistress nearby because of her own coldness to him. She was so stunned that she froze where she stood, unmoving. Was he only waiting for her to warm to him before he renounced other women?

She was terribly confused. Should she let the subject lie, or ask what she wanted to ask? "Let—let me remove your tunic," she said quickly, bending toward him. In doing so, her linen robe slipped open and Rolfe's eyes fastened on her beautiful breasts. He took a long, deep breath, his eyes moving slowly up to hers. She saw great longing there, and realized that he had been celibate since his injury. He was tired from the journey, but that did not seem to matter.

Heat stole up her cheeks and she pulled her robe together. This was not the time for a return of his amorous attentions. How could she ask him about his disturbing question if he continued to look at her this way?

Not knowing what else to do, she grabbed the hem of his tunic and pulled it over his head carefully, so as not to pull on his wound. She did the same with his undershirt, then moved away to the opposite side of the room so that he could stand up and remove the rest of his clothing.

The suspense was unbearable, and she finally blurted, "My lord, if—if I were to change . . . would you send Lady Amelia away?"

"No."

He spoke flatly and without hesitation, and a sick feeling gathered in Leonie's belly. She closed her eyes, miserable. Fool! She had asked the question she knew better than to ask, and received the answer she dreaded.

"What has the one to do with the other?" Rolfe demanded, his voice sharp.

"N-nothing, my lord," she whispered.

"Then explain yourself."

Leonie panicked. What could she tell him? She recalled Amelia telling her that Rolfe did not like jealousies. Was that how he interpreted her question, believing she was jealous? Of course she wasn't jealous. Why should she be when she did not love Rolfe? Lord, how she wanted to cry.

She said tonelessly, "I have had your ward on my mind since I saw her this morning, because I wondered why you did not include her on this trip. I thought perhaps you were angry with her."

He came and stood in front of her, his body tense. "I am not angry with her. There was no reason to bring her with us. She does not like court."

"*I* do not like court, but you dragged me with you."

"You are my wife!"

Leonie whirled around, her back to him. It would serve no purpose to let her own anger loose, but she was barely able to hold it in check.

"I thought you got along well with Amelia," he said, and she turned around slowly.

"Of course I do," she replied sharply. "Why ever should I not?" She was close to tears.

"Damn me, Leonie! What is this about? Have you had words with Amelia?"

She shook her head. "I would not hurt her, if that is what you fear."

"Hurt her? Why are we even speaking of her?" Rolfe's frustration was mounting rapidly. What was this all about?

"You want her sent away, is that it?"

"I did not say so. I asked if you would, and you said you would not, so that is that."

She tried to turn away again, but Rolfe's hands fastened tightly on her shoulders. He gazed into her eyes so intently that she couldn't look away. "You know! *That* is what this is about! Who told you?"

"My lord?" Leonie asked, then burst into tears. Shocked, he gathered her in his arms, holding her gently. "I swear you will drive me mad, Leonie. Why can you never speak plainly to me?"

She continued to sob. Let him think whatever he liked. She should not have said anything, and she refused to say any more. No one was going to accuse her of being a jealous wife.

He picked her up, carried her to the bed, and cradled her, rocking her gently until her tears subsided. His hand moved soothingly over her hair and back, lulling her. And then suddenly he was kissing her, but she managed to break the spell and push him back from her, denying her own needs as well as his.

"My lord, no, not now—please," she beseeched, bracing herself for his anger.

But he surprised her. "Just let me hold you then, dearling. I will do no more than that."

She very nearly cried again, he was being so kind. She bowed her head, and after he stretched out under the covers, he pulled her to him. It was a long time before she slept, but eventually she drifted into a dream-plagued sleep, pressed firmly against her husband.

Chapter 30

A FLUTTERING of movement woke Rolfe and he opened his eyes to see Leonie slipping out of bed. Their argument had caused him to lie awake half the night trying to piece together what had happened.

It was possible that she might learn what Amelia had been to him, but he didn't even want to think about that possibility. If Leonie insisted Amelia leave, how could he explain to her that Amelia must stay? He could not tell Leonie the other woman was to bear him a child. He had told her Amelia was his ward. If she learned about Amelia's child, he would lose any further chance to win her love.

He watched Leonie as she slipped into her blue linen robe and moved over to the small hearth. She sat down on a stool there to begin combing the tangles from her hair. The light from the window made her silken silver tresses shine. How lovely she was!

And she was considerate, a truly kind woman. She would not call for her maid as long as he was asleep. And she was as kind to the servants as she was to him.

What was it about this woman that turned him inside out? She caused him sleepless nights, made his temper run riot, caused him endless confusion, endless worry. Caused his hopes to rise, then to crumble. Would he ever be at ease with her?

Thorpe suggested he talk with her frankly, but Rolfe

wasn't willing to take that risk. In truth, he feared that the real reason she had been against him from the start was that she loved that craven knight, Alain Montigny. The sole reason for her hatred of him was that he now owned Montigny's land. Was that the truth? The last thing he wanted was to force such a confession from her. It would end his hopes.

Leonie felt him staring at her. She rose and went to him, looking worried.

"It is no wonder you slept so long. You have tried to do too much too soon, my lord," she scolded gently. "Let me see your wound now, will you?"

He nodded. Her silver-gray eyes met his. "My lord, I beg you to forget last night. I was overly tired and—and I am never myself when I am nervous. If I angered you, I am sorry."

"You are still so nervous about meeting Henry?"

She nodded and gave him a baleful look.

"Then we will return to Crewel."

She was stunned. "You would do that for me?"

"Of course," he said simply. "I didn't realize you were so frightened."

"It is not fear, exactly. More like . . . unease," she assured him. "I am sure it will pass." Knowing that he was willing to change his plans for her added greatly to her self-confidence. "It is too late to turn back now. The king expects us."

"Henry can be disappointed once in a while."

"No, my lord, truly, I will control my nerves."

"You are sure?"

"Yes. And the worst that will happen is that my old rash will reappear. It used to whenever I went to court as a child."

"That might not be so bad." He grinned. "Then I

won't have to worry that every knight in the kingdom is being smitten by you."

She shrugged. "I have outgrown my nervous rashes, so it will not happen."

Rolfe frowned. "Leonie, you had a rash on the day we married."

"Of course, my lord," she replied dryly.

"You mean you did *not* have a rash?"

Her eyes flashed. "You know why I was veiled. I do not wish to speak of it."

Rolfe stared incredulously as she got up and stalked angrily to the door. Did she really think he understood?

"Leonie!"

She turned only long enough to say furiously, "I will not speak of it! Now, stir yourself, my lord, or we will not reach London before nightfall."

She slammed the door, leaving Rolfe more bewildered than he had ever been in his life.

Chapter 31

BECAUSE Leonie had been confined so long at Pershwick and then at Crewel, she was fascinated by the journey to London, whereas Rolfe had traveled through France and England for so many years that he barely bothered looking around, leaving the enjoyment of the journey to her.

They passed through villages she hadn't seen in years, and she gazed hungrily at everything, from the mundane sights of peasants working their masters' fields to beautifully gowned ladies on horseback traveling with their guards. She was glad there was no older woman with her to scold, for she knew she ought not to be staring so avidly at everything around her. But she was enjoying herself tremendously, and she didn't give a hoot for convention most of the time as it was, she reminded herself.

They passed through a village just as the bells were ringing for Sixtus, and the midafternoon quiet touched Leonie's memory, bringing back the times she had finished with her lessons and been taken to her parents by her maid. From three until four o'clock was a sacred hour, when the three of them talked and, if the weather permitted, walked in the forest together. Nobody was ever allowed to intrude on their hour together.

With her mother's death, all of that peace, those joyous times, were swept away forever. *Damn her father,* she thought. Why hadn't he taken care of her after her mother's death? Why had he been so weak? In his place, she would have forced herself to rise above grief.

Leonie shook herself. When would she ever learn not to think about her father? The few moments she indulged in would cause a day or more of brooding unhappiness, she had learned that much—and she had enough to contend with in her present circumstances without grieving over her past.

She turned again to look around her, reminding herself to enjoy this treat because London was not, she feared, going to offer much enjoyment.

There were more than a hundred parishes in London, each with its own church, and the hundred church spires rising above the city walls was an awesome sight. Leonie well remembered her first journey to London as a child, and the most outstanding building seen from a great distance—Saint Paul's Cathedral, which rose high over the city, commanding with its mighty roofs and bays and Gothic arches.

The Palatine Castle, nearly a century old, was another formidable stone structure in a city built mostly of one-story frame houses. It was the only royal palace within the old Roman walls of the city, and it was where Leonie and Rolfe would be staying.

Leonie was glad. The king was in residence at Westminster Hall, which was outside the city, so she hoped to see Henry only once. She was to be presented to him the day after their arrival. Rolfe, however, would be seeing him on the evening they reached London.

As if Leonie were not anxious enough over meeting King Henry, London itself intimidated her. It was a full square mile of raucous cosmopolitan congestion, dedicated mainly to trade. There were mercers, grocers, fishmongers with their tally-sticks, every kind of merchant. The river Thames was clogged with wool barges and riverboatmen. And all of this noise and bustle was within the walls of London, whereas just outside those walls were plowed fields and vast forests.

As soon as she caught sight of Palatine Castle, Leonie remembered the terribly crowded conditions at court. She had been there when it was filled with servants, lords and their ladies, and the parasites who always stayed close to power, as well as dancers, gamesters, mountebanks, jugglers, even prostitutes and pimps—all of whom followed the king wherever he went.

She prayed that most of Henry's court would be staying with him at Westminster Hall and that she would not have to share quarters with others at the city palace.

What awaited her at the Palatine Castle was not nearly as bad as she had feared. Rolfe did not stay to see her settled, but she had known he would have to leave. He left Sir Piers and half of his twenty men-at-arms with her. Richard Amyas and the other ten men went with Rolfe. Sir Piers and Sir Richard were the only knights accompanying them to London, Sir Piers because Rolfe wanted him to guard Leonie when he was away from her, and Sir Richard because the young man was thrilled by court life.

Sir Thorpe had been left in charge of the siege of Warling Keep, and Leonie found herself missing him. She got along well with young Richard, but she did not like Piers at all. An older man, he would not unbend. She felt that he disliked her, tolerating her only for Rolfe's sake. Yet he did his duty well, scowling blackly at any man who even looked Leonie's way as they crossed the great hall of Palatine Castle.

Leonie was given a small turret room to share with

Wilda and Mildred. Rolfe and Damian, when they returned, would have to sleep in the same room. But at least there would be no strangers, Leonie told herself, relieved.

It was very late when Rolfe returned from Westminster Hall. Leonie was in bed, a candle burning as she lay listening to Mildred's excited chatter. The maid had seen a great deal of the castle, and had met an attractive guard, whom she planned to meet later that night when his duty ended. Wilda decided not to remain in the turret room, but to stay with a handsome knight she had met that afternoon.

Leonie chastised both maids, more than a little shocked, but she did not have the heart to deny them what they wanted, so she didn't forbid them their pleasures.

When Leonie heard Rolfe's voice shouting for her from a great distance, she hurried into her robe. Mildred was frightened of Rolfe, and Leonie didn't want to ask her to go to him.

"What can be wrong, my lady? He—he does not sound right."

Leonie frowned, hearing another bellow. "He is going to wake the whole castle!"

She ran out of the room to the top of the stairs. A wall sconce was lit, but it cast only gloomy shadows down the stairway. She heard her husband before she was able to see him there at the bottom, being supported by Richard Amyas. Both men were swaying, holding on to each other.

Rolfe's voice boomed again, monstrously loud as it resounded off the stone walls. "Leonie!" To Richard, he said, "If she is not here, I will tear this place—"

"I am here, my lord," Leonie called.

They looked up, Richard grinning sheepishly, Rolfe

happily. Leonie was reminded of the only other time she had seen her husband drunk, the day he was told of her beating. She had rather liked the idea that the knowledge had led him to drink.

"Will you tell me why there must be so much noise at this hour?" Leonie asked, and Rolfe held up a hand for silence, saying to Richard, "Find your room, my friend. My lady will see to me now."

"How?" Leonie called to him. "I cannot support your weight up these stairs." Was he truly too drunk to navigate?

"I can walk, dearling. You come down and lead the way, though."

Leonie sighed as Richard bowed to her and left, unsteady but moving in the right direction. When Richard let go of him, Rolfe leaned against the wall for support.

"This is not wise, my lord," Leonie said irritably as she ran down the stairs. She grabbed his arm and put it around her shoulder. "We will both fall down the stairs."

He chuckled. "You are no doubt under the misconception that I have had too much to drink. Let me assure you I have not. It was only that Henry was in a talkative mood and insisted I drink with him."

"And of course you could not refuse the king," she said sarcastically, sighing. "But surely he had an available bed. You should have stayed there, my lord, instead of riding back here. You could have broken your neck—not unheard of with those who imbibe too much."

She began to pull him up the stairs, but he yanked her back. "Do not scold, dearling. I do not feel drunk, therefore I am not. And I could not stay there because you are here."

She laughed. "Would that you could ride your horse up these stairs."

"Think I cannot climb the stairs?" he growled, and with that he grabbed her hand and ran up the stairs, dragging her behind him until they reached the top. Then he grinned at her.

"That was foolish, my lord," Leonie said, panting.

"Do not sulk, dearling."

"Oh!"

Exasperated, she jerked her hand away, but Rolfe threw his arm around her shoulder again, taking a few unsteady steps, leaning heavily on her. He chuckled when she mumbled a choice curse.

"Ah, Leonie, I do believe I love you."

Her heart jumped, but she quickly stayed the impulse to make a similar declaration. He was drunk. She could not afford to believe drunken nonsense.

"Do you, my lord?"

"I must," he said simply. "Why else would I put up with your sulkiness?"

"I have told you before, I do not sulk."

"And your disobedience," he continued as if she had not spoken. "And your willfulness."

"I did not realize I had so many faults," she said stiffly.

"You do, but I love you anyway." He swung her into his arms, squeezing the breath out of her. "Can you love me, dearling?"

"Of course—my lord."

"Ah, Leonie, would that you spoke the truth, but I know you are lying."

He was whispering into her ear, making her nerves tingle. It was always a churning experience, being so attracted to this man. She wished she were drunk. She wished she could let go of the tight rein on her emotions and savor her time with him. She wished . . .

She squirmed out of his tight embrace so that she could wrap her arms around his neck. "It is not impossible to love you. In fact, it is very easy."

Rolfe caught his breath. She was pressing her soft body against him, and he said huskily, "You humor me, dearling, but at least that is a start."

His mouth swooped down on hers, taking her lips in an exquisitely passionate kiss. That first violent shock stunned her, then melted into sweet sensations. She clung to his body, feeling every hard muscle, returning his kiss with her own passion. She was frightened by her desire for him.

Suddenly, to her amazement, Rolfe broke off the kiss and threw back his head, emitting a wild roar, like a war cry. It sent shivers through her. When he looked down at her, raw passion smoldered in those dark eyes. Very deliberately and slowly, he slid his hands down her hips, holding them firmly.

A core of heat burst in her loins, and suddenly her muscles had turned to water. Her legs were unable to support her. It must have showed in her eyes, for Rolfe smiled triumphantly, then scooped her up in his arms.

Leonie gasped. "We might get there safer, my lord, if you put me down."

He was too inebriated for this. "No," he said flatly.

She pointed at the open door a few steps away. "Over there."

He walked unsteadily into the small room. Seeing the nervous Mildred, he ordered her out. Leonie smiled at the look on poor Mildred's face as she ran out of the room, for she was sure the maid was only too glad to leave.

"Where is the other one?" he asked as he moved toward the bed.

"Wilda is sleeping elsewhere tonight."

He chuckled. "Wise girl."

"And what have you done with Damian?"

"Left him with his father, Lord Sutton. I desired privacy for us."

They fell heavily onto the bed, both laughing. He did not have to ask her to help him disrobe. In swift order she did it, the two of them laughing and teasing. Then her bedrobe was removed, and Rolfe's eyes kindled with desire. When he placed his hands on her breasts, she was jolted back into total awareness of her raging needs. They lay down on the bed together, clutching each other tightly.

His strength was a palpable thing, the corded muscles running along his neck, mounded across his chest. He was raw power held in check, and she accepted his gentleness as a gift. She touched those muscles, felt them move under her fingertips, felt the silkiness of the dark curling hair all over him, another aspect of his overwhelming masculinity.

He was all she could ever want—and she wanted him desperately, her eyes telling him so. He watched her fascination with him. He played with her lips then, nibbling, teasing her, knowing she wanted to be crushed. When he finally plundered, his tongue ravaging her mouth, a sound of pure pleasure was wrenched from her.

His caresses were sheer torture as he moved from her breasts to the core of her, his fingers opening her. She moved as close to him as she could, wanting more, and suddenly waves of heat converged in her loins to shatter the little control she had left. She tore her mouth away from his to cry out his name as the exquisite spasms washed through her. He mounted her then, before she had time to recover, his arms slipping under her to gather her to him more closely. The throbbing in her loins continued as he plummeted to her depths, and then the throbbing burst into flames again as the gushing warmth of his release filled her.

Leonie could feel the waves of pleasure running through him for a long, exquisite moment, and then Rolfe rolled over, taking her with him, his arms still wrapped around her. She lay across his chest, floating.

After a time she realized he was sleeping soundly. She looked up at him with a tender smile and then, carefully, tried to move off him. But Rolfe's arms tightened, wanting her close even in sleep. So there she settled, her head on his arm, her belly pressed to his side, one leg covering him. She slept a blissful sleep.

Chapter 32

"DO you know that wagers were placed last night after Sir Rolfe arrived? Half the guests here swear he killed you. The other half were divided between your lover being found and killed, and you getting a beating. What did happen, my lady?"

Leonie was speechless, hot color suffusing her cheeks. And for Wilda to have spoken as calmly as you please while she combed Leonie's hair made it that much worse. She was not prepared for something like this so early in the morning.

"How do you know there were wagers, Wilda?" she demanded.

"It is all they are talking about below, my lady." The maid shrugged, then grinned. "Everyone heard him calling for you, my lady. So they wonder what happened after he found you."

"I cannot believe that people think he killed someone just because he made too much noise."

"It was because of that last terrible roar, though not everyone heard that, my lord being up here by then. Those who heard that are the ones who swear murder was done."

"Enough!" Leonie snapped. "He drank too much, that's all. And he caused no trouble, Wilda, for me or anyone."

Wilda glanced at her mistress hopefully. It was her

fervent wish that things would work out between Leonie and her husband, for if they did not, she could see only years of unhappiness ahead for her lady. She truly loved Leonie.

"Mildred said he carried you in here," she ventured.

"Do not be impertinent, Wilda! Mildred says too much."

"Was he as masterful as—?"

"Wilda, stop it!" Leonie had a difficult time keeping from laughing. The maid was incorrigible, but Leonie knew Wilda wanted only to be reassured about her marriage.

She stood up to allow Wilda to finish dressing her, and just then the door opened and Rolfe came in, surprising the women. Under his arm was tucked a long narrow box, and in his hand was another, smaller box. He was just as surprised as they were, for Leonie was clad only in her sleeveless, knee-length shift. He stopped short and, with a dark look, turned abruptly and called out, "Richard! Close your eyes!"

The knight was directly behind Rolfe, laboring under a large chest. "Cover yourself," Rolfe said to Leonie, "until my friend here can deposit his burden."

Red-faced, Leonie quickly complied, incensed by Rolfe's unchivalrous behavior. How dared he barge in unannounced and then scowl at her for not being properly clothed?

She remained silent while donning her robe, but when she swung back around, there was a silver gleam in her eyes that spoke volumes. She found Rolfe smiling sheepishly, and Sir Richard grinning as he set the large chest down, bowed formally, then turned and left.

Rolfe wagged a finger comically. "Come and see what I have bought for you."

Leonie came forward hesitantly, wary as Rolfe opened the chest. Amazed, she knelt down and fingered the most exquisite gray silk. It was shot through with so much metallic thread, it gleamed like liquid silver. She had never seen anything like it.

But that was only the first of many surprises. There were ten lengths of cloth folded in the chest. There were silks in rose samite, violet sendal, and a heavy green and blue damask. Even more beautiful were three lengths of velvet in vibrant colors. Velvet very rarely appeared as far north as England, and it was so costly as to be seen only on kings and very wealthy lords. She had never thought to possess any, and she was overwhelmed.

"Where—where did you find these?" she asked in awe.

"Henry opened his stores to me," Rolfe said casually, though he was beaming at her pleasure.

"He *gave* these to you?"

"Gave?" Rolfe grunted. "What an idea! Henry does not give gifts unless he wants something in return. No, I told him what I was looking for, and he suggested I would find a better selection if I bought from his stores. He gets cargoes from the Far East that London merchants can only dream about."

"But—but these are worth a fortune." Leonie shook her head slowly, thoroughly confused. "You bought these materials for me?"

"Of course."

"Why?"

He grinned. "May I not receive a simple thank you? Must I have a reason for everything I do?"

She became alarmed then. Was she being rewarded for her behavior of the night before?

"If this has anything to do with last night..."

Leonie blushed, unable to finish in Wilda's presence. With a nod, she bid the maid leave them. When they were alone, Rolfe pressed her. "Did you do something last night to warrant—"

"Nothing to warrant gifts." She cut him off indignantly. "Why would you think so?"

"I did not think so. In fact, I meant to ask you about last night." He seemed a good deal less sure of himself. "I cannot seem to recall . . . I have no memory of leaving Westminster Hall, except a vague one of finding you at the bottom of the stairs here."

When she made no reply, he said, "Shall I assume I made an ass of myself?"

Leonie grinned. "If you are looked at strangely today, it is because you woke half the castle last night."

"And you, Leonie?" he said softly. "I would not like to think I offended you in any way."

Taken aback, she said, "You said much, but you did not offend me." Then she ventured, "Do you have no memory at *all?*"

"Pieces, dearling," he replied, looking at her thoughtfully. "But I am not sure if what I *do* remember was a dream or . . . did I carry you in here?"

Slowly, Leonie nodded, and then Rolfe's whole manner changed. He chuckled, and his eyes gleamed with masculine pride.

"That will teach me to drink so much." He grinned. "I waited for an eternity for you to let me make love to you again, and when you finally did, I could remember only half of it."

Leonie could feel the heat rushing to her cheeks again. She was beginning to think he said those things just to make her blush, for it happened much too often. Would she ever get used to his bluntness?

"The gifts, my lord," Leonie reminded him.

"So it is 'my lord' again?"

Leonie lowered her gaze.

Rolfe sighed. "These are for you as well." He handed her the two boxes. As the question leaped into her eyes again, he warned defensively, "Do not make the mistake of asking why I give these to you. It is a man's right to spend his money where he will."

"From Henry's stores too?"

The boxes themselves were beautiful. The long one was carved redwood, the smaller one silver, decorated with smooth enamels. She was almost afraid to see what they contained.

"I ordered those last week from the goldsmith here in London. I hope you will be pleased."

He did not wait to see if she would be, but turned to leave.

"I do thank you, my—"

Leonie caught herself before adding 'lord,' but not soon enough. Rolfe turned around at the door, his expression inscrutable.

"When you can finally bring yourself to use my name freely, then I think you will love me. I will wait for that day."

After he was gone she stared at the closed door, her confusion complete. Why did he so badly want her love? He had Amelia's. Was that not enough? Oh, such thoughts would only make her angry again, so she shook them off.

Such generosity! Inside the long box were two exquisite girdles. One was five feet of interlocking gold disks, each with a tiny flower engraved on its shiny round surface. The other was made of gold chains that hung in several lengths, connecting every three inches with a large ruby. There was a larger ruby to clasp the belt together. When she wore the girdle, the chains would flow all the way to her feet.

Inside the silver box were hundreds of precious stones, already in intricate gold settings. They could easily be sewn onto the clothes Leonie would make from the magnificent materials. She was holding a fortune in her hands.

She was stunned, awestruck, and thrilled. But even so, she found herself wondering if he had been equally generous with Amelia.

Chapter 33

WEARING her best bliaut of soft blue silk over a darker blue chemise, Leonie's confidence was nonetheless very low when Rolfe escorted her into the great hall at Westminster. Only the new girdle fit in with all the glitter of court dress.

She was taken into the presence of Princess Alice and her ladies and left there, as it was too early for her presentation to the king. Leonie did not know Princess Alice, Henry's reputed mistress, but she had met Queen Eleanor on one of her childhood visits to Court. It was said that Eleanor had instigated the rebellion of Henry's sons. Whether or not that was so, he had confined her to Winchester Castle. The fact that the queen was more or less imprisoned while Henry's mistress was by his side reminded Leonie too much of her situation with Rolfe and Amelia, and her spirits sank.

She was disappointed not to see the queen. A beautiful woman, with dark brown eyes and ivory skin, it was no wonder she had been wife to two kings. Her marriage to King Louis of France had been dissolved on grounds of their being related. But they were only fourth cousins, and the dissolution had been effected so that she could marry Henry.

Henry succeeded Stephen to the throne of England two years after marrying Eleanor. He was already duke of Normandy and count of Anjou, and with their marriage, Aquitaine was added to his possessions, making him ruler of all western France. Henry was the most powerful man in Europe.

Leonie remembered Eleanor as a gay, frivolous woman, a bit high-tempered, and truly vain. But Leonie's mother had sworn that Eleanor had mellowed since her youth. Eleanor was twelve years older than Henry, and possibly that was why he had put her aside for younger women.

King Louis' daughter, Alice, was no older than Leonie. She had been betrothed to Henry's son Richard, but that hadn't stopped Henry from making her his mistress four years ago, a fact he did not even try to hide after his queen was banished from court.

What was surprising was that Alice was not beautiful, not even terribly pretty. Her ladies-in-waiting were quick to point out that it was her wit Henry took pleasure in. Leonie was told, confidentially, how much Henry admired Alice's grace in walking and dancing. It seemed these beautiful ladies were making excuses for why their king did not prefer them, but the only reason needed was that Henry doubtless loved Alice, as she loved him.

Leonie might have warmed to the princess except that she saw Alice only as the other woman, and Henry as the unfaithful husband. When she looked at Alice, it was Amelia she was reminded of. So she was not in the best of moods when Rolfe came to escort her into the king's presence.

Henry had changed little in the six years since Leonie had seen him. He was still an intimidating man. His carelessness in dress had not changed either. He obviously found no time for tailors, for though his clothes were expensive, they did not fit him well.

"I did your husband a disservice in telling him that you were an uncomely child. I even tried to talk him out of having you. I can see I would never have been forgiven if I had succeeded."

Those were Henry's first words to her as he led her away from Rolfe. Leonie was not impressed.

"If that is a compliment, Your Majesty, then I thank you," she said tersely.

His gray eyes warmed. "Do you dislike me, my dear, or are you really as inflexible as Rolfe says?"

Leonie groaned inwardly. This was the king and she dared not offend him.

"I know not what he has told you," she said, forcing a smile.

"Oh, many things, many indeed—though I think he exaggerates. It cannot be true that you tried to kill him on your wedding night."

Leonie blanched. Rolfe had never discussed the incident with her, yet he could tell Henry about it!

"That—that was an accident, Your Majesty, caused by my nervousness and fear."

"I thought as much." Henry smiled disarmingly. "And I doubt you are as dissatisfied with this marriage I arranged for you as your husband seems to think. You might have objected at the start, but once you saw him, you were relieved, weren't you?" He did not wait for an answer. "Tell me, Lady Leonie, are you pleased with Sir Rolfe?"

"If it pleases you to think so, Your Majesty."

"That is not an answer."

"Then my answer is no."

"Now, see here—"

Her heart leaped into her throat. "You would not want me to lie, Your Majesty. You asked and I answered."

Henry began to chuckle. "So you did."

Leonie had forgotten his quick temper. She should have been watching his expression instead of keeping her eyes lowered. Fortunately, it appeared she had appeased him.

"This is most intriguing, my dear," Henry continued thoughtfully. "Your husband is a man the ladies find most attractive."

"So he is," Leonie agreed.

"Does he appeal to you?"

"I did not say he does not appeal, Your Majesty."

Henry frowned. "He is also a man of merit, and landed now, with wealth gained from prizes of war and tourneys even I cannot imagine. So will you tell me what exactly it is about Rolfe d'Ambert that displeases you?"

There was no way she could avoid answering.

She glanced around to be sure no one else would hear the confession of her shame.

"It is what I imagine many wives object to," she said lightly with a little shrug. "My lord Rolfe is not a faithful husband."

"After meeting you, I find that difficult to believe," Henry replied.

"I wish I had as much doubt," Leonie admitted.

There was a pregnant silence, and then the king said, "I remember your mother well, my dear. She brightened my court and did much to curb the queen's impulsiveness—for which I was grateful. I do not like knowing that her daughter is unhappy. Nor do I like seeing a man I am most fond of overset with confusion and just as unhappy. Can you not count your blessings and accept him the way he is?"

"I know I should, Your Majesty. And—and I will try if that is your wish."

"That doesn't sound very promising," Henry scolded gently. "If it is so important to you, I suppose I could summon Lady Amelia back to court."

Leonie flinched. She had not mentioned Amelia by name, and if the king knew of Amelia, then others at court must know as well.

"Your Majesty, that is something my lord Rolfe must decide for himself."

"As you wish, my dear."

Henry seemed relieved by her answer. He went on then to discuss things of a less personal nature. No doubt he did not really want to interfere in Rolfe's life. No doubt he preferred doing favors for his men, not for their ladies. Ladies were rarely in a position to return favors, and Henry was a crafty and political sovereign.

The hunt that afternoon in the nearby woods was less than stimulating, a stag and three boars brought down in short order and without much drama. If there had been more challenge to it, talk of a tourney might not have ensued. But the court was bored and restless, Henry having been in residence at Westminster longer than usual. Even Leonie felt a certain excitement when it was suggested. It was said again and again that Henry would never allow a tourney, yet she hoped he might make an exception when he heard that his lords were greatly in favor of it.

Leonie's excitement turned to anxiety that evening when Rolfe told her that Henry had surprised them all by giving his permission for the tourney, and that Rolfe himself would be participating. The tourney would be held the following day.

"But you cannot," she declared, forgetting her preparations for bed.

"Cannot? Why?" he asked, frowning.

"Your wound," she said. "It has not even been a fortnight—"

Rolfe laughed. "Your concern pleases me, Leonie, but it is no longer necessary."

"You scoff at me when I am serious," Leonie said tightly.

"Even you have said my wound is healed."

"I have not said so. I have said it is mending. There is a difference."

"Trust me to know if I am capable."

"You thought you were capable of this journey," she said sharply, "yet you forget how drained you were after only a day's ride. You have not your full strength back, my lord. To test your skills on the morrow would be sheer folly."

"It would be folly to listen to the worries of a woman," he returned just as sharply. "Tourneys were a way of life to me before I came to England. And these English knights are no challenge. Their skills have grown lax because Henry accepts scutage from them instead of calling up their forty days' service."

"My lord," she said succinctly, "your wound can be opened by one blow."

"Cease before I become angry, Leonie."

She should have remembered that Rolfe would not tolerate anger in the bedchamber, but she was reminded when he pulled her to him and kissed her savagely.

This is what Wilda saw when she reached the door. Swiftly, she managed to turn Mildred and Damian back around and close the door silently.

Leonie had forgotten the impending tourney. What

began in anger between her and Rolfe ended in sweetest passion. But later, awash in tender feelings for her husband, she determined to take the matter of the tourney out of his hands.

Chapter 34

"THIS is not right, my lady," Wilda said as she reluctantly handed the cup of wine to Leonie. "His anger will surpass anything we have seen before."

"What does that matter, as long as he is unharmed?" Leonie demanded.

"But to do *this*, my lady!"

"Hush, Wilda!" Leonie snapped. "He will return any moment and hear you."

"Better that than what will happen after the deed is done," Wilda muttered.

But Leonie was no longer listening. She opened her medicine basket and found the herbs she required. No sooner had she stirred them into the wine than Rolfe returned from mass with Damian. He eyed her darkly, knowing how she felt about the tourney.

"Will you ready yourself now, my lord?" Leonie asked.

"Will you help?" he rejoined skeptically.

"If you like."

Rolfe shook his head. "I swear I will never understand you, Leonie. Damian will dress me. From you, all I ask is that you have more faith in me."

"Your skill and ability were never in doubt, my lord, only your state of health. Please drink this and I will cease to worry."

He eyed the cup of wine warily. "I need no special potions, Leonie."

"It is only a few herbs to give you strength. Please," she beseeched earnestly. "This is the least you can do for me to relieve my mind. What harm can there be in a few herbs?"

He grabbed the cup from her and drank it. "Now will you cease worrying?"

"Yes," she replied meekly and handed the cup to Wilda, whose eyes rose heavenward over her lady's performance.

It was not long before the sleeping draught began to take effect. Damian became alarmed when Rolfe started swaying on his feet. Rolfe, confused by his sudden tiredness, allowed them to help him to bed. Relieved, Leonie thought that was the end of the matter.

But Rolfe grabbed her wrist before she could step away from the bed.

"What—what did you do to me, Leonie?"

His eyes, heavy-lidded, still managed to pierce her. He knew. There was no point in denying it.

She said staunchly, "I saw to your safety, my lord, since you would not."

"I swear . . . too far . . . this time."

His hand slowly released her and his eyes closed. His words had been jumbled, but she understood. She had gone too far.

"You did this, my lady?" Damian was staring at her incredulously.

"Yes."

"He will kill you!"

Leonie paled. Damian understood what she had done, but not why. Rolfe would know why, but he would not care. It would not matter to him that she couldn't bear the thought of his having another injury. He was under the misconception that no harm could come to him, and if he wouldn't admit that his strength was not fully recovered, he wouldn't admit that she was justified.

It was too late to regret her impulsive decision. Damian was right. He would kill her. Rolfe was a soldier. What she had done was unforgivable.

"I must speak with Sir Piers," Leonie said as she started for the door.

"Do not tell *him* what you have done!" Damian warned her. "He will strike you down."

"Then I will see the king."

It was Sir Piers who tried to stop Leonie from leaving the castle without waiting for Rolfe, and it was Sir Piers who finally escorted her to Westminster Hall when he saw that she would go alone if he did not accompany her. She told him nothing of what had happened, for she had no doubt that Damian was right about him.

The only thing she was able to do right that morning was to gain Henry's attention without the notice of any of the lords surrounding him. He was still dining in the hall when she entered with Piers. As it was his habit to eat standing up and moving about as he talked to his courtiers, it did not attract notice when he approached Leonie.

"Has your husband gone straightaway to the lists?" he asked.

Henry was in high good spirits, and she prayed that would aid her.

"He is not coming, my lord."

Henry frowned. "Whyever not?"

She explained, finishing, "I saw no other way to protect him."

"Protect him! I think he is in need of protection from you!"

"I did what I thought best, Your Majesty," she replied miserably. "I am not sorry I saved him from possible injury, only that it was necessary to do so."

Henry shook his head in amazement. "You do not know your husband, Lady Leonie. You have done him no favor. My son Richard is also a tourney follower, and he has told me he has seen Rolfe d'Ambert receive wound after wound, and still go on to win the day and a fortune in ransoms. There are few to equal him on the field. He can be near to death and he will still fight. That is his way—the way of the wolf. He did not get that name simply because of his dark looks, my dear."

"I—I did not know that, Your Majesty."

"He is not going to thank you, my dear," the king said, sighing.

"I know," she replied.

"I hope you have not come here to seek my protection?" he asked shrewdly.

"No, but I beg an escort to take me home, Your Majesty. I fear Rolfe's men will not do so without speaking to him first."

"You want to run from his anger?"

"Not . . . run, exactly. Merely give his temper time to cool before I must face it."

Henry chuckled. "It will not be as bad as all that, not unless he must go looking for you to hear your explanation. No, I will not help you run away from your husband, but I will give you an escort to return to him." With a flick of his wrist, Henry summoned three men to his side and gave them their orders. To her he added, "I suggest you tell him the truth. Perhaps he will overlook your foolishness this time."

"The truth? He already knows why I didn't want him to fight today."

"Ah, but the reason *behind* the reason, my dear. Tell the man you love him. It is astonishing what that single admission can do."

She was dismissed.

She took the opportunity to leave quickly before Sir Piers took notice and followed with more questions. Confess to a love she did not feel? No, that was not so. Confess to a love she—she was not going to think about it just then.

When she returned to the city palace, she found Richard Amyas in the stables. His impatience to be gone was obvious, and it was easy to convince him that Rolfe would be delayed for a while yet and that he should go on ahead to join Sir Piers on the tourney field. He left immediately, taking only two of the men-at-arms. That left Leonie the remaining eight, one of whom was the master-at-arms, Guy of Brent.

Leonie had never had reason to speak with him before. She did so now, using a tone that brooked no interference. He was not like Piers or Richard who would feel it was their duty to question her. Guy simply did as he was told and ordered one of the baggage wains readied. He sent men with her to collect her trunks.

Damian was more difficult to deal with. She did not want him to remain there to tell Rolfe she had gone, nor could she tie and gag Damian and bring him along. She waited until her trunks were removed and the maids gone before she launched into the lie that would delay Rolfe's following her.

"The king has bid me move to Westminster Hall until my husband is in a reasonable enough mood to listen to my explanation about what happened."

"That is wise, my lady," Damian replied solemnly. "So you have the king's protection?"

"Yes. Stay with my lord until he awakens."

She looked at Rolfe once more, knowing that the next time she saw him, his face would not look as peaceful as it did then. A shiver passed down her spine. Was she making it worse by leaving? She could only pray that time would calm him.

Chapter 35

LEONIE directed her escort off the main road and into the woods late that afternoon, despite the dire warnings of Guy who swore it wasn't safe to travel except on the main road. But Leonie was not worried about cutthroats or wild animals. She was buying herself more time, for Rolfe would go directly to Crewel, assuming that was her destination, while this route would take her around about, finally coming from the east to Pershwick. Oh, she would not compound her mistakes by pitting Pershwick against her husband, but hopefully he would think twice before beating her at Pershwick.

They made camp that night in the dense woods. Leonie could not complain, for she had brought it on herself. Wilda did complain, her grumbles continuous.

Rolfe would never forgive her. That thought carried Leonie into sleep that night. Sometime later, when a hand clamped over her mouth brought her awake, her first thought was that Rolfe had found her much sooner than she had anticipated.

She was dragged upward, an arm slipped beneath hers and across her breasts, gripping her firmly against a hard body. She was backed out of camp furtively, seeing by the light of the small fire that the rest of the camp was not disturbed, and that the guard at watch was not where he should have been.

But Rolfe would not take her away this way. He would have arrived with his wrath full-blown and awakened all with his booming voice. But if this was not Rolfe . . .

Leonie began to struggle, but it was too late. The grunt from the man behind her was not loud enough to carry back to camp. Her attempt to scream and to bite her captor's hand only made his grip tighten.

"Settle down, lady, or I will have to put my fist to you."

The gruff voice was speaking French, but it was not the fluid French of the nobility. As soon as she realized that, she realized he was not alone.

"Do we take her to the lord?"

"What did I wait around and snatch her for if not that?" the man behind answered irritably.

"We could keep this one for ourselves."

"That will not put gold in our pockets," was the quick retort.

"But this one is pretty, Derek." A beefy face loomed in front of Leonie.

"What does that matter when we need the pay?"

"We can have both." A third voice spoke. "Your lord will have his fun with her, Derek, so why shouldn't we as well? We took the risk of snatching her. I want her before we turn her over to him."

"Agree, Derek, or we do not leave here," the second man threatened.

The moment was tense. The other two men waited for Derek to decide. And then the quiet was broken by another man who burst through the brush, running.

"Osgar," the new fellow whispered excitedly, "the guard died without making a sound! I did a good job!"

"Quiet your fool brother, Osgar," Derek hissed angrily. "I swear I do not know why I use him."

"Because he does your killing for you," Osgar said smoothly. "Now—what about the lady? Does she pleasure us first?"

"Yes, but not here," Derek agreed. "And it must be done quickly. It is a long reach to the castle and her men have horses while we do not."

"We should have killed them all," someone grumbled.

"There were too many, fool. Now let us hurry if we are to stop before we reach the castle."

Leonie was carried along at a near run. She felt numb at first. This could not be real, could it? But the numbness began to wear off as Osgar and the others resumed speaking while they hurried through the woods.

"Will the lady be tortured like the others, Osgar?"

"You talk too much," Osgar growled at his brother.

"Will she?"

"If she does not admit who she is and arrange to ransom herself, yes, she will be tortured."

"Derek watches, doesn't he?"

"Idiot! Derek does the torturing. It is his lord who likes to watch."

Derek laughed, overhearing. "Did you tell him how often you sneaked into the dungeon to watch, too, Osgar?"

There was silence, then Osgar's brother asked, "Will she be kept for long in the dungeon, Osgar?"

"You ask too many questions."

"That merchant was killed even after his man brought the ransom. The merchant and his man were both killed."

"Quiet your brother, Osgar, before I do," Derek said angrily.

Leonie had heard of such happenings, but not since

the time of King Stephen when anarchy had prevailed. During King Stephen's time, even the poorest petty lord could collect riches and many did, extorting serf and freemen, even plundering churches. It was a common crime to capture anyone suspected of having even a little wealth. The victims were imprisoned and tortured until they were willing to give up all they possessed. No one was safe in those days, for there was no recourse to a king who was perpetually busy fighting to keep his crown. The true extent of criminality was realized later when all the unlicensed castles—more than a thousand—were ordered dismantled by Henry.

Leonie's fear became overwhelming as she considered all of what would happen to her when she was turned over to Derek's lord. But even so, those fears receded when the four men stopped, and she recalled what they planned.

Bile rose in her throat when Derek said gruffly, "I need a gag."

"Oho, so you want her too. And here you put up such a fuss—"

"A gag! Quickly!" Derek snapped. "I warn you, we have very little time. She needs to be locked away before her men come looking for her."

"We do not carry rags with us," Osgar grumbled.

"Your shirt will do. Give it over."

The second Derek removed his hand so that one of them could gag her, she let out an ear-piercing scream. It was cut off quickly, the stinking shirt yanked hard across her mouth. The shirt was tied behind her head so tightly, she thought the corners of her mouth would surely rip open.

The moment the gag was secure, Derek shook her hard. Pain shot up her arms where he gripped her.

"Stop, Derek, before you break her neck!" someone warned.

"Do you think they heard her at the castle?" Osgar asked.

"They don't care what happens in the woods," Derek told him.

"Then why are you so angry?"

"We are far enough away from her men, but not if one has awakened and come after her."

"We should have killed them one and all," Osgar said disgustedly. "There was no knight among them."

"And no sword among us but mine," Derek reminded them with contempt.

"Quiet! I hear something!"

Leonie heard it, too, growing louder by the second, the unmistakable sound of horses charging through the brush. Hope rose inside her, a living thing.

"You are saved for now, lady," Derek rasped angrily, "but I will make you pay for this later." To the others he ordered, "We cannot delay here now. Move quickly, but for God's sake do not make any noise."

"Derek, no," came an alarmed whisper. "There is the meadow to cross yet. We will be seen."

"Not if we wait by the meadow until all is quiet again. They will be spread out looking for her. If one comes upon us, we can kill him."

Leonie was propelled forward again. This time her arms gripped just above the elbows so that she couldn't reach up to pull out her gag. The other three men moved off ahead, but her struggle with Derek slowed him down. She tried jerking out of his hold, she tried stomping on his feet, she tried lifting her feet off the ground to pull him down. He was much stronger and none of it worked. He finally growled and hefted her up under his arm to carry her like a sack of meal.

She began feeling desperate again. The sound of hoof beats receded. Oh, she would have given her life for a chance to call out!

Derek stopped near a wide clearing that cut through the woods and was exceptionally bright compared to the woodland on all sides of it. The other three men were crouched down by the edge waiting for her and Derek, alert, nerves taut.

"What have you seen?" Derek demanded, scanning the clearing.

"No movement, but I thought I heard another sound down the way."

"Who else heard it?" No answer came, and Derek grunted. "It is as I thought. They will not come this far afield to look for her. We have only to cross the meadow and we will be safe."

"*I* will not feel safe until we are rid of her. This was not such a good idea, Derek. Our usual prey do not have such large escorts."

They moved out, keeping close together. But they were not even halfway across the meadow when a horse and rider moved slowly out from the trees facing them.

"Tell me that is your lord, Derek." Dread filled the voice.

"Of course it is not. He is not such a large man. But do not panic now," Derek warned. "This is a full-armored knight. She had no such knight with her."

"Why does he sit there and stare at us?" Osgar asked uneasily. "Why doesn't he move?"

"Wait, he comes now," Derek cautioned. He set Leonie down and shoved her at the others. "Hold her. I may have to fight him."

"*You* fight *him?*"

"With your help, fool," Derek hissed just as the

large destrier came abreast of them. "How may we serve you, my lord?"

"Show me what you have there."

"Just my lord's runaway wife. We are often sent to find her and bring her back. She is given to mental affliction."

"Strange. She looks so like my own wife. Of course, if I thought the lady of Kempston was being rough-handled, I would not like it."

Derek seemed to lose his tongue completely.

The large knight on the destrier eyed the rough man, waiting for him to speak.

"I think we are meeting the new lord of Kempston," Derek whispered.

"But the Black Wolf now has Kempston. You mean—"

"Yes. I think—I think this is his wife we have here."

"God's mercy, look at her eyes!" the third man cried. "She knows him!"

Osgar's brother started running before the words were out. The huge destrier cut off his flight in seconds, the flash of a blade felling the man. The blood-curdling war cry that followed set the other three to running, all in different directions. But it was only moments before the war-horse had run down two, the heavy sword following swiftly.

Osgar ran back the way they had come and would have escaped into the cover of trees before the destrier could cross the clearing, but another knight rode toward him from those woods and dispatched him with a spear.

Leonie could not move. The bodies of her four abductors were strewn around her, but she felt no relief. She was safe—yet not safe. A new ordeal was beginning.

"Finish here, Piers, and then send the men back to camp." As Rolfe spoke, more of his men rode into the clearing. "If one of those men is still alive, I want to know where they were going with her."

"Are you . . . ?" Piers began.

"I will be along shortly—with my wife."

Leonie had removed her gag, but she was too frozen with terror to speak.

Rolfe dismounted and came to stand before her. His face was hidden beneath his helmet, and she could not tell what he was thinking. Silence held her.

Finally, he asked, "Did they hurt you?"

How coldly formal he was! "They—meant to, but the sound of your horses frightened them." She looked directly up at him then, her eyes imploring. "My lord, I would speak with you—"

"Oh, we will speak, my lady. Do not doubt it."

Leonie gasped as he gripped her arm and propelled her toward his horse. He mounted, pulling her up into his lap. They rode off toward the woods, then—not toward camp, but away from it.

Leonie was in a misery of dread. She did not want Rolfe to hurt her. But he was going to beat her. Why else would he take her away from the others?

It did not seem as if he would ever stop, and she wanted it over and done with. She was being allowed too much time to be overcome by her fear. The farther he took her away from the others, the worse became her imagined punishment.

They came to another clearing, the ruins of an old tower centered in it. Rolfe rode toward this, stopping by the crumbling stones to set Leonie on her feet. The place was ominous, stark in the moonlight, but not as ominous as her husband dismounting. He removed his helmet and his gauntlets with slow deliberation. He moved toward her and stopped a foot away, his face hard.

"Who told you I was unfaithful?"

She started, disbelieving. The anger was there. His features were harsh with anger, too, his lips in a hard, straight line, but why was he asking such a thing?

"I . . . do not understand."

"What did you tell Henry?"

"I—" She gasped, recalling the conversation she had had with the king the day before. Anger rose swiftly. "He had no right to repeat my words!"

"The king's rights are not under discussion. Who told you I was unfaithful?" Rolfe asked again.

"No one had to tell me," she retorted. "Do you think I cannot see with my own eyes? Lady Amelia is not your ward. She was never your ward."

"She means nothing to me," he said swiftly.

"Is that supposed to set everything right?" Leonie cried. "A man will rut with the serving wench at his neighbor's house, and she means nothing to him, but that does not mean he is faithful to his wife! He is only more discreet than a man who keeps a mistress under his own roof—for all to see." She was close to tears.

"Damn me, Leonie, I have not touched another woman since we wed!"

That only stirred her anger. "You touched *me!* Have you forgotten you would have taken me to bed at Pershwick without knowing who I was?"

"So!" He looked at her hard, his eyes probing. "You still have not forgiven me for that."

"I mention it to prove the falseness of your words, my lord. You *have* touched other women. The fact that Lady Amelia was still sharing your chamber when I was brought back to Crewel proves it."

He came toward her then with a low growl, but Leonie stood her ground. Even when his fingers bit into her arms and he lifted her off the ground so that they were face-to-face, she did not flinch.

"Tell me why it matters to you, madame." Rolfe's voice was dangerously calm. "Did you not say that you did not care how many women I bedded?"

"With discretion."

"I did not realize there were conditions," he said sardonically. "So you truly do *not* care?"

A lump rose in her throat. "I do not."

He set her down and turned away. Leonie bit her lips, despising herself.

"Why do you want me to care?" Her voice turned soft.

"A wife should care," he said quietly.

"A wife should not be insulted with the presence of her husband's mistress."

Rolfe swung back around, his body taut with anger. "There was never any insult intended. I have told you she is no longer my mistress."

"If you wanted me to believe that, my lord, you would send her away."

"Do not ask that of me, Leonie."

She swallowed her pride. "I *am* asking. If she means nothing to you, then you have no reason to keep her."

"She does not . . . want to go," he said tightly.

He might as well have struck her. "You put her wants above mine?" She waited for him to speak, to promise to send Amelia away. She waited, and when he did not speak, she said, "Then all you will have from me, Rolfe d'Ambert, is my contempt."

"I will have more than that, madame." He dragged her to him, his mouth coming down hard on hers, his kiss leaving her weak and shaken. She could not let him overpower her again, not let him bring forth those impossible feelings.

"I hate you," Leonie whispered, the words sounding less than convincing even to herself.

"Then I will love you despite your hatred."

He kissed her again, and the traitorous flame leaped within her, drawing her to him despite everything. She fought and fought, and what she was fighting against wasn't him, but her own desire.

Chapter 36

A MANGY hound sniffing at their feet woke Leonie and Rolfe. Rolfe rose with a roar, pretending to charge the animal. The dog simply stared at him. Leonie giggled, and Rolfe turned on her with an indignant look.

"Perhaps you could just *ask* him to leave?" she suggested, laughter in her eyes.

"You are welcome to try that," he said.

She did. The dog simply stared at her. "I think we should let him stay," she allowed.

Rolfe chuckled. "I think he will do just that."

He bent down and drew her head up for a light kiss, his eyes smiling warmly into hers. Then he left her to relieve himself, and Leonie lay back on his mantle with a lighthearted sigh. They had spent the night wedged between fallen rocks and what remained of a tower wall. She had slept contented and secure in Rolfe's arms, all of her anger and hurt washed away by his desire for her.

That was the one thing she could not discount. No matter what else stood between them, Rolfe did want her. His own anger couldn't even withstand his desire. And knowing that was a sweet balm to Leonie's pain.

For a while last night he made her believe that he loved her. She gloried in that feeling and all the other feelings he ignited in her. She blushed, recalling Rolfe's impatience. He undressed with her help, and she with his, and they made love slowly, savoring every moment, and each gentle caress. Never could she have imagined such a terrible day to end the way it had.

"Your blushes give your thoughts away, dearling."

Leonie turned redder and Rolfe laughed, delighted. He helped her to her feet and patted her backside in a blatantly possessive way.

"Go and do what you have to," he told her with a grin. "We have delayed here longer than anticipated."

She hurried off, still flustered. When she returned, Rolfe was readying his horse. His back was to her, so he did not hear her approach. She paused, hesitating. Anxiety was returning. It was inconceivable that Rolfe was going to dismiss the matter of her drugging him. She hated to think of his anger returning.

She took the few steps that brought her to Rolfe's back. Still he did not turn around, and she clutched her hands uncertainly.

"How did you find me so soon?" She tried desperately to sound casual.

"Inquiries produced results. You were seen leaving the main road. Your direction was clear, so it was not difficult to find your camp, even after dark. I did not expect to find you missing from it, however."

He turned around slowly and eyed her.

"I—I am most grateful, my lord, that you found me when you did."

"Do you know where they were taking you?"

"To a castle nearby. To a lord who practices extortion by using torture." She shuddered. "I am certain you saved my life."

"They wouldn't have killed you, Leonie. Hurt you, but you are too valuable to kill."

"They didn't care who I was, or know my value. I'm sure of that."

"They would have known your value once you told them your name."

He said that so matter-of-factly, but what did he mean? Hers was not a name to be reckoned with. Then she recalled the reactions of the men when they realized who Rolfe was. Even the overconfident Derek had lost his courage when he realized he had taken the wife of the Black Wolf.

Leonie said reflectively, "I see now I was too isolated all those years at Pershwick. I had no idea such things could happen."

Rolfe grunted. "How could you not know? Your neighbor was one of the worst of that kind."

"Neighbor? Who do you mean?"

"Who else?" Rolfe said, disgusted. "Montigny and his son. No doubt his vassals were involved as well. It would help to explain why those vassals were so afraid to accept me. They undoubtedly thought I was there to see *full* justice done."

Leonie stiffened. "I do not believe it! I have known the Montignys all my life. Sir Edmond was a good neighbor, and Alain—"

"Do not mention the boy to me," Rolfe cut her off sharply. "And whether you believe it or not, Leonie, the Montignys were guilty of many crimes. They were careful. Their victims didn't know where they were taken, or who collected their ransoms. And of course those who were killed could not carry tales. But Henry has received complaints from the midlands for a long time. It was only recently that he had names to match to the crimes."

"It is unfair of you to malign a man who is dead and cannot defend himself."

"How do you think he died, madame? There were finally enough good men aware of his activities to swear against him. He was killed resisting his arrest. His son fled before he could be brought to trial."

"But none of this makes sense. Sir Edmond controlled all of Kempston. What need had he of unlawful gains?"

Rolfe shrugged. "He had many more keeps in Stephen's day, keeps he was forced to dismantle. I suppose he resorted to unlawful means to re-create the wealth he was accustomed to. The man always lived extravagantly."

Leonie recalled hearing just how extravagantly Sir Edmond had lived.

She remembered, too, vague talk of things she had not wanted to hear about. Had those rumors been true? She found it hard to believe, especially of Alain. Alain's father may have been corrupt, but timid, fainthearted Alain? No.

But this was a poor time to begin an argument.

"Should we be going, my lord?" she said.

"I suppose Guy has been kept in suspense about his punishment long enough. Yes, let us go."

He mounted, then lifted her up onto his horse, holding her steady as they began to move.

"What punishment? What has the master-at-arms done?" she asked.

"He put you in danger." The destrier moved into the woods.

She gasped. "But he only followed my orders!"

"That is not the point. You were in his charge. He knew better than to lead you off the main road. He is lucky I did not kill him last night. He will receive twenty lashes tonight when we reach Crewel, and he will be grateful that is all he will get. He knows he did wrong."

She was horrified. "I wish you would not punish him, my lord. No one must suffer for what was my fault." She was shouting over the horse's hoof beats.

"You can accept the blame, Leonie, and rightly so, but you will not interfere in my judgment. The man will be punished for his carelessness, and nothing can prevent that."

"What will be my punishment, my lord?" she asked.

"I hope you learned an important lesson last night."

"Should you not whip me as well?" she demanded. "I was just as careless as the master-at-arms."

"Do not tempt me, Leonie. You were more than careless," he said in a hard voice. "Because of you I nearly came to blows with the king."

Leonie groaned. "No."

"Yes. I called him a liar when he insisted you were not hiding under his protection."

"Sweet Mary!" Leonie lost her color. "I told Damian I was going to the king only to delay your following me. I did not think you would disbelieve Henry when he told you I was not there."

"Sir Piers swore he had not seen you leave Westminster Hall. If he had not realized half my men were missing and told me so, I would have torn Henry's hall apart looking for you."

"You—you did not really call Henry a liar, did you?"

"I did."

"God's Mercy, he will never forgive you! What have I done?"

"He has already forgiven me," Rolfe said a little less severely. "He is not an insensitive man. He allowed my behavior was understandable. He even told me of your conversation with him, to help me understand your behavior. I was furious, knowing you could tell Henry why you will not accept me, but you could not tell me."

There was a silence, and then he said, "Now I find it was not even the truth, what you told Henry."

"It *was* the truth."

"Was it? You swore last evening that you do not care."

Leonie opened her mouth, then thought better of speaking. They had been through this and gotten nowhere. He had made his position clear. He would not give up Amelia. She would not ask him again.

Rolfe sighed. "Do not drug me again, Leonie. And never run from me again either."

"Yes, my lord."

He said no more.

Chapter 37

HARVESTING had begun on the Crewel manor lands, that portion of the lands devoted to the lord's use. But Crewel lacked a bailiff to oversee the villagers' work, and although Leonie was able to do the overseeing, she recalled the animosity of the villagers to her and decided not to try. She did appoint an acting bailiff, however, the village headman. It was an unheard of choice, but a logical one, for the serfs would listen to him.

She had made the decision on her own, because Rolfe was away. He had been gone for all of the two weeks since their return from London.

His absence was only one of the difficult things Leonie had suffered since the night Guy of Brent received his twenty lashes. Rolfe left directly after the punishment for the siege at Warling, and hadn't returned since.

Warling Keep was nearly fifteen miles north of Crewel, a long distance. She understood that he couldn't come home, but she missed him. She caught herself listening for the sound of horses approaching, and even considered riding to Warling herself, but she knew Rolfe wouldn't approve.

Missing Rolfe was not the only unhappiness in her life, either. There was the endless presence of Lady Amelia.

One evening, at dinner, Sir Evarard was called away from the table, which left the two women with only his empty chair between them.

Although Leonie had every intention of being civil to Amelia, it was not easy. The other woman positively radiated smugness. Leonie was perplexed by this. What could be the reason for Amelia's attitude?

That night at dinner, when Sir Evarard was gone, Amelia asked Leonie for a potion to quell nausea.

"Should you not be in bed if you are ill?" Leonie asked her.

"Heavens no!" Amelia laughed. "There is nothing wrong with me that another month's time won't cure. I have this difficulty only at meals."

Leonie grasped the meaning then. "You are insinuating something, Lady Amelia. What is it?" She meant there to be no mystery about this.

"Surely Rolfe told you!" Amelia seemed aghast. "It is hardly something that can be kept secret."

"You are saying you will bear my husband a child?" Leonie said levelly.

"The babe is Rolfe's, yes," Amelia replied. "He does not deny it."

So much fell into place in that moment. No wonder Rolfe refused to send Amelia away! It was almost a relief to understand this.

Leonie's gaze moved down over Amelia's figure, as pathetically thin as ever, and she said icily, "When did you conceive?"

"What difference—?"

"Answer me, Amelia!"

Amelia shrugged. "It has been a month."

Leonie figured swiftly. It had been a month since she was brought to Crewel to live. She could remember clearly the night Rolfe left their chamber angrily. Amelia had been in exceptionally good spirits that next morning.

Leonie left Amelia without saying another word. What was there to say? But that night was the most miserable of her life. Alone, she cried and stormed, cursing Rolfe for his weakness and his lying. But she cursed herself as well—because it mattered to her, it mattered much too much.

When another note arrived from Alain Montigny the next day, Leonie was too distracted to think about it. She tucked it away with some other papers and forgot about it. She sank into a terrible melancholy all the remainder of the week, an unhappiness caused by the shock of learning that she, too, was pregnant.

The fact that the babies would be born about the same time was most telling. It was not unusual for a lord to ask a new wife to raise his bastard children if he had any. The wife had no grounds to refuse because those children had been conceived before her marriage to their father. But it was another thing entirely to accept children conceived by other women after the marriage.

Leonie did not think Rolfe would ask her to raise Amelia's child. But she had little doubt that he would want to keep both child and mother near him. This would not be the child of a serf. A serf could be expected to give up her child because the father would give it a better life than she could. But such was not the case with Amelia. Amelia would never give up her child, and so Rolfe would never give up Amelia.

The future looked progressively grimmer. She no longer had the hope that Rolfe would send her away one day, not if she had his child. Rolfe would never let her go if he knew there was a baby on the way.

She was not going to tell him. She could hope to

leave him before her body gave the truth away. Perhaps she could lock herself away in Pershwick until after the child was born. She would not, she determined, give him an excuse to keep her.

Leonie could share some kinds of love, could share her gift for healing, but she could not share her husband with another woman. Always there had been the hope that Amelia would leave. Now that hope was gone. It seemed her heart flew out of her, for she bore an ache in her breast that did not diminish, even with the passing of many days.

Sir Bertrand and his oldest son Reginald came to Crewel late one afternoon with news that Rolfe had sent for them to meet him at Crewel. Bertrand was Leonie's own vassal at Marhill Keep, one of her holdings. Why her husband should ask to see Bertrand was a mystery.

All she could think about was that Rolfe would be home soon. She managed to ask the proper questions about Marhill, about the harvesting there, but she could not later recall what was told her. Her mind was in complete confusion over Rolfe.

It was a busy time. She entertained her guests as best she could, with Sir Evarard's help. Thankfully, Amelia kept herself absent from the hall. It grew late and still Rolfe had not come. Leonie readied rooms for her guests, but the men preferred to remain in the hall, curious as to what Rolfe wished to see them about.

Sounds of his arrival were heard at last, and Leonie quickly excused herself, retiring to her room. She had finally concluded that she could not face Rolfe without her resentment bubbling over, and to let that happen in front of her vassal was unthinkable. Safe here in their room, she did not have to conceal her feelings.

There was no time, however, to prepare herself for what she assumed would be a full-fledged battle. Rolfe came to her immediately, so quickly that she realized he could not have spared more than a moment's greeting for their guests below. What might excuse such rude behavior? After all, he had sent for the two men.

Her brows narrowed suspiciously. "You have not shamed me, have you, my lord?"

"How so?"

Rolfe tossed aside his helmet and gauntlets, but his eyes did not stray from Leonie. She kept her position by the hearth, standing stiffly at attention.

"You sent for Sir Bertrand and his son. What can they think of your ignoring them?"

Rolfe grinned, moving to close the distance between them. "I told them I was tired and would speak to them in the morning. They understood."

"How could you?" Leonie hissed. "You must go below and speak to them now!"

"They have already retired, dearling, and—"

He fell silent as Damian came into the room. Leonie swallowed her ire and turned her back while Damian assisted Rolfe with his heavy hauberk.

It did not take the young squire long, and it was only moments before Rolfe said agreeably, "Off to bed with you, lad."

Openmouthed with surprise, Damian left the room. Never had Rolfe spoken to him so pleasantly. It was amazing how the sight of his wife could change his manner completely.

Leonie waited only until the sound of the door closed before she swung around, ready to get everything off her chest at once. But the sight of Rolfe in only shirt and chausses stopped her. The thick muscles straining on his long legs, the breadth of chest—always startling because it was just as wide with his armor removed—his hair curling riotously about his head, all of it brought out the man and the boy in him at once. It was unfair that he could affect her so powerfully that she couldn't even remember what she'd been about to say.

"You have missed me, dearling."

"I have not, my lord," she said stiffly.

"Liar." He had moved over to her before she could move away. He tilted her chin up and gazed into her eyes. His eyes were velvety brown, yet intense. "You are angry because I stayed away so long."

"There are many things I am angry about, my lord, but that is not one of them."

"You may tell me what they are tomorrow, Leonie, for this is no time for anger."

She tried to move away, but Rolfe caught her to him and kissed her.

"I missed you, Leonie. God, how I missed you," he exclaimed as his lips trailed along her cheek to the soft contours of her neck.

She was nearly lost. She could not let him do this to her again, but already her desire was ignited, despite all her misery and bitterness. "If—if you must have a woman . . . go to your other lady . . . I cannot—"

"I have no other lady."

She leaned into him, pliant. She could not fight their passion, and for the time being, she gave up trying.

Chapter 38

ROLFE leaned back in his chair and fixed Thorpe with a steady gaze. It was always good to consult his old friend. The talk with Bertrand of Marhill and his son Reginald had gone well. They had begged off staying any longer once the meeting was over, because they had left guests of their own in order to meet with Rolfe. Rolfe was well pleased. It was as Henry had said. Bertrand had several sons that Rolfe could make use of, and that was just what he needed. Rolfe's own men were loath to take the responsibility of governing his remaining keeps. They preferred soldiering.

"What do you think of Sir Reginald? Will he make a good castellan of Warling?"

"He seems eager enough, overeager in fact," Thorpe replied thoughtfully. "Until now he had only the prospect of Marhill, and that only after Bertrand dies. I think he will serve you well, if only to prove he is worthy of Marhill when the time comes."

"I agree. Now we have only to win Warling."

"Another week or two, and the walls will give," Thorpe predicted confidently. "The tunnel at Blythe is in the works as well. Kempston should be well secured before the first snows. And what will we do then? We will have peace across your lands, and nothing left to do."

Rolfe grinned. "Let me enjoy peace for a while, before I go looking for another war."

"You may come to like being a landed lord too well to go hieing off to war."

Rolfe said nothing. He was considering the truth of that statement, and Thorpe knew it.

Thorpe grunted. "At any rate, I see your point. It was wise to sound out Sir Bertrand and his son before you actually need them. To tell the truth, I thought you were only using this meeting as an excuse to see your wife."

Rolfe grinned, and Thorpe guffawed. "Damn me! I was right!"

"Whatever brings me back here is welcome." Rolfe shrugged.

"And what did she think of your enlisting two of Bertrand's sons for your own keeps? He did say he had another son who would do well for Blythe Keep?"

"Yes, but I have not told Leonie yet."

Thorpe rolled his eyes heavenward. "What can you be thinking of, my friend? Sir Bertrand is *her* man."

"I know."

"You should have consulted her before you made him the offer."

"I meant to, but last night . . . was not the time. And this morning"—he smiled fondly—"she was sleeping so peacefully, I couldn't waken her. But what can she object to? I have simply bound the family more firmly to us. The father will work for her, the sons for me."

"A woman can be more jealous of what is hers than a man would ever be."

Rolfe frowned. "How is it that you know so much about women all of a sudden?"

"I know a good deal more than you do, apparently."

Rolfe grunted, stretching his arm to reach the cold

meat on a platter which the young serving maid was just bringing to the table. Rolfe noted her smile and his eyes followed her as she walked away.

"If you know so much about women," he demanded of Thorpe, "tell me what the devil has plagued the women around me. I do not mean my wife."

Thorpe choked on a bit of bread. "What women?" he managed without grinning.

"All of them! The servants, the wives of my men. For weeks every one of them behaved as if I were diseased. Now suddenly I get smiles all the time. Lady Bertha even rode over to Warling to bring me a fruit pie, and Warren's wife sent flowers—flowers!"

Thorpe could not hide his amusement any longer and laughed with delight. "They are doubtless trying to make amends for thinking it was you who beat your wife on your wedding night. Lady Leonie was the one who corrected the mistake. I hear she was quite angry when she learned you were being blamed for what her father did."

"She was beaten. Who says so?"

Thorpe's humor fled. Rolfe had paled, and his body was still as death. "Damn me, Rolfe, do you mean you didn't know? But you spent the night with her. How could you not know?"

"Who?" Rolfe repeated. His voice was a whisper.

"Lady Roese caught a glimpse of her face the next morning when the ladies came for your sheets," Thorpe said uneasily.

"How badly was she beaten?"

Thorpe realized he had to tell all he knew. "Apparently it was a harsh beating. I heard it said Lady Leonie's face was swollen grotesquely and blackened with bruises. That is what shocked Lady Roese so badly. Thinking you were responsible, she did not keep quiet about the beating."

"You knew all this, and you never spoke to me about it?"

"I thought surely you *knew.* I would not have mentioned any of this now except for the gossip and . . ."

Thorpe watched as Rolfe leaped from his chair and bounded out of the hall in six strides. A few moments later, he jumped as a door slammed shut upstairs.

Chapter 39

LEONIE looked up in dismay as her husband towered over her, in a rage about something, glowering in a terrifying manner.

"Why did you never tell me what was done to you?"

"Done?" Was he drunk again? "You will have to be more specific if—"

"You were beaten severely! Was everyone to know of it except me?"

Leonie stiffened, her eyes turning a stormy silver gray. This was not a subject dear to her, but then he already knew that.

"I have told you before that I will not speak of what happened," she said frostily.

"Damn me, you will! You will tell me what you gained by hiding your beating from me!"

"Hiding it!" she came back furiously. "There was nothing to hide, except from Sir Guibert, and that was to prevent murder being done. *You* knew! Judith admitted to me that she told you. Why else do you think I stabbed you that night? I awoke in pain, caused by your touch on my bruised face. It was a thoughtless, normal reaction. You must have understood that, since you never mentioned the stabbing to me."

Rolfe's anger was tempered somewhat by hers, but only somewhat. "I never mentioned that little prick you made with your knife, Leonie, because that is all it was. And your stepmother did warn me you had to be forced to marry me, but she didn't tell me how you were forced. I thought you were denied a few meals, the standard practice for reluctant brides."

"There was no time for that, my lord," she said bitterly. "My father did not tell me I was to marry until the day before the wedding. As usual, his drunkenness made him thoughtless."

"Does drunkenness excuse him?"

"*I* do not excuse him!"

"For your beating, or because you are now married to me?" he asked harshly.

Leonie turned her back, but Rolfe whirled her around, his fingers biting into her arms, his eyes black with rage.

"Why, Leonie? Why was I so abhorrent to you? Why did you have to be beaten before you would consent to marry me?"

He was shouting at her, stirring her already churning emotions. Never mind that she was beaten. Never mind that she had suffered. His vanity was wounded, and that was all that concerned him!

"I was afraid of you, my lord. I had been told you were a monster, and that was all I knew of you. I thought you wanted me only for revenge, because of the trouble you felt I had caused you. A beating was easier than what I believed you would do to me." Reflectively, she added, "I thought I could withstand a beating, but I was wrong. The cur would have killed me had I not sworn on my mother's grave that I would wed you."

This was uttered with all the hatred she felt for Richer Calveley. Rolfe thought it reflected her anger at being forced to marry him.

"So you thought me a monster?"

"I did."

"And still do?"

"I did not say so, my lord."

"No, of course not, but I must assume it is so. Why else do you still scorn me? Why else do you refuse to be my wife in truth?"

Something in his tone made her wary. What kind of confession was he looking for? And then it struck her. He wanted to hear her rail at him again about his mistress. How appeased his vanity would be to have her act the jealous wife. She would not give him that satisfaction.

She dropped her eyes. "I do not scorn you, my lord. Whyever would you think so?"

"Do you not?" he said harshly. "You are just cold by nature then?"

"Perhaps," she agreed glibly.

He turned away from her. "Or perhaps you love another!"

"Another?" she replied incredulously, her temper flaring despite her resolve. "Look who talks of another! I take marriage seriously, my lord, even if *you* do not!"

"Be damned if you do, or you would have renounced your first love and accepted me. Well I would hear the truth now, madame, and have done with it. No longer will I let these suspicions gnaw at my insides."

Leonie found it hard to believe what he was saying. How dare he accuse her of infidelity when he . . .

She drew herself up sharply, eyes a wintry gray. "If you are searching for an excuse to send me away, my lord, you need not go to so much trouble. I will be more than happy to leave."

His eyes flared before his lips tightened into an ominous line. "No doubt you would like that, wife."

"Indeed," she retorted, her anger flaring. He was

going to sever their relationship. How easy everything was for men!

He took a step toward her, and she thought for certain he was going to strike her, so black was his expression. He towered over her, body rigid, fists clenched, eyes like hot coals.

"If it has been your hope that you can still have him, you hope in vain," he rasped furiously. "I may indeed grow tired of your icy demeanor one day and have done with you, but you will never have him. I will kill him first!"

"Who?" she shouted.

"Montigny!"

Leonie was so surprised she might have laughed. It was unfortunate she did not, for Rolfe saw only her surprise and it inflamed him.

"You thought I did not know it was that young ne'er-do-well? I knew it before I wed you!"

Leonie tried to comprehend but couldn't. She said simply, "You are wrong, my lord."

"You have always loved him, madame. It is why you set your people against me. It is why you refused to marry me. It is why you hate me still, because I have you, while you yearn for him!"

Leonie did laugh this time, and it was Rolfe's turn to be bewildered. She couldn't help herself. He was jealous of poor Alain. How absurd.

She smiled at her husband. "I do not mean to take this matter lightly, for no doubt you have harbored these suspicions for some time. But you see, Alain is only a friend. I did once fancy he might do as a husband, but that was long ago when he was the *only* young man I knew and I despaired of ever having a husband, confined as I was to Pershwick. But it was only a fancy, and quickly forgotten. Alain grew to be a man sadly lacking in character, and I no longer yearned for a husband by then anyway. Yet I could not forsake him simply because he had a few weak traits, so we remained friends."

Rolfe was still scowling. "You expect me to believe you would set your people against me for the sake of—of friendship?"

"Would you not go to war for a friend?"

"You are a woman."

Leonie kept a rein on her temper. "I will not argue that point with you, my lord. The fact is I did not set my people against you. The day Alain told me what had befallen him, and that you were coming here to take his lands from him, I wished a pox on you. There, I have finally confessed what I did," she said, relieved. "I thought the worst of you, and my people took this to heart."

Rolfe did not know what to think. He wanted to believe her, but if she did not love Alain, then why would she not love him?

"If all you have said is true, Leonie, then there is no reason for you to still hate me."

"But I do not hate you, my lord."

"But you will not accept me, either."

Leonie lowered her eyes and said softly, "I could accept you, my lord, if it were *only* you. But you ask more of me than that I accept only you."

"Is that supposed to make sense to me, woman?" His voice rose in frustration.

Leonie did not look up. Rolfe stared hard at her for several moments more, then turned and stalked out of the room. Seeing Thorpe waiting for him downstairs reminded him of what had set him off, and his frustration over his wife's cryptic remark turned once again to burning anger. He had to put an end to these secrets and confusions and upsets, and he believed he could end the turmoil by going back to its beginning.

Chapter 40

JUDITH rolled her head back, giggling as Richer's thick beard began to tickle her breasts. He had come upon her in the storeroom and proceeded to play his little games with her, refusing to take no for an answer. Backing her into the meal sacks, he thrust his body against her, stilling with his lips her protests over the hour and place.

How forceful he was, this cruel man. And he was cruel. She could see in his eyes, when he touched her with a gentle hand, that he desired to hurt her instead, as he did his other women. But he did not dare use rough ways with her. They both knew he did not dare, but knowing what he was capable of made him all the more exciting to her.

When he began to lift her skirts, Judith gave another token protest. It was what he liked, her resistance. It always fired his blood. When they met at agreed-upon places, she was usually too ready for him, too eager. He liked to catch her unaware, to take her in unlikely places where he knew she would fear discovery and try to put him off.

"Can you not wait until this evening, Richer, and come to my room as we planned?"

He grunted. "I do not like taking you with your husband snoring drunkenly beside us."

"But that is what is so exciting, love," Judith purred. "If he wakes, he thinks he is having another delusion."

He glowered at her, but she knew it rather suited Richer's dark sense of humor to cuckold his lord right in front of him. It suited her, as well, for she hated William more every day. It was thrilling to have another man mount her while her besotted husband slept beside them.

"I will have you now, and then again later." Richer grinned darkly, pressing the lower half of his body firmly into hers.

His flames of desire were well met by hers, as he knew they would be. Her thighs parted to accommodate him, even as she sighed and said dramatically, "You will do as you will, Richer. You always do."

He laughed, but his laughter was cut short by a whining servant's voice outside the door. "My lady?"

"What?" Judith shrieked.

"My lady," quavered the voice. "Your son-in-law is here. Rolfe d'Ambert awaits your pleasure."

To Richer she said curtly, "Let me up, love. You must wait for this evening after all. Faugh! What the devil does he want?"

Judith made haste to straighten her bodice and her hair. She shouted to the servant that she would greet their guest momentarily.

"I will make myself scarce," Richer said, "in case he has brought his lady with him."

Judith glanced over at him, startled. She had never heard uneasiness in Richer's voice before.

She frowned, a touch nervous herself. "Yes, that would be best. If the lord of Kempston has gained any fondness at all for my stepdaughter, it would not do to remind her of you. She might talk to her husband about you, and there is no telling what would come of that."

In the great hall of Montwyn, Rolfe d'Ambert stood waiting with two of his knights. This was not a simple courtesy visit, and Judith became frightened immediately upon seeing Rolfe's menacing countenance. There was not a cordial line in his face, not even a feigned smile of greeting as she approached. At least Leonie was not with Rolfe, she noted, hoping her absence would make him a bit less confident than he seemed.

Judith graciously nodded to him. "Lord Rolfe—"

"Your husband, madame. How long will he keep me waiting here?"

"Waiting? William is indisposed, Sir Rolfe. The servants know they must not disturb him."

"Then I suggest you disturb him, madame."

She gave him her most beguiling smile. "Surely you would not mind spending time with me instead? I will tell William later that you were here."

"I think not," Rolfe said. "It is your husband I wish to have words with, not you. Will you rouse him, my lady, or shall I?"

"But he truly *is* indisposed," Judith insisted worriedly. "I—I doubt he would even know you, my lord."

"He is already drunk at this early hour?" Rolfe growled in disgust.

Judith shrugged. It was just as well he knew, for then he would not bother her again. "It is an unfortunate truth, my lord, that William is very seldom sober."

"I see."

Rolfe turned to his men and said, "We will stay here and see the man wrung out to dry. Send word to Sir Thorpe that we will not return today. He might as well go back to Warling—Damn me!" he said explosively. "There is no telling *how* long this will take!"

Judith was finding it difficult to hide her increasing fear. "What is it you want with my husband, my lord?"

Rolfe's black eyes fixed on her. "That is not your concern, madame."

"But—but you cannot simply—"

"No?" he interrupted, his voice low. "Perhaps you like having a sot for a husband?"

"Of course not." She managed to appear most affronted. "I have tried to stop his drinking, but he cannot function without it. I have been unable to help him."

"Then you will thank me for taking a hand. I will soon see him functioning well and understanding me perfectly. Now please lead the way. I would begin this distasteful duty immediately."

Panic mounted in Judith and grew steadily worse as days passed and Rolfe d'Ambert stayed doggedly at the task he had set for himself. She even considered killing the arrogant lord, or killing William, but the former was impossible and the latter, well, if William died, Leonie would inherit everything. Judith would be cast out, penniless. Leonie would do her no good, that was certain.

If only she knew what it was that had brought the lord of Kempston there, but he continued to ignore her pleas to explain. Richer insisted she worried for nothing, but why was Rolfe d'Ambert so angry, and why did he have a ruthless determination to see William coherent and sensible?

The lord of Montwyn was bathed and sheared and bathed again countless times despite his curses and attempts to ward off his persecutors. He was stuffed with food, only to retch it up. He was denied all but milk or water to drink. He was ignored when he screamed for something more potent, ignored when his body shook uncontrollably. And all the while d'Ambert's anger was a palpable thing, held in check only by heaven knew what.

Judith could only stand by helplessly and watch all that she had accomplished over the years being undone. Her only hope was that William was too far gone to remember any of the recent past, and that once d'Ambert left them alone, William would run back to his drink.

Chapter 41

ROLFE rubbed his face wearily. He was sick of this room, sick of the pathetic man who had drunk his life away.

"If you meant to kill me, why couldn't you do it quickly?"

Rolfe had heard that lament a dozen times in the last grueling days. William of Montwyn was feeling deeply sorry for himself, and hurting miserably. But his hands no longer trembled quite so much, and his nightmares had begun to lessen.

Rolfe decided he had waited long enough. He finally replied, calling across the room, startling Montwyn and his servants, Rolfe's men, and Lady Judith. "Because, my lord," Rolfe drawled, "I want you to know why I wish to kill you."

The voice was so emotionless that William did not quite credit the statement. His eyes, still slightly streaked with red, fastened on Rolfe. He had been fully dressed that morning despite his protests, and forcibly seated at a table where a feast of wholesome foods awaited him. He ignored them, staring hard at the man responsible for his miserable condition.

"Do you, indeed, Sir Rolfe?" William asked sarcastically, his voice cracking. "Be so good as to tell me why."

"William, no!" Judith rushed forward, alarmed. "Do not provoke him!"

"It is you who provoke me, madame," Rolfe said harshly as he rose and came forward. "Out, all of you," he ordered, nodding to Sir Piers to indicate that Judith would need help in leaving.

"You take too much upon yourself!" William blustered, but he did not even rise.

Rolfe waited until the door was closed before his eyes pierced William. "You know me now?"

"Of course I know you. I just married you to my daughter. God's pity for that."

"Just?"

"What do you mean, sir?" William demanded.

"It has been a full three months since I wed your daughter. Do you know that?"

"Three?" William deflated. "Where has—the time gone?"

"Do you remember the wedding?" Rolfe's voice was coldly menacing now.

"Well, most of it."

"And before?"

"You signed the contract."

"Before that," Rolfe hissed, leaning across the table. "Before you came to Crewel."

"Now, see here." William sighed, exasperated. "If you have something you want to say, then say it. Do not keep prompting me. I am very tired."

"I want to know exactly what you remember doing to your daughter!"

Confused, William rubbed his temples, trying to think. What could he have done to so incense his son-in-law?

"Ah, yes, I do recall she was very upset with me, and with reason," William admitted frankly.

"Upset?" Rolfe growled. "What you did merely upset her?"

"I make no excuse for myself," William said contritely. "I gave her no warning about the wedding because I did not remember it myself. In truth, I still have no memory of receiving the king's order that insisted she marry you."

"Damn me!" Rolfe shouted furiously. "You speak of trifles after the brutal beating you gave her!"

William came slowly to his feet, his fact mottled with rage. "What knavery is this? How dare you suggest—"

"She *was* beaten, my lord, forced to marry me, as she has finally admitted to me. I did not know it myself, but God knows everyone else did."

The crimson turned to pallor. "It is impossible."

"Impossible that you do not remember, or that you did the despicable deed?"

William shook his head. "I tell you, whether I could remember or not, I would never hurt that child. She is all I have left of my Elisabeth. I could not hurt her. I love her too dearly."

"Love her?" Rolfe was truly astonished. "You love her so much you banished her from here and forsook her for years?"

"What lies are these?" William demanded. "I . . . sent her away for a time, in the agony of my grief, yes, I remember that. But not for long. I could never be long away from my only child. She was—" He pressed his palms to his temples, trying to remember. "Judith swore . . . Leonie was busy . . . I . . . Judith swore I . . . God in heaven!" He moaned. "I did not recognize her that day at Pershwick! *I cannot remember* seeing my Leonie grow up!" He looked at Rolfe, stupefied, as though expecting some clarification from him.

Rolfe frowned. Something was not right. The man's anguish was genuine.

"What are you saying, Sir William?" Rolfe asked carefully. "That in your drunkenness, you thought Leonie was still here with you?"

"She was." The voice had weakened to a whisper.

Rolfe sighed, disgusted. "If you had been sober when I came in here, I would have killed you for the pain you have caused your daughter. Now I can feel only pity for you." He turned slowly and moved toward the door.

"Wait! I do not know who has told you these lies about my Leonie, but Judith can tell you—"

Rolfe swung back around, eyes flashing. "Fool! It is Leonie who told me."

"No! God's mercy, no! May my hand be struck off if I ever hurt her. I swear—"

"Let me think!" Rolfe bellowed, and William subsided.

"Who else was with you when you told Leonie she must marry me?" Rolfe asked.

"I can barely remember being there, and you expect—"

"Think, my lord!"

"There were servants . . . Leonie's man Guibert . . . my wife."

It made no sense. Leonie's people would not hurt her, and Judith wasn't strong enough to do Leonie harm. Sir Guibert wouldn't have hurt her.

"What did Leonie say when you told her the news? Did she attempt to leave Pershwick?"

"I have already told you she was upset. She said

not a word to me but fled to her room. If she came out before the next day, I do not know."

"You didn't even try to talk to her?" Rolfe demanded. What was wrong with this man?

William dropped his head abjectly. "Judith felt it would do no good, after my unpardonable forgetfulness had caused Leonie's dismay. She insisted I leave the matter . . . to her." William's voice faded again. "She pointed out that I would be in the way of the preparations. She had Guibert amuse me with a hunt. You see? I am beginning to remember things."

Rolfe stepped to the door and called for Sir Piers. "Where did you take Lady Judith?"

"Below."

"Bring her back—quickly." To William he said, "She is a woman. What man here would do her bidding without question?"

"All," William admitted. "I am ashamed to say I cannot remember the last time I dealt directly with my people for anything."

"Do you tell me your wife has had full control of Montwyn for a matter of years?" Rolfe asked incredulously.

"I . . . she must have," William whispered.

William's mind was still very slow, but one thing was becoming crystal clear. If he could believe all that his son-in-law had been telling him, then Judith was not simply guilty of tricking him into marrying her—and yes, he did remember that—but she had also kept him separated from his daughter. He didn't know how she had done it, but she had.

Leonie's husband was enraged over the pain inflicted on her because of the wedding, but William was devastated by the pain she must have borne thinking her father had abandoned her for so long. And he had abandoned her, in truth, abandoned her to his grief, to his weak will, and to a woman who manipulated and lied to him so easily, for so long.

He was remembering too many things all of a sudden, and the blackest rage engulfed him from deep within himself. He was to blame. He had let it happen, let his scheming wife take over his whole existence.

When she stepped into the room, Judith was met by such a murderous look from her husband that she knew she had been found out in some way. She couldn't brazen it out with lies, for William was sober and in control of himself. She hadn't seen him like this since the time he discovered she had tricked him into marrying her. He was looking at her as if he wanted to kill her. She would have to throw herself on his mercy and play for time until they were left alone and she could get him to drinking again.

Her fear was real enough as she threw herself at her husband. Tears came quickly, and she looked up at him beseechingly.

"William, whatever you think I have done, I am still your wife. I have served you well and—"

The back of his hand sent her sprawling to the floor. "Served me well? I am nearly dead from what you have served me!" he spat.

Judith's fingers touched her burning face, her stomach twisting in knots, remembering the last beating he had given her. She was no longer aware of Rolfe. Her husband's hate-filled eyes impaled her. He would show no mercy, she knew that. She would have to save herself with lies after all.

"No one could have stopped you from drinking yourself into oblivion, William," she said. "I did not like it, but what could I do?"

"Liar!" he hissed, and she cringed as he took a step toward her. "You encouraged my drinking. Do you think I don't see that now? And the one person who could have helped me wasn't here. You made certain of that. You made certain she did not return here, while you lied to me, convinced me I saw her often. Why did you keep Leonie away from me?"

Judith froze in terror. How had he figured so much out already? Desperate, she latched on to the first thing that came to her. "I did it for you, and for her. Can you not see how devastated she would have been to see you as you were? I tried to save you from shame. And I tried to protect her innocence."

"By Christ's holy blood! Do you take me for a complete fool?" William snarled. "The only one you were protecting was your despicable self! You knew I wanted none of you. You knew you would have been cast out if I had come to my senses. So you kept me senseless. And I believe you kept my daughter away by making her think she was not welcome here." He saw the truth of this in Judith's eyes, and he reached for her.

Rolfe stopped him. It was not in him to stand by and watch a woman beaten, though he knew how William would deal with her later, when there was no one to stop him.

"My lord, I would have a word with her." Rolfe's tone implied *before you do what you will.*

William forced himself to muster some control. He owed Rolfe whatever he could give him.

Rolfe extended a hand to Judith, and helped her up. "Why did you have my wife beaten?"

His voice was deceptively calm, and Judith's eyes flew to William, looking for his reaction. But his face registered nothing. Had he already known about the beating? She looked back at Rolfe.

"It was necessary," she said defensively. "She refused to marry you. Do you think I wanted us to go against the king?"

"You took it upon yourself—without your lord's consent?" Rolfe ventured softly.

"I could hardly depend on him to get her to the altar," she said with a glance of contempt at William that she failed to hide. "The king must be obeyed."

"There were other ways!" Rolfe said furiously. "You could have sent me word and left the matter to me!"

Judith stared at him incredulously. "You dare to quibble about the means, when you were only after her land. I *told* you she was forced to wed you. You got what you wanted. What difference does it make how you got it?"

It took every bit of self-restraint Rolfe possessed not to strike her. "You know nothing about it."

"Not so!" she said, sneering. What was he making this fuss about? She had enough to deal with already. "You offered for Pershwick before you offered for Leonie. When I refused both offers, you asked the king's help!"

The words out, Judith paled. "I—I mean—I—"

"Judith." William interrupted her stammering with a weary sigh. "How many offers have you refused in my stead? How long would you have kept Leonie unmarried?"

"She did not want to marry," Judith asserted. "I saw no need to give up . . . her lands were well run. Why should someone else profit from them?"

The two men stared at her silently.

"What did I do that was so wrong?" Judith demanded. "I tell you Leonie did not want to marry. Why else would she flatly refuse Lord Kempston?"

"She had reasons for refusing me of which you know nothing," Rolfe interjected coldly. "Madame, what you have done to Leonie warrants . . . but you are not my concern. All I demand from you is the name of the man who follows your orders, any kind of orders."

Her chin jutted out stubbornly. "There is not a man here who would hesitate—"

William hit her again. "Tell him what he wants to know, or by God—"

"Richer Calveley!" Judith threw the name out for whatever leniency it might bring her. She didn't give Richer another thought, and would never have considered protecting him. "He—he is my master-at-arms and was the logical one to force Leonie because she knew what he was capable of."

Rolfe turned and left the room, leaving William to deal with his wife in whatever way he would.

When he found Richer Calveley in the barracks with his men, a change took place in Rolfe's countenance. His fury hid itself deep within him. The man was huge and brutish, the arms and chest beefy, the hands enormous. Leonie's beating must have been brutal. His little wife was incapable of defending herself against a man this size. How brave and foolish she must have been to think she could withstand this monster! She never had a chance, and so Calveley would have no chance.

When Richer saw Rolfe d'Ambert's eyes he knew instantly why he had been sought out. He spared a moment to curse the faithless lady who had thrown him to the wolves. But he had known when she ordered him to beat Lord William's daughter what might come of it.

He had enjoyed that experience because the lady was a noblewoman, but her status was also what condemned him. It didn't matter who had ordered him to do what he did. There was not a lord in the realm who would hesitate to kill him for raising his hand to a lady. And this was the lady's husband.

Richer began to sweat, wondering in what manner his death would come, for death is what he saw in the lord's eyes. His death might be the most horrible imaginable, torture to last indefinitely. No one would prevent it. He was surrounded by men who followed his orders, yet not one of them would dare defy a man of d'Ambert's stature. It was a putrid feeling, the fear that took hold in his gut, knowing there was nothing he could do to stop what would happen to him.

"Richer Calveley?" Rolfe did not wait for confirmation, for he could smell the man's fear. His voice was curiously flat, making it sound all the more ominous. "For what you did to my lady, I am going to kill you. Draw your sword."

It took a second for Richer to realize his good fortune, and then there was a rush of giddiness as he realized his death would not be drawn out after all. The lord was not going to take advantage of his rank. He was going to give him a fair fight, more than a fair fight, because he was not wearing armor, though Richer had at least a modicum of protection in his thick leather jerkin.

There was a chance for Richer to win, a good chance, but it was set somewhere in his mind that he was going to die, and that destroyed his chance, worked against him, and undermining his skill. Once his sword was in his hand, he swung wildly.

Rolfe's sword found its mark with his first effort, sliding smoothly through flesh and bone to pierce the heart. No pity stirred in Rolfe's own breast, no regret for killing a man. In his mind was a picture of his Leonie suffering under those brutish hands. He turned and walked away before Calveley's large body had collapsed to the floor.

Chapter 42

THE pasture was abloom with summer flowers warmed by the midafternoon sun. By contrast, the surrounding forest was dark and gloomy. The forest kept the eight men and their horses well hidden.

Alain Montigny was satisfied when he looked their way that his seven men could not be seen. A group of ragtag thieves and landless knights like himself, they were Alain's following, their needs paid for with the money the Crewel steward had stolen for Alain. But that easy money was no longer available since Erneis had been found out. Alain had dispatched him quickly, his usefulness over. It still rankled Alain that Leonie had been the one to catch his man.

Alain needed money desperately now. The few travelers his men and he had robbed produced light purses, and there wasn't enough money to keep his band of men fed. The men wanted to move on to the better traveled routes, farther south, but Alain had his own personal reason for being where he was. He had no intention of leaving until he found his chance to kill the man responsible for his terrible reversal of fortune. He had almost succeeded when he'd set the Crewel mill on fire and drawn his prey to where he could take a good aim at him. What an unexpected bit of bad luck that his arrow hadn't found a vital spot.

It was taking too long, waiting to find Rolfe d'Ambert away from his army, or separated from his escort. If only Alain could catch him unprotected, d'Ambert could be overcome by Alain's men and easily killed. Then Alain could marry Leonie and have back all that was his, all that he had lost.

It was Erneis who had told him that Leonie's people were harassing the Black Wolf. How Alain had loved Leonie for that! It was also Erneis who told him that she was being forced to marry d'Ambert. At first, Alain was enraged. But then he decided it was a good thing, for Leonie would so hate being forced that she would hate her husband as much as Alain did. She would make a good widow. She would marry Alain, and with her support, Alain would petition the king for a pardon. The plan would work, all of it, for what man, even the king, could resist Leonie's sweet charms, or her sweet body, if it came to that?

Alain watched the woods like a starving hawk. This time, she had to come. It was not easy getting messages to her, for the villagers were content under their new lord. There was only one man willing to deliver his messages to Leonie. The other men remembered Alain's heavy hand too well and were likely to report his presence to d'Ambert. Alain vowed he would remember that once he was master of Crewel again.

Leonie had not responded to his first two notes, but it was doubtless difficult for her to come to him alone as he'd requested. Well, d'Ambert was away from Crewel, so Alain waited eagerly to see her . . . eagerly and very anxiously. The men were very restless and bad-tempered. It was getting harder and harder to convince them that they would possess greater wealth if they would only be patient a little longer.

A large ransom would solve one of Alain's problems, and keep the men pliable for a while. Should he tell Leonie that he intended to ransom her? If she agreed to come away with him peacefully it would make his life easier. After all, he didn't have to tell her everything. He might tell her only part of his plan.

The sound of horses coming from the wrong direction threw Alain into a panic, but then he saw her. She was leaving the woods with her escort, but coming from Pershwick. Her men-at-arms were her own, wearing Pershwick colors.

Leonie had left immediately for Pershwick when Alain's third message came. Once there she dismissed her escort, telling them she would use a guard from Pershwick to bring her back to Crewel, as she planned to stay the night at Pershwick. She wanted none of Rolfe's men to be able to tell him she had met a man in a field. But she wanted no more notes from Alain, either, and the only way to stop them was to talk to him.

It was impossible to leave Pershwick alone, for Sir Guibert insisted she take at least six men, and he could not be talked out of it. But they were her men, and when she told them to wait for her at the edge of the woods, no one argued.

Within plain sight of her guard, she rode slowly toward Alain. Her heart beat harder as she approached the man she hadn't seen in half a year. It seemed even longer than that, for she had been through so much and seen more of the world in that time than in all the rest of her life. And Alain, how had he fared since leaving? She supposed his presence in the region meant one of two things. Either he was no longer running, had perhaps reason to believe he might be given a royal pardon, or else he was so desperate that he felt in no more danger there near his old home than he did anywhere else. Poor Alain.

When they'd last met, a cold winter sun had lit his blond hair to gold and turned his cheeks ruddy pink, making him look younger than twenty. As she neared him, she was dismayed to see how haggard he looked. There was a deep weariness in his features, and his eyes glinted with a cunning that made her wary.

"Alain." Leonie kept her greeting reserved as he lifted her down from her horse. "I thought you meant to remain in Ireland."

He smiled bitterly. "I did. But when I arrived there, I found my kin were staunch supporters of Henry's. Not one was willing to incur his displeasure by harboring me. They assisted me in leaving as soon as I arrived."

"I am sorry," Leonie said sympathetically, but she needed to come to the point. "You never did tell me what you were accused of, Alain, and I have heard things—"

"Lies," he said quickly. He smiled warmly. "It is so good to see you, Leonie. Is all well with you? You do not seem to have fared badly with the Black Wolf."

She answered stiffly, "He does not mistreat me, Alain. But I will not talk of him. Why have you come here?"

He appeared crestfallen. "Can't you guess? When I heard of your marriage, I grieved for you. I thought you would welcome my help."

"Thank you, Alain, but I do not need help," she said as courteously as she could.

"You are *happy* with him?"

She looked away sadly. "I cannot say I am happy, but nothing can change my circumstance."

"You could come away with me, Leonie."

Leonie turned toward him again, startled. She had thought of fleeing, but until Rolfe was willing to let her go, he would be sure to track her down. What she needed was sanctuary, and Alain could hardly give her that.

"Where is it you plan to go, Alain?"

The question was simple curiosity, but he interpreted it to mean acceptance.

"You will not regret your decision, Leonie." He smiled, wrapping her in his arms. "I swear I will make you happy!"

"Alain!" She gasped, trying to push him away. "I am married."

He held her tightly. "A mistake that will soon be corrected."

Leonie grew very still. "What do you mean?"

"Your husband risks his life daily," Alain answered carefully. "Even now he wars with my vassals."

"Your father's vassals."

"The same thing," he said curtly. "Such a man, a man of war, will die—and soon."

Sudden understanding made her feel sick. Alain's first message had come not long after Rolfe's injury. Alain might have been there. He might have been the one who unleashed the arrow.

"Alain," she began carefully, "you—misunderstood—"

"Quiet!" he hissed, his body tensing. She followed his gaze toward Crewel, horrified to see her husband break through the woods, alone.

"Keep your men out of this, Leonie," Alain said excitedly. "My own men will take him easily."

"What?"

She could see no other men in or near the clearing. But when Alain let out a shrill whistle, she knew Rolfe was in danger.

"Alain! You must not attack Rolfe!"

"Hush, Leonie," Alain said confidently. "This will be easy." He called across the clearing, "Stay where you are, d'Ambert. You have lost what is yours."

Rolfe had already seen the lovers standing close together, embracing. This was the truth he had dreaded. He had returned to Crewel to tell Leonie the truth about her father, only to find that she had gone to Pershwick. Then he found a message from Alain Montigny left carelessly on the writing table. A search produced another note from Montigny. Two notes were enough to declare her guilt, and what was before him was the damning confirmation.

"Let her go, Montigny!"

"She is leaving with me," Alain taunted.

Leonie gasped, outraged. But then everything began happening so fast that she had no time to deny Alain's claim.

Her own men had mounted and were riding toward them. Much closer, Alain's men came bursting through the trees. All seven of Alain's men charged Rolfe, who drew his sword like lightning. His battle cry resounded in the clearing, bringing some of the attackers up short so that only four of them actually met Rolfe head-on.

Leonie screamed for her men to hurry, but no one realized she meant for them to help Rolfe. Alain, confident of his plan, believed she meant for her men to attack Rolfe.

"Never fear," Alain assured her, relishing his triumph, "he is strong, but he is outnumbered."

"Fool!" Leonie cried, and Alain's smile vanished. "I would kill you before I would let you kill him!"

"You will thank me . . ."

He went silent as his men turned and fled back into the woods—five of them, while two lay dead in the meadow. When he saw why, Alain gripped Leonie's wrist and pulled her toward their horses. Rolfe had not come alone after all, but had only raced ahead of his men in his haste to reach Leonie. Two knights and a half dozen men-at-arms were with Rolfe now. And Leonie's own men had joined their lady.

Rolfe did not move, but faced Alain from yards away. "If you go with him, Leonie, I will hunt him down and kill him."

Alain let go of her instantly. "He wants you so badly, he can have you," he told her fearfully. He mounted his horse, glancing at Rolfe to see if the larger man would stop him.

"He believes the worst," she told Alain. "You must tell him . . . Alain! Come back!" He rode into the forest in the direction his men had taken. Leonie called his name once more, but Alain did not even look back.

She swung around to face her husband. His eyes were black with fury, his expression cruel as he slowly walked his horse toward her.

"My lady, do we fight your husband?"

She had barely noticed her men gathering around her. What could she tell them? What must this look like to them? She did not want to be left alone with Rolfe, but of course there was no question of a battle.

"Answer them, madame," Rolfe ordered.

"My lord, you must let me explain," she began.

"Answer them!"

She took a deep breath. "My lord, you must tell them you mean me no harm."

"I will tell them only that no one keeps me from my wife. I will kill anyone who tries. If they wish to die, then they may fight me."

She faced her guard. "Return to Pershwick. I go with my husband willingly."

"But, my lady," the youngest man said uneasily, casting a glance toward Rolfe. "Sir Guibert will kill us if—if anything happens to you."

"Tell him only that you escorted me home to Crewel." The man did not move. "I will not have Guibert Fitzalan riding on Crewel to rescue me, do you understand? I will flay you myself if he learns what has happened here. Now go." The man still did not move. Leonie sighed. "He is my husband. I *must* go with him. Do not make it more difficult, I beg you."

She signaled to him to help her mount, and he did so, reluctantly. She then rode out of the clearing without waiting for anyone. She rode in the direction of Crewel Keep. It did not take Rolfe's men long to catch up with her.

She did not turn around once to see whether Rolfe was behind her.

Chapter 43

THE next week passed in a torrent of emotions, and she spiraled between deep depression and impotent fury. Rolfe indeed followed her back to Crewel and dragged her up to their room. She expected the worst, but what he did was to lock her in. Later she learned he had drunk himself into oblivion that night.

He released her the next day, but nothing had changed. He wouldn't listen when she tried to explain about meeting Alain. He wouldn't listen when she said there had been no question of her leaving with Alain. He wouldn't listen. He would not speak to her. The servants avoided her for fear of his anger.

The worst was that Wilda and Mary were sent away, leaving her bereft. There was no one at all for her to talk to.

If he would leave, the tension might become bearable, she told herself. But he did not return to the siege at Warling. He did not even leave the keep to hunt. He stayed near Leonie, yet away from her, as if he did not trust himself to be with her, yet could not leave her alone.

She knew exactly what he thought. He expected her to flee, and he was there to make certain she didn't. Finding Alain's two notes together and crumpled on the floor the day Rolfe locked her in the room told her how he had found her and what conclusions he had drawn. She knew how damning that scene in the clearing had been, but there was no way to put things right when he wouldn't listen to her.

He would not even sleep with her in their bed, but was sleeping on a pallet in the antechamber, like a guard outside her door.

She knew she could not go on that way much longer. Frustrated and angry, Leonie threw open the door that separated her from her husband. His eyes were open. He was staring at the ceiling. He was ignoring her and it sent her over the edge. She looked around the antechamber for something to throw at him.

"Do not, Leonie." His voice was low and menacing.

"Why not?" she demanded furiously. "Then you could beat me and we would have done with this!"

"Beat you?" Rolfe sat up on his pallet. "I killed a man for doing just that and you dare to think I—"

"What?"

"Calveley is dead by my hand," he told her tonelessly. "I could not let him live after what he did to you."

Leonie was stunned. "How did you know? I never said—"

"The last week I was gone from here I spent with your father, rendering him sober enough to accept my challenge." As her eyes reflected panic, he said irritably, "I did not kill your father, woman. He was not the villain I believed he was. He had his wife turn him into a drunk. He was weak, and hardly guiltless, but he did not order you beaten, Leonie. He did not know anything, did not even know you were at Pershwick all these years," he finished a bit more gently.

"How . . . could he not know?" she whispered, nearly in shock, and Rolfe explained all of it.

"Right now he is overcome with remorse for failing you so terribly," he finished.

She was sickened. Why had she not once tried to force her way in to see him? She might have saved herself and her father so much misery. She might have learned the truth sooner.

"I shall go to him now!"

"No!"

"No?" she cried. "How can you say *no?*"

"Give the man a chance to regain his self-respect, Leonie," Rolfe said adamantly. "He will come to *you* when he is ready. You may be certain he will."

She glared at him, near tears. "Do not wrap your refusal in noble sentiments! You say no to keep me imprisoned here. Why deny it?"

"Damn me!" Rolfe exploded. He reached her in two strides, taking no notice of his undressed state. "I returned here to tell you all I learned about your father, and found you run off with your lover!"

"He was never my lover!"

"Liar!" His hands bit into her shoulders. "I would not be surprised if you left his note out on purpose so that I could be drawn into his trap. You *did* know he had men waiting to attack me?"

"I know it now, but I did not know it then. How could I? I had not seen him before that day, I swear it."

He was so furious, he shook her. "There were two notes!"

"There were three!" she shouted back. "But I paid no attention to the first two. I wanted only to see what Alain was doing here. He was so insistent about seeing me. And why would I leave notes for you to read when you told me you could not read? If anyone is a liar, you are!"

Rolfe sidestepped that issue entirely. "What did he tell you, Leonie?" he asked her darkly.

She wasn't fooled by the softer tone. "That he wanted to help me, that he thought I was suffering living with you." She lowered her voice too. "But I don't think that is really why he drew me out there. I think those men who attacked you were there to assist him with me if I did not agree to go away with him. I think he meant to hold me for ransom."

She lowered her eyes. That was a mistake, for suddenly she was very much aware of his nudity. Rolfe became aware of it too. He didn't know whether he ought to believe her, but he desperately wanted to.

When he gathered her into his arms, she was shocked. How could anyone be so changeable? She tried to pull away.

"Rolfe, no!"

He crushed her to him. "Unfair, Leonie. You use my name to weaken me."

"How can you—"

"How can I not? God help me, I want you. I cannot fight it and I will not try anymore."

Rolfe didn't know it, but those words worked magic on her, making her suddenly realize that he did love her—he was just too stubborn to admit it.

In truth, all Leonie had ever wanted from him was his love. Having that, she would give him everything, her heart, her life, her children.

She gave him passion to match his own, and Rolfe was nearly undone by her response. He picked her up and carried her to the large bed she had not been able to sleep in alone. There he made love to her with his hands, his lips, all of his body, showing her with his desire what was in his heart.

And Leonie loved him in return, with no thought for any time but the moment. He was hers, and she let her joy guide her, exalting in having all of him.

Chapter 44

WHEN Leonie awoke the next morning, Rolfe was gone from their room. But as that was his habit, she gave it little thought. So she was shocked later to learn he had returned to his army and was not expected back soon. How could he leave without even speaking to her? Was everything settled between them? She wasn't sure. She even began to wonder if she had imagined all those wonderful feelings of the night before. Had she only heard in his words what she wanted to hear?

She retired to her room and did not set foot from it for two days. She might have died for all the attention she stirred in the household. Food was left at her door, but that was all. What did it matter to these people that she still felt a stranger here? She felt like an intruder and it was destroying her! She couldn't live this way, simply could not.

When she did venture forth to ask a servant to order a bath, she discovered that Amelia was still in residence, and still acting the lady of the keep. It was the last blow. She was leaving. Just let Rolfe try and bring her back.

She packed, taking only one trunk so as not to be obvious, and ordered it taken below. That was as far as she got. Sir Evarard had orders to supply her with a fifteen-man escort if she left the keep. The men were not to leave her side until she returned. Evarard was loath to let so many men leave Crewel for anything but an emergency. The garrison was depleted, he informed her, all spare men having gone with Rolfe's army. He was adamant in his refusal to let her go.

When Leonie found Amelia, she came right to the point. "I am leaving. I shall not be back, no matter the inducement. Does this suit you, Amelia?"

The older woman was too delighted to pretend otherwise. "It suits me very well."

"So I thought. Then will you help me? Sir Evarard will not release the number of men Rolfe insists I have for escort. He seems kindly disposed toward you. Can you persuade him to change his mind? Tell him I will be gone no more than a few hours."

"But if the escort are needed here—"

"They will return here once I am safe inside Pershwick," Leonie assured her.

"Pershwick? But Rolfe will find you there. Can you not leave England instead?"

Leonie sighed disgustedly. "It is not my intention to hide, Amelia. It doesn't matter if Rolfe finds me, for Pershwick will be closed to him."

"Oh." Amelia smiled. This was even better than she had hoped for. For Rolfe's wife to pit her men against him would sever their relationship for good. He would not want her back after such an action. "You may leave Evarard to me," she said graciously.

Evarard allowed Leonie to leave Crewel, however much his sour countenance spoke of his reluctance.

The usually short ride to Pershwick took longer because of the baggage wain carrying Leonie's trunk. And when she arrived it was to find Sir Guibert absent for the day. That was just as well, for he would disapprove, she knew that, and might even try to prevent her. There would be little he could do when he returned to find the deed done and Leonie firmly ensconced in Pershwick.

She herself gave the orders to secure the keep. Her escort might have become suspicious over all the activity, but Leonie kept herself from them and there was nothing they could do when those suspicions were borne out. The major preparations finished, she had them removed from the keep, explaining only that she would not be returning to Crewel, and ordering them to return without her.

Aunt Beatrix was sympathetic. Wilda, on the other hand, showed surprising objections. She was disgusted that Leonie would let Amelia have Rolfe without a fight. Her feelings where Amelia was concerned were quite strong, and she revealed that it was Amelia who had ordered her and Mary whisked out of Crewel. If Amelia could use foul means to get whatever she wanted, why couldn't Leonie show some of her fighting spirit? Leonie simply kept Wilda busy so that she would not have to listen to her.

She could not do the same with Sir Guibert. When he arrived that evening and was told her plans he was furious. He strode into the hall to find her, glowering as he approached.

"Have you taken leave of your senses?" he demanded without even a nod of greeting. "You would make war against your own husband? I cannot—"

"Not war," Leonie interrupted. "I just refuse to abide with him any longer."

"You cannot do that!" Guibert sputtered. "God's mercy, Leonie, he is your lord now. You are bound to him in every way!"

Truth or not, the saying of it grated on her. She would not give in. But she needed Guibert's support, so she did something she had never done before. She burst into tears, gauging the effect it had on the man who had been like a father to her. In between heart-rending sobs, she confessed everything to Guibert, sparing nothing, not even that she was carrying her husband's child—his second child.

But the revelations she made about Amelia were not as shocking to him as she had hoped they would be, for she had forgotten that her situation, though painful, was not unique.

"You are not the first woman who has been asked to raise her husband's bastards, Leonie," Guibert scolded gently. In truth, he was shocked at Rolfe's behavior, and he hurt for Leonie, but coddling would do her no good now.

"If it were only that, I could live with it," she said. "But my husband will not send this child's mother away. I have asked him and he refuses. He flaunts her in my home. He gives her responsibilities that are mine by right. I feel like a second wife!"

"You exaggerate, Leonie."

"I do not! I have told you plainly how it has been. I tried to live with it, Guibert. If—if my feelings were not entangled, perhaps I could. But—"

"You love him?"

"Yes," she said, sobbing in earnest now. "I fought against loving him, I did. I knew it would cause me only pain. And he expects me to continue sharing him with that woman. I cannot do it anymore. It is killing me, Guibert."

Guibert sighed. "I do not see what you hope to accomplish by coming here, Leonie. The man has besieged stronger keeps than this and won them."

"He would not do so here!" Leonie told him. "I am his wife."

Guibert shook his head at her. "You think that will stop him? That is the very reason he will not turn away from our closed gate."

"No, Guibert," she said confidently. "Rolfe has two keeps to secure yet. He will not take his army away from victory there to come here. He will come himself, yes, but I will tell him plainly how I feel—if I have to shout it from the walls. He will have to accept my decision."

"Does he know of your condition?" Guibert asked shrewdly.

"No," she admitted, glancing at him and then away. "I will not give him that excuse to force me to return to Crewel."

"I pray he will let you go," he said, sighing. "If not"—he shook his head—"God help us."

Chapter 45

LEONIE worried over Guibert's misgivings for days to follow, for she had believed that Rolfe would come to Pershwick immediately, but she was quite wrong. Days turned into weeks, and still he did not come. She was as miserable as she had ever been.

After two weeks, Leonie opened Pershwick again, allowing things to take their normal course. She sent back the extra men she had requested from her other keeps, but kept her men-at-arms ready. The stores were full with the recent harvest, so she had no worry there. Time dragged by, taking with it the remains of her good humor. Nearly four weeks had passed since she left Crewel. She was two and a half months into her pregnancy, with a thickened waist her gowns could barely disguise. She was disgusted, having wanted to give Rolfe her ultimatum without bringing their child into the argument.

One unseasonably warm day, she stood on the parapet and watched her husband approach the keep. Four of his knights rode directly behind him. But beyond that was a sight that froze her where she stood.

"Sweetest Mary, he's brought his whole army!"

There seemed to be a thousand men moving toward Pershwick. The army stopped well out of range of Pershwick's weapons. Did that mean Rolfe truly expected a battle?

"I warned you, my lady," her friend and vassal said dolefully.

Leonie tore her eyes away from the horrifying sight below and made no attempt to hide her fear from Sir Guibert.

"I will have the gate opened," he said.

"No," she returned, and his face collapsed into a picture of misery.

"God's mercy, Leonie, what can you be thinking? This is no longer a woman's whim. Your lord is serious!"

"I tell you he will not attack us," she insisted. "He has brought his army only to frighten me."

"You would risk all our lives on an assumption?" he cried.

"Guibert, please," Leonie pleaded. "This is my whole life that will be decided here. Let me at least hear what he has to say. If you give me up to him without even that, he will never believe he must take my feelings into account."

Guibert looked out again at the men. A man did not order a paid army to follow him unless he meant to make use of that army. She was fooling herself. The Black Wolf was prepared to attack.

"You will talk to him yourself?" he asked, and when she said "Yes," he asked hastily, "You will not provoke him?"

Leonie shook her head. "I will be careful, but he must know I am firm. How else can we come to terms? But I swear, if it does not go well, I will surrender."

"Very well." Guibert sighed heavily. "But remember a man's pride, my lady, and do not push him too far. Pride can make a man do things he doesn't really want to do, for honor's sake."

Rolfe and his knights had ridden to the gatehouse

and halted. Rolfe slowly surveyed the manned walls to each side of the gatehouse, the weapons trained on him, the closed gate. Tension crackled in the air.

Rolfe demanded entrance and was refused. Leonie held her breath, waiting for his reaction. How far, indeed, would Rolfe go for honor's sake?

"My lady wife is within?"

"I am here, my lord," Leonie called down to him.

"Lean forward. I cannot see you, madame," he shouted up.

She leaned forward. She could see him fully. He wore full armor, and because he didn't remove his helmet, even his eyes were hidden.

Rolfe moved his destrier so that he and the horse were standing directly beneath her. "You have readied Pershwick for war?"

"Keeps should always be kept in a state of readiness," she said evasively. "I would as well ask you why you have brought your army here."

"Why, to please you, of course," he called. "Isn't war what you want?"

Leonie gasped. "I take precautions, my lord, nothing else."

His voice whipped out fiercely. "Against me!"

"Yes!"

"Why, Leonie?"

The answer was too embarrassing to be shouted down at him, but shout she must.

"My lord, I will abide no more at Crewel with your . . . with Lady Amelia in residence."

"I cannot hear you, Leonie."

She had heard *him* plainly enough. Did he mean to shame her?

Leonie steeled herself and leaned farther over the

parapet. "I said I will no longer abide at Crewel with Amelia there also!"

"Is *that* what this is about?" He sounded quite incredulous.

"Yes."

And then the unthinkable happened. Rolfe began to laugh. He removed his helmet and his laughter grew louder and louder. It carried over the walls into the quiet keep.

"Your humor is misplaced, my lord." Her tone was bitter. "I mean what I say."

There was a moment of silence and then, harshly, he said, "Enough, Leonie. Order the gate opened."

"No."

His expression was darkly turbulent. "No? You have heard me say that no one will keep me from my wife. That includes you, wife."

"You also said you would kill anyone who tried. Does *that* include me, my lord?"

"No, indeed, Leonie, but if you force me to break down these walls, I doubt there will be many left alive to rebuild Pershwick. Do you want your people dead?"

She gasped. "You would not!"

Rolfe turned toward his knights. "Sir Piers, order the village torched!" he shouted.

"Rolfe, no!" Leonie called.

Rolfe turned back to Leonie, waiting

"You—you may come inside, my lord—alone. And only to talk. Do you agree?"

"Order the gate opened," he said coldly.

Leonie's features marked her defeat. Rolfe had called her bluff. Her advantage was lost and they both knew it. He knew he was safe inside her keep, for he had an army outside.

"Do as he says, Sir Guibert," Leonie said quietly. "I will await him in the hall."

"Do not take it so hard, Leonie," he said gently. "Perhaps he will give you what you want, now that he knows how strongly you feel."

She nodded sadly and left.

Guibert's temper rose as he watched her go. He could not bear seeing her so desolate. He didn't approve of what she had done, but her motives were understandable. Angrily, he went to meet Rolfe d'Ambert.

Chapter 46

ROLFE rode into the bailey and dismounted from his large war-horse. He was furious. He had left Crewel with a light heart, deciding to believe that Leonie loved him. After all, how could she respond to him so passionately if she really loved Montigny? he had chided himself.

The question was as irrelevant now as Alain was dead and buried. Rolfe hadn't been there to see it, but he had been told about it. In the stupidest action imaginable, the young fool had managed to enter Blythe Keep and incite the besieged occupants to attack Rolfe's small camp outside the keep. He had then led them on to Warling, thinking the occupants under siege there would come out and join the battle. They did not, but it truly would have made no difference if they had. Either Montigny was simpleminded, or he had greatly underestimated the size of Rolfe's army. There was no real battle at all. Montigny had gathered less than a hundred men. They were quickly overcome, and many died, including Alain Montigny.

The occupants of besieged Warling, witnessing the slaughter, quickly came to terms of surrender.

Rolfe had not been there to see this astonishing turn of events because he was called away to Normandy only a few days after leaving Leonie. He had spent the last weeks tending to his late brother's estate.

It was an unsettling time, trying to sort out his feelings for his brother. He finally realized he had none. He felt no particular grief over the death. He did find, however, that he had no desire to ignore the widow and her children. Altogether it was a trying time.

And then! To come home and learn that Leonie had been closed up in Pershwick all that time, that she was prepared to fight him to stay there! Once more, she had made a mockery of his trust. He decided this was the last time she would hurt him. If she was so set against him as to do such a thing, then he did not want her back. That decision was firm.

Or so he'd believed. For three days he resisted all impulses to change his mind. The problem was, he *did* want Leonie back, and at any cost, too. He'd even brought his army to prove that to her. And now, to find that all this drama was motivated only by jealousy! He didn't know whether he wanted to shower her with kisses or throttle her.

He did know one thing. She would not come out of this free of retribution. She had to be made to see that she couldn't run to her vassals every time he and she disagreed.

If Rolfe's anger had simmered to mild exasperation, it did not stay that way. Sir Guibert met him in the bailey and told him flatly that Leonie would not leave Pershwick at all unless she left willingly. He was prepared to support his stand with all necessary force.

Rolfe was livid. "Do you understand in what cause you are prepared to die?"

"I do, my lord."

"Do you know also that my wife's jealousy is unfounded? There is a good reason for Lady Amelia's being at Crewel. *I* do not prefer it that way, but so it must be."

"We are aware there is a child involved," Guibert replied, undaunted.

"We?"

"Lady Leonie would not take this hard stand if she had only suspicions."

Rolfe glowered. "I told you her jealousy is unfounded. The child does not concern her because it was conceived before I wed her."

"Then you must convince her of that, my lord, for she surely believes otherwise."

Rolfe was brought up short. The statement was made matter-of-factly. It was bad enough that Leonie had learned of the child when he had hoped to spare her that knowledge as long as possible. But for her to think . . .

"Take me to her," Rolfe demanded, angry anew over the foolish notions in Leonie's mind. It showed clearly what opinion she had of him. He remembered now the doubts he had had about letting Amelia remain at Crewel, but even so he'd never guessed what conclusions Leonie might draw from his leniency with Amelia.

As Leonie watched Rolfe cross the hall toward her, she was surprised by her fear and, just below the surface of her fear, her terrific pride in Rolfe. She had to respect a man who held to his purpose so tenaciously.

The truth was, she hadn't wanted him to give in to her demands if his giving in would leave him with a longing for Amelia. That would do no good. Leonie wanted the issue settled forever.

Rolfe came to a halt several feet away from Leonie, studying her position and demeanor. She was standing behind a chair, her fingers gripping the high backrest as if to keep the chair between them. Her chin was raised defiantly, but her eyes were uncertain and fearful.

"Was it necessary for you to come here with an army, my lord?" she asked, seizing the opening.

He might have laughed, for there were a dozen armed men about the hall, as well as her stalwart vassal and a goodly number of brutish-looking serfs who didn't even attempt to conceal their dislike of Rolfe d'Ambert.

"Be glad I did, wife, for if I had come here alone, you would have stood fast to your foolishness and forced me to resort to harsh measures later on."

She bridled. "It is hardly foolish to—" She clamped her mouth shut. "I will not argue about that. What do you wish to do now?"

"Take you back."

"And if I refuse to leave? Will you attack my keep?"

"I will leave not a single stone standing," he answered. "I am tempted to dismantle Pershwick anyway." His face hardened. "You cannot come here and pit your people against me every time you are upset with me, Leonie. If you ever do this again, I will not hesitate to destroy Pershwick. You belong with me."

"But I am not *happy* with you!" She flung the words at him.

She might as well have stabbed him. He told himself not to open his heart to her if all she wanted was to trample on it.

"I had hoped in time you would come to love me, Leonie, or at least to find life with me . . . pleasant. I regret that you cannot." His voice was funereal.

Her heart dropped into her belly. "You—you will give me up?"

Rolfe's eyes narrowed darkly. So that was what she wanted. "No, madame, I will not give you up."

Joy leaped into her breast, and she cautioned herself against revealing too much of herself to him.

"What of Amelia?" she asked evenly.

He sighed wearily. "She will be moved to another keep."

"To another of *your* keeps? What real difference will that make?"

"Do not be heartless, Leonie," he growled. "You know she is with child. Would you have me abandon a pregnant woman?"

"I would never ask that of you!" she cried. "But must you keep her always within reach, so that she is there to comfort you whenever you are angry with me?"

"Damn me, where have you gotten this notion? The woman was my mistress, yes. I regret that a child was conceived. But I have not touched her since I wed you, and I am mystified by your implying that I have—or shall."

"Lady Amelia says differently, my lord," she informed him.

"You mistook her," Rolfe replied rigidly.

Leonie turned her back to him, so furious she wanted to hit him with something. Sweet Mary, how could she love him when he made her so furious? He was lying. He surely was!

"Gather what you will, Leonie." Rolfe addressed her stiff back. "We are leaving. Now. And if you value Sir Guibert's life, you will tell him you are going willingly."

She swung back around. "I am not going willingly, but you won't have to drag me away or kill anyone," she hissed at him.

She swept past him to order her trunk packed. Then she conferred with Guibert, who was greatly relieved to know that she had agreed to go home with her husband.

"He is not angry with you?" Guibert asked doubtfully as he eyed Rolfe pacing the hall impatiently.

"His anger does not frighten me," Leonie lied bravely.

"He refused to send the other woman away?" her vassal asked hesitantly.

"No," she said with a sigh. "He agreed."

Guibert frowned. "Then you should be pleased, my lady."

"Indeed—I should be. But I am not."

Guibert shook his head as he watched her flounce away.

Chapter 47

BUT things were to resolve themselves in a manner no one could have expected.

No sooner had Leonie returned to Crewel and entered the master bedchamber than a maid frantically sought her out.

"My lady, she is dying! You must come—please," Janie cried.

"It's a ruse," Wilda said quickly. The young maid was Amelia's own servant, and not part of the Crewel household. "The woman has learned that she will be sent away, and she means to prevent it by claiming illness." She cast a triumphant look at Janie.

Wilda stood firmly planted between Leonie and Janie, and Leonie was gratified that Wilda was trying to protect her, as she so often did. If nothing else had been accomplished by going to Pershwick, at least she had been able to bring Wilda back with her.

"Go back and tell that woman we are wise to her," Wilda ordered brazenly, and Leonie saw she would have to put a stop to this.

"Tell me what has happened," she demanded, and Janie wailed, "She will be so angry that I have come, because she wants no one to know what she has done. But she is bleeding and it won't stop. She is dying, my lady, I am sure of it!"

"*What* has she done?" Leonie insisted.

"She—she took something. She said it was to make everything right again."

Leonie paled, understanding at once. "God's mercy, this is my fault. I had such bad feelings about the child because of the mother, and—"

"My lady, will you come?" Janie begged again, and Leonie shook herself. This was no time to indulge in remorse.

"Wilda, get my medicines, quickly."

To Leonie's surprise, Sir Evarard was waiting outside Amelia's door. He looked very unhappy.

"There is something seriously wrong with Amelia?" he asked dejectedly.

"You are fond of the lady, Sir Evarard?" She had no idea what else to say.

"Fond? I love her!" he said emphatically.

Leonie smiled at him. "I will do all I can."

"Will you?" he asked more anxiously than diplomatically. "I know you have no liking for her, nor she for you. And she can be childish and petulant, but—but she is not all bad, my lady."

"Sir Evarard," Leonie said gently, "please go below. If I can help Amelia, I will. You may believe that."

Amelia's quarters were larger than Leonie had expected, and cluttered with objects, most of which reminded her of Alain. He had always liked ornate things, and he had left most of his possessions behind when he fled Kempston.

The room reeked of sickness. The sheets had been changed recently, but the bloodied ones were left in a pile in the corner.

With just a glance at the gaunt figure in the bed, Leonie's suspicions were confirmed. The face was a sickly gray, and there were huge dark circles under her eyes. Amelia's body was racked with pain, and in her half-conscious state, she thrashed around, whimpering and moaning, while the two maids standing near the bed looked at Leonie helplessly.

Leonie pulled down the sheet. Amelia was lying in a pool of blood. With the maids' help, Leonie changed the linens once more and cleaned Amelia, packing her with bandages to staunch the flow of blood. She then forced Amelia to drink a syrup of marsh woundwort, hoping that would stop the hemorrhaging.

In a vial on the candlestand beside the bed was the decoction Amelia had taken, which Leonie had known would be spurge laurel, commonly used to aid the bowels and known to cause abortion. Too large a dose could violently flush the body with vomiting and bloody stools, and often proved fatal. The vial was nearly empty.

Amelia's eyes, when she opened them, were wild with confusion. She saw Leonie standing beside her bed and whispered, "What are you doing here?"

"How much of this did you take?" Leonie asked, holding the vial up.

"Enough. I have used it before, but—but always when I first suspected. Never this late."

"*Why,* Amelia?"

The older woman was startled by Leonie's obvious concern. "Why? What do I want with a child? I detest children!"

Leonie's sympathy began waning. "So you would kill my lord's child?" she asked in disgust. "If you never wanted it, then why did you wait so long."

"I needed it to . . . but with you gone . . . oh, leave me alone!"

"I am tempted to do just that and let you die from your own foolishness!" Leonie's voice crackled with emotion.

"No, please, you must help me!" Amelia cried. "I have lost the child already, and now he will send me away."

"Are you so sure of that?" Leonie wanted to know.

"Rolfe did not want me after he wed you," Amelia moaned. "I thought he would, but he didn't."

"Explain yourself, Amelia."

"I did not want to return to court," Amelia gasped. "You don't know what it's like there, do you? Having to compete with younger women, always having to—"

"Tell me about Rolfe," Leonie insisted, her voice rising.

"I lied to him," Amelia said. "I told Rolfe there was a child when there was not." She looked Leonie full in the face and told her the whole truth.

"The child is not Rolfe's, but Evarard's. I used him to conceive the child in case Rolfe took too much time growing tired of you. I really thought he would. When he came back here and didn't go to Pershwick after you immediately, I was sure that was the end of his love for you, so I no longer needed the child as an excuse to stay here."

Leonie warned herself not to react, keeping her features set. Her rival's revelation had fired her love for Rolfe anew, made her want to rush to him and throw her arms around him. But she would not allow Amelia to know how much those words meant. There had to be, when all was said and done, some dignity left to both of them, so she told herself not to permit any show of emotion.

Deciding a swift change of subject was the only route, she said, "Evarard is terribly upset. Fool that he is, he loves you."

"Love?" Amelia replied bitterly. "What is love? My

first husband loved me too—until he wed me. Then only other women interested him. Why do you think I was so sure Rolfe would want me after you married him? Men have no care for their wives."

"I do not think that is always so, Amelia."

Amelia sighed. "Rolfe certainly cares for you."

"And perhaps Evarard would care for you, if you gave him a chance. He is not blind to your faults, but he loves you. Did he know about his child?"

"No. I would have told him, yet let him think it was Rolfe's. I kept putting it off, because I did not really want to hurt him."

Amelia had had no such hesitations about hurting Rolfe and her, Leonie thought wryly. But she began to believe she could be forgiving in light of what she had just learned.

"Then I see no reason for him to know too much about this," Leonie told her.

"And Rolfe?"

"I am not so impartial where he is concerned. I will not tell him. You will."

"But he will kill me if he knows how I have lied to you both!"

"I think not, Amelia. I think he will be relieved to learn the truth. But if you do not promise to tell him, I will leave you here to . . ."

"You are cruel, Lady Leonie."

"Not so. I simply love my husband and will not have him grieving over a child he thought was his."

Chapter 48

THE little boy was beautiful. Leonie saw him the moment she came downstairs after leaving Amelia's bedchamber. Rolfe was standing near the boy. The child had thick black curls, and the darkest brown eyes, which regarded her shyly as she approached him. He was an eight-year-old replica of Rolfe.

She turned a questioning gaze on Rolfe, and he said, "Before you reach the wrong conclusion, he looks like me because he is my nephew."

Leonie smiled. "How could I have thought otherwise?"

Frowning, Rolfe introduced her to Simon d'Ambert, then pulled Leonie aside. "I sent him to Lady Roese these last few days because I was in no mood to have him with me. But now you are here, so—"

"But you didn't tell me he was coming to visit."

"My brother is dead," Rolfe said simply, "and the child is not here only to visit. My brother and I had no great love for each other, but that is neither here nor there," Rolfe went on gruffly. "His widow was concerned for her children's welfare, and she sought me out. She left Gascony when my brother died and took refuge with a friend in Normandy. That is where I have been this last month, Leonie."

Her eyes widened. "Then that is why . . . I did wonder why it took you so long to come to Pershwick. So all that time you did not even know I was there?"

"Not until I returned to England. Sir Evarard sent messengers, but they didn't find me. My brother's widow was near undone with worry. She trusted no one. She feared that powerful lords around Gascony would attempt to take control of her children or her in an effort to rape my brother's holdings."

"Was that likely?" she asked softly, glancing over at the child.

"No. The family lands in Gascony were held directly through the queen, and therefore through Henry. She need only have applied to Henry for a guardian."

"Or contact you."

"Yes, well, I have in fact agreed to take on the responsibility. I sent my three nieces back to Gascony with their mother, but I decided to keep the boy with me for a time. My brother had little time for him and he has been around women too long."

"There are women here, my lord," she teased.

"I want to get to know him, Leonie," Rolfe said brusquely. "Do you object?"

Leonie looked down at the floor, hiding her smile. "Of course not, my lord."

Rolfe shook his head. What had brought about this change in her? Where was the hot-tempered woman of only that very morning? She was so subdued, so agreeable.

He continued warily, "I must find a man I can trust to send to Gascony to oversee the estates and keep a watchful eye on the widow and my nieces until they are ready for marriage."

"Might I suggest Sir Piers?" Leonie offered. "He is the perfect one to supervise a household full of women.

He might even take a liking to the widow and think of marriage."

"*Piers?* Think of marriage? Never!"

"You never know, my lord. But now, please, leave Simon here in my care while you visit Lady Amelia."

Rolfe frowned. "I will tell her soon enough that she must leave here. You need not think I have forgotten, Leonie."

"I did not think it, my lord. But she is—ill. I have warned her to stay abed for some days, perhaps a week."

He looked shocked, and before he could speak, she said firmly, "Go to her, my lord, for she needs to speak with you. But when you are finished"—she paused here—"come to me, for I have much to say to you."

Rolfe was so confused that he decided not to argue. He turned and went toward the stairs, and she watched him.

Leonie sat in the hall with Simon, talking gently to him. He was shy, and spoke very little. She tried to make him feel at ease, but that was awfully difficult because she was so jumpy herself.

Rolfe returned to the hall thirty minutes later, his temper nearly beyond his control. He said not a word to Leonie as he grabbed her arm and dragged her out of the hall and all the way to the garden. There he let her go, and actually kicked at the dandelions at his feet.

"Do you know how much I resented this garden of yours when you took it in hand?" he stormed. "Amelia told me you could not be bothered with the running of my household, yet you could waste time here! Many times I thought of setting my horse loose on these blasted plants!"

Leonie nearly choked on her laughter. "Your horse

would have gotten very sick, indeed, if you had, my lord."

He glowered. "Do not jest, Leonie. Why did you think I asked you to clerk for me when I could have managed myself? I thought it was the only thing you could not refuse to do for me. You had refused everything else. And when it would have meant the world to me to know that you had made my home livable, you let *her* take the credit! Why, Leonie, why?"

"Well, you were fool enough to believe she was capable of putting this place to rights," she said archly.

"I a fool, madame? What does that make you for believing the absurdity that I would not want you to run my household?"

"Another fool," she said.

"Damn me, I find nothing amusing in any of this! Why did you never once mention to me the nonsense she was telling you? She would have been proven a liar if you had spoken to me, and then you might have believed me when I told you I did not love her."

"I could ask you the same question. You believed her nonsense as much as I did."

"That is beside the point!"

"Is it?" She moved closer and hesitantly placed her hand on his chest. Eyes soft and luminous, she asked, "Why are you so angry, my lord?"

He lost himself, gazing into those eyes. "Because—because I finally believe you love me . . . yet you have never said so. I have told you I love you—"

"When did you tell me?" she cried.

"That night in London."

"You were drunk," she insisted.

"Not so drunk I can't remember that. And I asked you if you could love me as well. It—it is your answer I cannot remember."

Joy washed over her, glorious waves of joy. "I said then that it would be very easy to love you," she said softly. "And so it was. I love you, my lord."

"Rolfe," he corrected automatically, even as he gathered her into his arms.

"Rolfe." She sighed breathlessly, and then her husband kissed her with all the warmth and love he felt.

He picked her up and carried her back through the hall and up to their chamber. Everyone who watched them pass smiled, but no one spoke. It was time to stop gossiping about the lord and his lady.

As Rolfe swept her up the stairs and into their room, she held him tightly and smiled, thinking how stubborn he was—as she was—and how gentle he was, yet how strong. Later, she would tell him about their child, and about the foolish pride that had kept them at odds for so long. Later.

For the time being, she wanted to think only about their love, and show him how deeply and passionately she loved him.

Enter the World of Johanna Lindsey

Welcome to the world of Johanna Lindsey, and enter into a fantasy of your choosing. Immerse yourself deep into times when men were warriors, tamed only by very special women, and romance reigned supreme. Whether it is against the backdrop of glamorous Regency England society, the pageantry of a medieval court, the wild wilderness of the American West, or any other you can imagine, Johanna Lindsey knows how to make a love story come alive. Enjoy!

Captive Bride

Johanna Lindsey touched deep into the soul of her readers with her first romance. The world realized a new star was born with this tale of an arrogant Arab prince cut down to size by a strong-minded English miss.

Philip Caxton saw Christina as soon as she entered the room. She turned away with contempt when she saw him. Well, he didn't expect an easy conquest. She had seemed to hate him last night.

He sighed, cursing the lack of time. But perhaps Christina Wakefield was just playing hard to get. After all, young women came to London to look for husbands. And he wasn't such a bad catch. But still, with only one day's acquaintance, the odds were against him. Damn, why hadn't he met her sooner?

Anne Shadwell drew Christina toward Philip. "Miss Wakefield, I would like to introduce—"

She was cut off abruptly.

"We've met," Christina said contemptuously.

Anne Shadwell looked startled, but Philip made an arrogantly graceful bow, took Christina's arm firmly, and walked her out onto the balcony. She resisted, but he was sure she wouldn't cause a scene.

When they reached the railing, she whirled to face him defiantly.

"Really, Mr. Caxton! I thought I made myself quite clear last night, but since you don't seem to understand, let me enlighten you. I don't like you. You are a rude, conceited man, and I find you quite intolerable.

Now if you will excuse me, I am going back to join my brother." She turned to leave, but he grabbed her hand and pulled her back to him.

"Christina, wait," he demanded huskily, forcing her to look into his dark eyes.

"I really don't think we have anything to say to each other, Mr. Caxton. And please refrain from using my first name." She turned to leave again, but Philip still grasped her hand in his. She faced him once more, stamping her foot in fury.

"Let go of my hand!" she demanded.

"Not until you've heard what I have to say, Tina," he answered, pulling her closer to him.

"Tina!" She glared at him. "How dare—"

"I dare anything I damn well please. Now shut up and listen to me." He was amused at the disbelief written on her lovely face. "Tina, I want you. I would be honored if you would consent to be my wife. I would give you anything you want—jewels, beautiful gowns, my estates."

She was looking at him in a most unusual way. She opened her mouth to say something, but the words wouldn't come out. And then he felt the sting of her hand across his cheek.

"I have never been so insulted in my—"

But Philip didn't let her finish. He gathered her in his arms and silenced her words with a deep, penetrating kiss. He held her tightly against him, feeling her breasts pressed against his chest, crushing the breath from her body. She was struggling to free herself, but her efforts only increased his desire.

Then, unexpectedly, Christina went limp in his arms and threw him off guard. Philip thought she had fainted but winced when he felt a sharp pain in his shin. He released her instantly to grab his leg, and when he looked up, Christina was running into the drawing room.

He should have known better, Philip told himself.

He should have gone to her home in Halstead and courted her slowly. But that wasn't his way. Besides, he had never courted a woman before. He was used to getting what he wanted immediately, and he wanted Christina.

A Gentle Feuding

Sheena Fergusson is the most prized beauty in Scotland. Every man wants to possess her—except for Jamie MacKinnion, the avowed enemy of her clan. But when the proud laird finally lays eyes on Sheena, his warrior's heart is conquered by the ethereal magnificence of this woman.

James MacKinnion moved slowly. An enveloping mist still clung to the dewy ground, and he was sopping wet from crossing the second of the two Esk rivers. He was tired from lack of sleep and the rough ride south. There was something wrong in all this, but he didn't know what it could be.

The mist swirled and parted before him in a gentle breeze, revealing for a moment a wooded glen not far ahead. Then the mist settled again, and the vision was gone. Jamie rode for it; the trees were a pleasant change from the barren moors and heather-clad hills.

He had never been this far east on Fergusson land before. He had never raided Lowlanders in the spring before, either.

Jamie's anger warred with his common sense. Dead men demanded he ride to avenge them. A scrap of plaid demanded he ride south. Yet . . . why? He would have given anything for more evidence. The act bordered on insanity. Was he sure of what he was doing?

The mist was rising steadily as Jamie entered the wooden glen.

Then he heard a sound, and in a flash he slid off his

horse and ran for cover. But when he listened again, he recognized the sound as a giggle, a feminine giggle.

Leaving his horse behind, he moved stealthily through the bracken and trees toward the sound.

When Jamie saw her, he wasn't quite sure he believed the vision. A young girl was standing waist-deep in a small pool, the mist swirling about her head. She looked like a water sprite, a kelpie, unreal, yet real enough.

The girl laughed again as she splashed water across her naked breasts. The sound enchanted Jamie. He was mesmerized by the girl, rooted where he was, watching her play. She was frolicking and having a joyous time of it.

She was like nothing he had ever seen before, a beauty, and no mistake about it. In a moment she faced him, and he saw nearly all of her loveliness. Pearly white skin contrasted starkly with brilliant, deep red hair. Almost magenta, it was so dark and gleaming and long. Two strands waved around her breasts and floated in the water. And those breasts were tantalizing, round, high and proud in youthful glory, the peaks sharply pointed because of the caress of icy water. Her features were unmistakably delicate. The only thing not clear to Jamie was the color of her eyes. He was not quite close enough to see, and the reflection of the water made them appear a blue so clear and bright as to be glowing quite impossibly. Was his imagination running wild? He wanted to move closer and see.

What he really wanted was to join her in the water. It was an insane idea, born of the strange effect she was having on him. What if she let him come to her, let him touch her as he ached to do? He had to leave before common sense completely fled. As if to point out his folly in tarrying, the first rays of sun broke through the glen, showing him the time he had wasted. His brother and the others would have all returned to the men by the river. They would all be waiting for him.

Jamie was suddenly sickened. Watching the girl, being transported to what seemed a sphere outside reality, he was appalled by the contrast between the lovely scene before him and the bloody one he would see in just a short while. Yet he could no more stop the one that was soon to happen than he could forget the one he was watching. Both seemed inevitable.

Jamie's last look at the girl was a wistful one. Beams of sunlight dotted the pool, and one touched the girl and lit her hair like a burst of flame. With a sigh, he turned away. That last vision of the mystical girl would be etched in his memory for a long time to come.

Love Only Once

With Love Only Once, *Johanna Lindsey introduced her beloved Malory family. The romances of these outrageous and outspoken sensualists, set in the ever-popular Regency era, are pure magic. Nicholas Eden, the rakish fourth Viscount of Montieth, is as enchanted as readers during this first encounter with Regina Ashton. Having just discovered that he has accidentally kidnapped the Malory ingenue, he is now setting her free. But if he is expecting anger from his unintended hostage, he's in for a surprise.*

She stood framed by the window, gazing at him in a startling direct way. There was no shyness in her look and no fear either on that exquisite, delicate, heart-shaped face. The eyes were disturbing, with an exotic slant. Such dark blue eyes in that fair face, so blue and clear, like colored crystal. The lips were soft and full and the nose was straight and slender. A thick fringe of sooty lashes framed those extraordinary eyes, while black brows arched gently above them. Her hair was raven black, too, in tight little ringlets surrounding her face, giving her fair skin a glow like polished ivory.

She was breathtaking. The beauty didn't stop with her face, either. She was petite, yes, but there was nothing childlike about her form. Firm young breasts pressed against the thin muslin of her rose gown. He wanted to pull the rose muslin down a few inches and watch those lovely breasts spring free. He received another jolt then, feeling his manhood rise against his will. Lord, he hadn't lost control like that since his youth!

Desperate to bring everything under control, he cast about for something—anything—to say. "Hello."

His tone implied "What have we here?" And Reggie grinned despite herself. He was gorgeous, simply gorgeous. It wasn't just his face, though that was striking. There was a sexual magnetism about him that was quite unnerving.

"Hello, yourself," Reggie said impishly. "I was beginning to wonder when you would realize your mistake. You certainly took enough time about it."

"I am just now wondering if I have in fact made a mistake at all. You don't look like a mistake. You look very much like something I did right for a change."

He quietly closed the door and leaned back against it, those beautiful amber eyes boldly moving over her from head to foot. It was not at all safe for a young lady to be alone with a man of his stamp, and Reggie recognized that. Yet for some reason he couldn't fathom, she wasn't afraid of this man. Scandalously, she wondered if it would be such a terrible thing to lose her virtue to him. Oh, it was a reckless mood she was suddenly in!

She eyed the closed door and his large frame blocking that only exit. "Fie on you, sir. I hope you don't mean to compromise me more than you already have."

"I will if you will let me. Will you? Think carefully before you answer," he said with a devastating smile. "My heart is in jeopardy."

She giggled, delighted. "Stuff! Rakes like you don't *have* hearts. Everyone knows that."

Nicholas was enchanted.

Hearts Aflame

Kristen Haardrad has been imprisoned by the Saxon warlord Royce when her shipmates dared to attack Royce's lands. The Viking maiden has been searching for a man who could stir her senses and make her blood sing, and now she's finally found him in Royce. So with the full force of her Viking determination she sets out to win the heart and love of her captor.

Kristen had been stretching when she heard the steps crossing the floor, coming from the entrance. She jumped up curiously, her heartbeat quickening when she saw Royce coming out of the shadows, his direction not the stairs, but toward her, straight to her.

She did not move, waiting for him to reach her. His expression was intense, harsh, and her heart beat even faster, not in fear but in expectation. When he stopped, she felt only a moment's surprise when his hand went to the back of her neck, his fingers gripping her hair to yank her head back. She held her breath as his eyes moved angrily over her face.

"Why do you tempt me so?" He asked this not of her but to himself.

"Do I, milord?"

"You do it apurpose," he hissed before his mouth slashed down over hers.

Kristen had waited for this, to know the feel of lips, to be able to touch him. She had wanted this to happen, but she had not guessed how devastating the actuality would be. Nothing could have prepared her for such a violent jolt of desire, when she had never felt desire before.

His mouth moved over hers brutally in his anger. He gripped her hair, holding her still for this ravishment, yet he did not touch her otherwise. Kristen was the one to lean into him, until she could feel the full length of his body and knew the extent of his desire. This inflamed her more. She didn't care that this was not what he wanted, that he was kissing her against his own will and probably hating her more because of it. She wrapped her arms around his back, moving her hands up over the hard muscle there until she gripped his shoulders, holding him tight to her.

She heard him groan at her complete acceptance of him, and his other arm slipped about her waist, crushing her tighter to him. His tongue plunged into her mouth and she drew on it, capturing it like a prize, refusing to let go. God in heaven, this was wonderful, more thrilling than anything she had ever felt before. She would have let him take her there, in the hall, on the table, the floor—she didn't care. She wanted to make love with him now, before he came to his senses and stopped.

He did stop, and Kristen sighed miserably when his lips left hers. He looked down at her, his eyes fierce, filled half with passion, half with fury. She met his look boldly, but this served only to anger him more.

With a snarl, he shoved her away from him. "My God, you have no shame, do you?"

"I feel no shame in wanting you," she told him softly. She smiled then at his snort of disbelief. Deliberately, she added in a teasing tone, "You are my heartmake, Royce. Begin to accept it. You will eventually."

"You will never count me as one of your lovers, wench," he stated emphatically.

She shrugged, the sigh she gave louder than necessary. "Very well, milord, if that is your wish."

"Not my wish, the truth," he insisted. "And you will cease to use your tricks on me."

Kristen could not help but laugh at this order. "What tricks are those, milord? I am only guilty of looking at you, mayhap more than I should, but I cannot seem to help myself. You are, after all, the most splendid man here."

He drew in his breath sharply. "God's mercy, are all Vikings as brazen as you?"

"What you call brazen, I call honesty. Would you rather I lie and say I hate you, that I despise the sight of you?"

"How can you not hate me? I have enslaved you. I keep you shackled and I know you hate the chain. I think you do hate me, that you tempt me apurpose, hoping to have revenge by bewitching me."

Her eyes narrowed at him. "I am through telling you what I hope for, through speaking the truth to you when you will not believe it. Think whatever you like."

She turned her back on him, but was tense, waiting for him to walk away. He did not do so immediately. She imagined he was fighting to control a new fury that she would dare dismiss him like that. She would have been much appeased if she had seen that his eyes had simply moved over her, revealing for one unguarded moment the yearning in his soul.

Once a Princess

What woman hasn't dreamed of being Cinderella, of being rescued by a handsome prince to a better world than the one she lives in? In Once a Princess, *that fantasy comes alive for Tanya, but the lovely orphan isn't quite ready to believe that fairy tales can happen for her.*

Tanya couldn't hold back the incredulous thought any longer. "Do—do you know who my parents are?"

"It is possible—if you carry a certain—birthmark that is—hereditary."

She didn't even notice his hesitation over those pertinent words. She was trying to tamp down her excitement, because what he was suggesting was just too unlikely to be true. And yet—ever since she'd found out that she was unrelated to Dobbs and Iris, she'd wondered about her real parents, where they came from, what they were like, *who* they were.

Other girls had backgrounds, rich in detail and color. Her life was a blank page begun in a tavern. Now here were four strangers hinting at knowledge she craved as much as, if not more than, her independence. To finally have a real identity, a family history, possibly even relatives still living—a birth date! It was just too wonderful to be true, and if she allowed her hopes to be raised, she'd be doomed to disappointment. And to have it all hinge on a birthmark?

"We are certain of your identity, mistress. The mark that will prove it should be found on the underside of your seat, on the left cheek. It will no doubt require a mirror for you to examine it, but go and do so now, and do so carefully, so you may return and describe the mark to us."

"And if I won't?"

"Then you may possibly be offended when we locate the mark ourselves, to end all doubt, you understand."

She was quickly learning that Stefan could be cruel in his remarks. Her cheeks flaming, she hissed, "You bastard," but he merely crooked a brow at her, showing her how little it mattered to him that he'd insulted her—again. "What happens if the mark *is* there?"

"Then you will return with us to Cardinia."

"Where is that?"

"It's a small country in Eastern Europe. It's where you were born, Tatiana Janacek."

A name. Her name? God, this was becoming real again, her hopes soaring again. "Is that why you're here? To take me back?"

"Yes."

"Then I have family there? They sent you to find me?"

"No." His tone softened for the moment. "Regrettably, you are the last of your line."

Up and down, these hopes. Why did she let herself be lured in by possibilities? All right, no family. But a name, a history—if they were telling the truth, and if she had the mark.

"If I don't have any family left, then why did you bother to find me?"

"These questions are pointless, mistress, until you prove to us all, yourself included, that you possess the mark that names you a Janacek."

"I don't care how pointless you find my questions, I'm not moving an inch until I know the real reason you came here."

Stefan took a menacing step closer, but she didn't budge. He growled down at her, "For no other reason than to collect you and return you—"

"Why?"

"For your wedding!"

"My what?"

"You are to marry the new King of Cardinia."

Angel

Angel never thought of himself as a hero. He was just a man with a gun and a reputation who had always walked a solitary path. But when a debt lands him in a marriage with a refined young woman who interferes in everyone's life, including his own, the inscrutable loner finally learns what it means to need someone.

"Are we divorced yet?"

Cassie woke with a start, that soft drawl echoing in her ears. "What?"

"Are we divorced yet?"

She knew instantly who he was, she just couldn't believe he was there. "Angel?"

His hand slipped into her hair as his body moved to cover hers. "Just answer the question, Cassie."

"We're not. I just haven't had the time—"

His mouth came down to cut off the rest of her explanation. Obviously, he wasn't interested in her excuses just now. But what he was interested in was bundled up in warm flannel.

"How come you don't sleep naked?"

It was a question born of frustration, not one for a lady to take seriously. Cassie answered anyway. "I do in the summertime."

He groaned, knowing full well an image of her naked was going to haunt him now. And his tongue slid in deep, eliciting an answering groan out of Cassie. It was a while before they drew breath.

"You got the sweetest, softest lips I ever did taste," he said against them.

"Your voice makes me tingle, Angel."

"What does my mouth do to you?"

"It makes me weak."

His mouth moved up to suck on her earlobe. "What else?"

"Hot," she whispered.

"Oh, God, Cassie, I'm going to burst if I can't get inside you right now."

"Then what are you waiting for?"

He laughed and kissed her again. Then he rolled to her side to shove the covers off her. She tore the top of her nightgown open, popping off three buttons in her impatience to get it off. He yanked his shirt out of his pants and sent his buttons to join hers on the bed and the floor. In seconds he was back, pressing her into the mattress. Her arms and legs wrapped around him, locking him in place. And then he was inside, deep inside, and that familiar throbbing came so quickly, bursting on his senses, pulsing around him, drawing his own climax to mesh with hers.

Cassie lowered her legs slowly. Her toes slid against leather. Angel was still wearing his boots and his pants. She wanted to laugh, but she felt like crying.

God, how she hated the reality that surfaced after the passion was spent. She resented that. She resented Angel, too, at the moment. And she particularly resented the fact that he hadn't taken off his boots.

She let him know it with the curt admonishment, "Next time take off your boots."

"I'll take them off now."

"No, you won't. You aren't staying."

"I'm not ready to leave yet, Cassie. And that was too intense. We're going to try it again, slow and easy."

Her stomach fluttered in response to those words. She suppressed the feeling.

"No, we aren't," she told him stiffly. "You're going to get out of here before my mama hears you and comes charging in with her gun blazing."

"Where is she?"

"In the next room."

"Then we'll have to be quiet, won't we?"

"Angel—"

His mouth was back, slanting across hers with tantalizing skill. She couldn't let that work this time. She couldn't.

She did. She'd missed him too much, wanted him too much, to be sensible about it. And there had been the thought, haunting her ever since he'd ridden out of her life, that she'd never know his touch again.

Now his touch was breaking the last of her resistance with a slow sweep of his hand over her breasts and belly. Gooseflesh followed in wake; nipples tingled to hardness. She'd just had the most incredible explosion of pleasure imaginable, but her body was firing up to experience it again. And in no way did Angel hurry her toward that end. He'd said slow and easy, and that was exactly how he proceeded.

It was nearly dawn before Angel finally got his fill of her. Cassie was too sated to feel any more resentment. And he'd been right. The first time had been over with too quickly. The rest . . . Lord love him, the man was as good at loving as he was with a gun.